THE SUBLIME AND SPIRITED VOYAGE OF ORIGINAL SIN

Visit us at www.boldstrokesbooks.com

What Reviewers Say About Bold Strokes Books

"With its expected unexpected twists, vivid characters and healthy dose of humor, *Blind Curves* is a very fun read that will keep you guessing." – *Bay Windows*

"In a succinct film style narrative, with scenes that move, a character-driven plot, and crisp dialogue worthy of a screenplay … the Richfield and Rivers novels are … an engaging Hollywood mystery … series." – *Midwest Book Review*

Force of Nature "…is filled with nonstop, fast paced action. Tornadoes, raging fire blazes, heroic and daring rescues… Baldwin does a fine job of describing the fast-paced scenes and inspiring the reader to keep on turning the pages." – *L-word.comLiterature*

In the Jude Devine mystery series the "…characters seem fully capable of walking away from the particulars of whodunit and engaging the reader in other aspects of their lives." – *Lambda Book Report*

Mine "…weaves a tale of yearning, love, lust, and conflict resolution … a believable plot, with strong characters in a charming setting." – *JustAboutWrite*

"While these two women struggle with their issues, there is some very, very hot sex. If you enjoy complex characters and passionate sex scenes, you'll love *Wild Abandon*." – *MegaScene*

"*Course of Action* is a romance … populated with a host of captivating and amiable characters. The glimpses into the lifestyles of the rich and beautiful people are rather like guilty pleasures a most satisfying and entertaining reading experience." – *Midwest Book Review*

The Clinic is "…a spellbinding novel." – *JustAboutWrite*

"*Unexpected Sparks* lived up to its promise and was thoroughly enjoyable … Dartt did a lovely job at building the relationship between Kate and Nikki." – *Lambda Book Report*

"*Sequestered Hearts* … is everything a romance should be. It is teeming with longing, heartbreak, and of course, love. As pure romances go, it is one of the best in print today." – *L-word.comLiterature*

"*The Exile and the Sorcerer* is a mesmerizing read, a tour-de-force packed with adventure, ordeals, complex twists and turns, and the internal introspection of appealing characters." – *Midwest Book Review*

The Spanish Pearl is "…both science fiction and romance in this adventurous tale … A most entertaining read, with a sequel already in the works. Hot, hot, hot!" – *Minnesota Literature*

"A deliciously sexy thriller ... *Dark Valentine* is funny, scary, and very realistic. The story is tightly written and keeps the reader gripped to the exciting end." – *JustAbout Write*

"*Punk Like Me* ... is different. It is engaging. It is life-affirming. Frankly, it is genius. This is a rare book in that it has a soul; one that is laid bare for all to see." – *JustAboutWrite*

"*Chance* is not a novel about the music industry; it is about a woman discovering herself as she muddles through all the trappings of fame." – *Midwest Book Review*

Sweet Creek "... is sublimely in tune with the times." – *Q-Syndicate*

"*Forever Found* ... neatly combines hot sex scenes, humor, engaging characters, and an exciting story." – *MegaScene*

Shield of Justice is a "...well-plotted...lovely romance...I couldn't turn the pages fast enough!" – Ann Bannon, author of *The Beebo Brinker Chronicles*

The 100th Generation is "...filled with ancient myths, Egyptian gods and goddesses, legends, and, most wonderfully, it contains the lesbian equivalent of Indiana Jones living and working in modern Egypt." – *Just About Write*

Sword of the Guardian is "...a terrific adventure, coming of age story, a romance, and tale of courtly intrigue, attempted assassination, and gender confusion ... a rollicking fun book and a must-read for those who enjoy courtly light fantasy in a medieval-seeming time." – *Midwest Book Review*

"*Of Drag Kings and the Wheel of Fate*'s lush rush of a romance incorporates reincarnation, a grounded transman and his peppy daughter, and the dark moods of a troubled witch—wonderful homage to Leslie Feinberg's classic gender-bending novel, *Stone Butch Blues*." – *Q-Syndicate*

In *Running with the Wind* "...the discussions of the nature of sex, love, power, and sexuality are insightful and represent a welcome voice from the view of late-20-something characters today." – *Midwest Book Review*

"Rich in character portrayal, *The Devil Inside* is an unusual, unpredictable, and thought-provoking love story that will have the reader questioning the definition of right and wrong long after she finishes the book." – *JustAboutWrite*

Wall of Silence "...is perfectly plotted and has a very real voice and consistently accurate tone, which is not always the case with lesbian mysteries." – *Midwest Book Review*

THE SUBLIME AND SPIRITED VOYAGE OF ORIGINAL SIN

by

Colette Moody

2009

THE SUBLIME AND SPIRITED VOYAGE OF ORIGINAL SIN

ISBN 10: 1-60282-054-6
ISBN 13: 978-1-60282-054-8

This Trade Paperback Original Is Published By
Bold Strokes Books, Inc.
P.O. Box 249
Valley Falls, NY 12185

First Edition: March 2009

CREDITS
EDITORS: SHELLEY THRASHER AND STACIA SEAMAN
PRODUCTION DESIGN: STACIA SEAMAN
COVER ART: BARB KIWAK (WWW.KIWAK.COM)
COVER DESIGN BY SHERI (GRAPHICARTIST2020@HOTMAIL.COM)

Acknowledgments

This book is dedicated to Laura, who never stopped telling me that I was capable of accomplishing this, and who was my tireless font of feedback, even when my requests went well beyond the boundaries of what was reasonable and humane.

Also to Radclyffe (for her accommodation and faith), Shelley (for her patience and astounding tenacity), as well as everyone at Bold Strokes who contributed to the final product—especially Barb, who produced such breathtaking cover art.

And to you, the reader, thanks for picking this book up. If from reading it, you get even a fraction of the enjoyment that I got from writing it, then it will have been completely worthwhile.

Dedication

For Nando, Addison, and Brontë.
I miss you every day.

CHAPTER ONE

May 1702

A s the sailor's dirty finger squeezed the trigger, the blunderbuss exploded, scattering shot and smoke in all directions. An instant later the blade of a cutlass, steeped in blood, pierced his abdomen. He toppled backward, clearly surprised, the crimson fluid flooding the ship's deck.

Ellis Churchill crouched and jerked his cutlass from the dying seaman's gut. "Bloody bastard," he spat, wiping the blood off his prized weapon and onto the British naval uniform of the man he had just run through.

He took in the rest of the ship's deck and at last saw no movement. The Royal Navy had caught up to *Original Sin* with a faster, more diminutive sloop, and her small crew had boarded them with relative speed, though a few well-placed cannon blasts had certainly cut into the size and power of their attack.

"Churchill!" someone called urgently from within the captain's quarters, and he dashed over, cutlass at the ready. Crossing the threshold of the room, he saw Captain Malvern badly wounded, his head resting in the lap of his daughter Gayle.

"He's taken some shot to his chest." Gayle's voice was filled with panic. "Have we dispatched the navy?"

"We have." Churchill dropped to his knees to examine the captain's chest wounds. "Neptune's balls. This looks bad."

"Go get Poole. Tell him to prepare for surgery. Father's losing blood fast."

Churchill grimaced. "Poole is dead."

"Buggar!" Gayle tried to apply pressure to her father's wounds, though they continued to ooze blood liberally. "Bring me whoever is left and healthy."

Churchill scrambled back out to the open deck of *Original Sin* and quickly assessed the results of their devastating battle with the Royal Navy. Many were wounded, but he commanded two of the more able-bodied seamen to follow him. Churchill knew that he and these two crewmen—Abernathy and Dowd—would have to find a new surgeon, one who could keep the captain from bleeding to death.

Gayle wiped her forehead on the sleeve of her linen shirt and cursed softly. This had been the worst attack on their ship that she could recall. When they had caught wind that the Royal Navy was patrolling the eastern Florida coast, no doubt devising a plan to invade this Spanish-ruled territory, her father had unsuccessfully tried to elude them, hoping that once night had fallen they could dissolve into the fog and steal safely away. Instead, before the sun had completely set, the navy had spotted and overtaken them.

Churchill and his two recruits appeared in the captain's quarters. "Is the navy sloop salvageable?" Gayle asked as she packed her father's wounds with more cotton cloth to stanch the loss of blood.

"She's hurtin', ma'am," Abernathy, a seasoned pirate who loved his rum, answered. "But we can get her up to speed, I'd wager. Her sails and masts are mostly intact."

"Good. I know this battle has taken quite a toll on us, but the life of the captain is a higher price than I'm willing to pay." Gayle glanced through the open door and squinted at the horizon. "The sun is already setting, and we're too far out to take the skiff. Take whoever you need to man the *Abigail Lee* and obtain a doctor from the mainland. Leave me the rest of the wounded and I'll tend to them as best I can while you're gone."

"You're leaving yourself a sittin' duck," Dowd, a dark, stocky fellow, asserted. "I'll not leave the cap'n here with naught but a woman and a pack of wounded men to defend him."

"What would you have me do?" Gayle asked. "*Original Sin* cannot sail into harbor crippled, even in the dead of night. If we stay here, our chances of remaining unmolested are greater."

"She's right." Churchill sounded resigned. "We'll grab a few more lads and be off. We won't come back without help for the captain. You have my word on it."

It was well after dusk and past time for Dr. Phillip Farquar to finish up for the night. He drew his pocket watch out of his waistcoat and examined it. Yes, he was definitely done for the day. No more house calls to the populace and no more admitting sick visitors into his home. All these simple Spaniards did was whine and complain about their conditions, when he had things to do and places to go. Public service was such a burden. He sighed loudly.

Damn his father for insisting that he trade his life of entitlement for this parade of open lesions and gout. Phillip still recalled his parent's horrifying final words on the subject. "Until you can learn to care for people as much as you care for a bloody farthing, you'll never inherit so much as a lump of my spittle."

Had Phillip known that a doctor saw such disgusting things, he might have chosen to be a blacksmith instead, but he worried the physical labor might chap his skin.

Now half of his bargain with his father was completed. He had secured a position (though hopefully a temporary one) as a physician in San Augustin, Florida, after being unceremoniously dropped not far off the eastern seaboard and set adrift by an angry British ship captain who, in Phillip's assessment, lacked complete breeding and judgment. After all, any reasonable person would have understood that amputating the captain's diseased penis was the only viable course of action. It made perfect sense.

At any rate, instead of arriving in the Province of Carolina as planned, he was placed in a skiff with his belongings and left to drift for several days. Based on the horrible things he had heard about the Spanish, when he realized he finally had made landfall in Spanish territory, he was worried that he would be instantly killed and eaten. It was fortunate that once he was able to help the inhabitants of San Augustin understand that he was a doctor, they were interested enough in his services to ignore his nationality—just as his desire for food, shelter, and wine helped him ignore theirs.

To fulfill the second part of the bargain, he now had to marry and create an heir, a surprisingly challenging task. These Spaniards simply didn't appreciate his gentility, and his poor command of their language didn't help. It was astoundingly difficult to woo a lady who thought he was either trying to purchase a chicken or a few tomatoes from her, or ask her for directions.

The only thing that had kept him from leaving town was the tailor's bewitching young daughter, one Celia Pierce. She was the loveliest lass in East Florida, and it didn't hurt that she and her British father were the only other people in San Augustin who spoke fluent English. Thank God she had accepted his proposal of marriage. Otherwise the last four months in this hellhole would have been completely for naught.

She had dark hair, eyes seemingly cut from sapphire, and the most voluptuous figure he had seen in a good, long while—and he had seen his share of figures, though he was unable to inspect some as closely as he would have preferred. Phillip was tall, but the top of Celia's head nearly reached his jawline. And since she was the tailor's daughter and a fine seamstress, she sported the most beautiful gowns in town.

At times, her mere presence made him lose his ability to form words, and he would simply stare into her décolletage, his mouth agape. True, these were not among what he considered his best moments, but they were definitely more interesting than having one more peasant hobble into his office with the Devil's Pox.

Good Lord, he could scarcely bear these people, with their oozing sores and dirty, common ways. He hoped within a few years to journey north to a cultured city such as Philadelphia with his beautiful and, with any luck, somewhat sexually deviant wife, where he could relish living the life of a wealthy doctor. He saw himself attending lavish parties, eating the most sophisticated and succulent fare, being the center of aristocratic attention. He could certainly do with a little more of that and a little less of the dropsy.

He jumped as a sound startled him from his ruminations. His fiancée stood there, absolutely stunning in a billowy gown of blue and green. Obviously his servant had barely mumbled the usual announcement as he had let her in.

"Hello, Phillip." She greeted him with a bright smile.

"I have told you, madam. It is improper for you to refer to me so informally before our wedding. Please, call me 'Doctor.' After all, I didn't spend all that time in the hallowed halls of Trinity College so that I can be addressed like any street peddler or fishmonger."

He thought back to his university days. He had hoped to venture to Italy to pursue his studies, and if it hadn't been for them speaking that damned Italian all the time, he was certain his dream would have come to pass. As it was, he had been barely able to keep up with all the body parts, fluids, and various diseases in English, let alone once they were translated into a bloody Romance language. He was thankful that his father had enough money to make sure that he secured his degree, as he had less than a natural proclivity for science and struggled with its terminology constantly.

Celia pursed her full lips slightly. "Yes, Doctor." Her voice was tinged with a hint of irritation. "At any rate, I've brought your coat for tomorrow night's engagement party. I would like for you to try it on to ensure it fits properly, as I've spent the better part of the day altering it." She produced a beautiful navy blue topcoat with large, flared double cuffs and elaborate embroidery.

Phillip was almost awestruck at the sight of such a garment, but collected himself and turned around with a sudden flourish so she might help him slip it on. The soft, rich fabric felt marvelous as he fingered it. This was how clothing should be, he thought. It should make a man feel that he was worth a king's ransom. He started to spin giddily, until he self-consciously remembered Celia stood there watching him preen.

"How does it look?" he asked.

A smirk passed over her features and disappeared just as quickly. "It seems to be long enough. But is it too tight through the shoulders?"

He froze, concerned that his magical coat might be flawed in some way. "Is it?"

She scrutinized it more closely. "Hold your arms out to the side," she instructed, and he rapidly did so out of concern. "Hmm, it could be roomier through here. But that's easily fixed. Did you receive the matching breeches I sent this morning?"

"I did, but I've had no time to do anything today but administer the occasional bloodletting. Wretched peasants."

"Your selfless devotion to curing others overwhelms me, Doctor," Celia said sarcastically. "Such compassion is so very attractive."

As she'd expected, Phillip's chest swelled slightly with pride. He was always oblivious to her ridicule.

"I find you attractive as well, my cabbage."

She fought her natural urge to grimace at his unpleasant metaphor. "Cabbage? Might you compare me to a vegetable with a slightly more palatable smell?"

His brow furrowed. "My little…mushroom?"

"You would liken me to a fungus?" Celia laughed. "Such wooing, sir. You might make my heart burst within my breast."

Phillip eyed her with belated suspicion. "Are you mocking me?"

"I? Your devoted mushroom dares not," Celia replied insincerely. "Were I perhaps a potato or a leek, however, I would be brimming with mockery. They, sir, are victuals of the trickiest sort and are not to be trusted."

Phillip seemed befuddled by this logic. He stood inertly, as though the activity of his brain stalled the functioning of every other limb.

"Now go and try the breeches on as well, Doctor," she said. "I'll wait out here for you."

As he disappeared into the back room, Celia momentarily dreaded her future. While she supposed that she should be excited about her betrothal, and thrilled with the promise that a life as a married woman offered, thus far she simply did not care much for Dr. Phillip Farquar.

Not only was he gangly and rather plain, but he possessed no discernable sense of humor and no visible chin. He was also as vain and obsessed with his appearance as the most conceited of females, and it rather unsettled Celia that he often focused inextricably on her bosom.

She knew she was more decoration for him than a mate. He made that abundantly clear with his obvious disinterest in most of what she had to say—unless, of course, it was about him. He also seemed to view her father as quite beneath him and spoke down to him on the few occasions he deigned to address him. She wasn't sure if Phillip's objections were rooted in the fact that her father had married a Spanish woman, or if he genuinely did not care for him.

Celia furrowed her eyebrows, a habit she tried to suppress, well aware that female frowns suggested bad temper or, worse, an opinion. If she knew of anywhere she could simply live as a seamstress and thrive as part of the community, she would pack her things right now. But she doubted such a place existed. She could aspire to no more than becoming the wife of a wealthy man who was not unkind. Phillip was at least somewhat wealthy. As for his lack of kindness—perhaps his nature had not fully revealed itself, and once they were man and wife he would prove to be wise and thoughtful.

Her own loud scoff of skepticism brought her back to reality. Somehow she could not imagine Phillip as the benevolent husband of her girlish dreams. Her cousin had already suggested Celia would simply have to take a lover, like most women who married for reasons of practicality. Who knew? Perhaps Celia could become a patron of the arts and have many lovers. Perhaps her life would be filled with romance and intrigue. The soldiers and settlers around here didn't have much time for the arts, so perhaps she would become a world traveler.

The thunderous sound of Phillip breaking wind from the next room shattered her reverie. So much for a life of romance and intrigue. She would obviously have one of dyspepsia and intestinal distress instead. She winced. One was hardly an adequate replacement for the other. She was brooding on this sorry fact when the door to the sitting room fractured open with a loud crack and three rather seedy pirate types greeted her coarsely.

"The doctor has closed for the night," Celia said.

One of the motley specimens drew his cutlass and flashed it malevolently. He was older than the others and had a red, bulbous nose. "We've special business for the doctor."

"But he has gone already." She was alarmed, though a bit excited. Had the god of irony just answered her wishes for intrigue?

"Gone where?" rumbled a dark, heavily muscled man menacingly. He stepped toward her and leered as if her beauty had overwhelmed him.

"He has left town, you see." She felt suddenly weak when she realized she might have found more adventure than she'd hoped for. And she really needed to work on her lying, she thought—especially when she finally took all those lovers. "He had to tend to someone several townships away. They sent a carriage for him. Spotted fever, I believe."

"And who might you be, lass?" growled the most physically imposing of the three grubby intruders, continuing to devour her with his eyes.

"Celia Pierce," she replied softly, sensing that this man could be dangerous. Surely Phillip was listening and would come to her rescue if things took an ugly turn. "I'm his seamstress."

"A seamstress, eh?" the obvious leader of the group asked with some interest. "And are you a very good one?"

"They say I'm the best on the coast," Celia said coolly. Phillip was coming out to save her, wasn't he? Any time now would be suitable.

"Then you'll have to do." The leader grabbed her by the arm, and his hulking companion gagged her and tied her hands together behind her back, albeit he was not as rough as Celia feared. To her left, the pirate with the red nose stuffed a nearby black leather bag as full of medical supplies as possible.

"Don't get any wise ideas about trying to call for help, or we'll slice your bleedin' heart out." The brawny one tossed a sack over her head. "Just come help us out a mite, and we'll let you go unharmed." He picked her up, slung her over his shoulder, and whisked her off into the night.

Nearly twenty minutes later, Phillip quietly poked his head out of the back room. He carried a fireplace poker in his trembling hand and searched about for any sign of the intruders, then sighed with relief when he saw they had taken nothing of real value.

"I told you to bring a doctor." Gayle stared in disbelief at the kicking petticoats of a woman draped over Churchill's shoulder. "What the hell is this?"

Churchill snatched the sack from the woman's head, exposing long, dark hair in disarray, wide panicked eyes, and a rather inelegant gag propping open her mouth. "The doctor wasn't to be found. We nabbed the town seamstress instead."

"The seamstress?" Gayle was afraid for a moment that the sheer force of her frustration might make her head come clean off her shoulders, but when she touched her forehead she found it was still attached. Whether this was a blessing or a curse, she was unsure. "Who will take out the musket balls?" she shouted. "Who will cut off the limbs shattered by cannon shot? Who will tend to the lads bleeding into their bloody bellies? This dressmaker?"

"Aye," Abernathy said, tossing the medical bag onto the deck beside her. "And I lifted plenty of supplies, though I found no drink there, as I'd hoped. She'll do a fine job of stitching up the cap'n and the men, I reckon."

Gayle expected the dressmaker to either faint, cry, or scream like some prissy governor's wife. Instead she simply stood there, then slowly closed her eyes. Maybe she could be of some value, Gayle thought.

Dowd untied her gag and ogled her. "It was this girl or nothin'. There was no time to gather a proper doctor."

Gayle studied the hostage before her. She was tall and dark-complexioned, with beautiful features. Her eyes were surprisingly blue, and she seemed strangely confident, not at all like someone who should fear for her life. "Have you ever seen a surgeon work before, good woman?" she asked.

"My name is Celia, and I have seen my fiancé remove a musket ball," the seamstress said matter-of-factly. "Of course that was from the rump of an ox, but I daresay the procedure can't be that different for a man."

Was their unwilling captive actually offering to help? "Then come with me, Celia," Gayle said, pointing toward the captain's cabin. She picked up the medical bag. "Churchill, direct the men to take whatever is salvageable from the *Abigail Lee*, then cast her off and help the others tend to the wounded. We will be with the captain."

She sliced through the ropes binding Celia's wrists and motioned with her dagger that she follow. Celia did so, gently rubbing her rope burn.

The cabin was lit dimly by a small oil lantern suspended from the ceiling. On the bed Gayle's father lay very still, his skin clammy and pale, his breathing shallow.

"Go in," Gayle instructed, then closed the door behind them.

"This is your captain?" Celia asked tentatively.

"Aye," Gayle answered. "He cannot die. It is not yet his time."

Celia assumed that this woman must be the captain's courtesan, though she wasn't dressed in the extravagant fashion for which courtesans were known. This one wore a man's shirt and breeches. She was a commanding presence, with her fiery red hair and full lips. But surely no pirate crew included a female. Celia knew that would never be accepted. In fact, if memory served, someone had once told her that it was considered bad luck for a woman to even be on a ship.

The redhead rummaged through the medical bag and pulled out a scalpel and some small forceps. She took out some antiseptic powder and shook it onto the captain's chest. Thankfully, for his sake, he had lost consciousness. "Light that lantern and bring it here so I can better see," she said, gesturing to an unlit oil lamp.

Celia did as she was bid and increased the length of the wick to get as much light from it as possible, then propped it beside the wounded man.

The woman passed the medical bag to her. "See if you can find some surgical thread in here. We'll have to trust what I remember from assisting Poole and what you remember from the ox's ass."

CHAPTER TWO

By the time Celia had treated all the casualties aboard *Original Sin*, the sun was high in the sky. She had slept no more than fifteen minutes at a time all night, and now she was feeling the effects.

They had lost only one of the wounded, and while she had never watched a man die, she was relieved that he was the only one to expire on her watch. The corpse was moved to an area on deck with the rest of those who had perished in the battle. She had learned from Abernathy, the man with the red, bulbous nose, that their dead would soon be buried at sea.

Celia had also never sewn flesh before, but she was a specialist after tending to twenty-eight injured men—some barely grazed and some so profoundly injured that she found it hard to treat their gashes and powder burns without flinching. Somehow, she had managed to persevere.

The courtesan had been absolutely amazing. She had fished musket balls and bits of cannon shot from wounds, which she then cauterized. She had cleaned lacerations thoroughly and dressed them, removed a shattered and now-useless hand from a lad and kept him from bleeding to death, and in general kept up the spirits of the wounded and the well alike. How a common prostitute managed to command a pirate ship confused Celia, as the men seemed to obey her every order, though she might have simply been too tired to see things clearly.

As Celia sat down on the deck tiredly, the puzzling woman appeared beside her with a ladle of drinking water.

"Thirsty?" she asked, extending the large wooden dipper.

"Among other things." Celia brushed a strand of hair out of her eyes before she drank the water slowly and handed the ladle back.

"I owe you," the redhead said softly. "When the lads first brought you, I didn't think a seamstress would be helpful." She sat down next to Celia and folded her legs up beneath her. "You've proved yourself as valuable as anyone else on board. Thank you."

Celia grinned. "Well, I'd be lying if I said I wasn't as surprised as you are, er…"

"Gayle," she said. "Sorry. I'd have introduced myself sooner, but we had so much else to do. I don't have much patience for formalities."

"How did you end up here, Gayle?" Celia was truly interested.

"The captain is my father. I've lived on board *Original Sin* for nearly twelve years."

"Ah, that changes a few things." Celia mentally shifted her preconceptions. "And the men here accept you like any other seaman?"

"Hardly. My father brought me aboard when I was thirteen. Had he not been captain, the crew would more than likely have raped me repeatedly and then killed me. Father protected me and, more important, as time passed he taught me how to protect myself. I'm now the quartermaster on this ship, and senior officer as well. Churchill, the navigator, is the only man who's been on board anywhere near as long as I have and the only one I totally trust, other than Father. I've put in my time and hopefully proved myself to be a valuable crewmember."

"But what caused your father to dare have you live aboard a ship at thirteen?"

Gayle stared at the deck pensively. "Mother had never hidden from me who my father was. Every couple of years he would head back into port and see us. I had his hair color and his dark, cinnamon eyes, so I guess he felt a connection to me. When Mother finally died of consumption, Father came 'round to pay his respects. He really cared for her, you see. He knew I had no other family, nowhere else to go. I think he struggled with the dilemma but decided he could give me a better life under his protection, rather than to toss me a gold sovereign and let me fend for myself in the city. He didn't want to see me end up as a whore, and neither did I."

"Good motivation to learn how to tie knots, I suppose," Celia observed aloud.

"Verily. Father has always tried to keep a rather low profile as a raider. He says the greedy pirates and privateers are the ones who get done in. They earn a horrible reputation, and then everyone and their minions are out chasing them, hunting them down for the bounty on their heads."

"What name does your father go by? Perhaps I've heard of him."

"Madman Malvern."

Celia gasped. "I have most certainly. Didn't he cut out a man's eyeballs once and save them in a jar?" she asked, with a mixture of excitement and horror.

"Totally exaggerated. He did blind a man once by shooting him in the face with a flintlock," Gayle answered casually. "But he didn't harvest any organs as trophies. That would be rather depraved. It's amazing how legends like that get started."

"I see," Celia whispered, marveling at how blinding a man could balloon into the collection of optic booty. Wait a second—blinding? Was that what they were talking about? "So how is the captain doing?" she asked nervously, hoping to change the subject.

"I checked on him a bit ago," Gayle answered, pulling her red hair out of her eyes and refastening her hair ribbon. "His color is better, but he's still not as stable as I would like. He's lost a lot of blood. We need to get him to a place where someone can tend to him properly."

"My fiancé should be back by now. You can take your father to see him."

"Your fiancé?"

"Yes. Your crew came for him last night before they settled on me."

Gayle's eyes narrowed. "I guess you didn't realize it, but we're already bound for medical care."

"Are we? Where?"

"Did you not notice that we've been under way all night? We're heading to the Bahamas. I've some friends in New Providence who'll lend us a hand and ask no questions."

Celia scowled. "But I thought after I helped you and your crew, you would return me."

"I will," Gayle reassured her. "But I first have to ensure the crew gets suitable medical attention. I don't know your fiancé, but I doubt his willingness to aid the people who kidnapped his betrothed."

Celia contemplated the man who had hidden in his own back room, breaking wind while she—naïvely trying to save him—had been abducted.

"I doubt his willingness to aid anyone but himself," she said aloud. "He's probably not even missed me."

Gayle's deep sepia eyes warmed. "Then he is most assuredly a half-wit."

"No argument," she answered, then paused. "Unless I told you that you were being too generous. He may be closer to a quarter-wit—or even an eighth of a quarter-wit."

"He sounds like quite the prize," Gayle said. "Then you won't mind a jaunt to the islands before we return you to the mainland. Consider it a wedding gift—a proper send-off."

"I thought that type of thing was only for the groom."

Gayle beamed, which Celia found unexpectedly striking. "You'll find *Original Sin* to be a rather unconventional vessel. We're not big on propriety or decorum."

"I noticed that right after that bastard put a sack over my head."

"Very intuitive of you," Gayle retorted. "So a send-off you'll have. We'll fill your final days as an unwed woman with the kind of adventure most people only read about."

Celia sighed and became more serious. "I *would* like to let my father know that I'm all right. He must be mad with worry."

"Unfortunately, by the time we get a message back to him, you'll be standing next to the courier. We'll be in New Providence in two, perhaps two and a half, days, weather permitting. For now, you should get some sleep."

Celia looked around warily. "I'm exhausted, that's true. But I don't think I'll be able to sleep here." She leaned toward Gayle and spoke softly. "Some of the men are eyeing me a bit hungrily, shall we say. Especially that burly dog who slung me over his shoulder."

"That would be Dowd. Well, it's no wonder. That frock of yours is quite…flattering."

"Thank you," she said. "I made it myself."

"We should get you into some proper sea clothes," Gayle said as she stood. "That clingy dress won't be comfortable for you here. You can sleep in my quarters. That should offer you a bit more privacy."

Celia stood as well, for the first time feeling her body weight as a tremendous burden. "But where will you sleep?"

"I'll make temporary accommodations in Father's quarters. I'll need to tend to him anyway." She motioned to a short lad of only fourteen or so. "Hyde."

The young man shuffled over, a small bandage wrapped around his temples. "Yes, miss?"

"Hyde, take our hostage—I mean, our guest—to my quarters and set her up there. She'll need some more comfortable clothes."

"Yes, miss."

"And, Hyde," she added sternly, "no one is to disturb her there."

The lad nodded and headed toward the rear of the ship, motioning for Celia to follow him.

She muttered a word of thanks to Gayle before she wearily followed Hyde and thought how strange it was to be thanking her kidnapper. Then the notion blurred into another one concerning the engagement party she had planned to attend with Phillip this evening. What an unexpected diversion she had fallen prey to.

When they reached a door across from the captain's quarters, Hyde stopped. "Here it is, miss," he said matter-of-factly as he opened it.

The room, no more than three feet by six feet, contained only a small cot and an undersized trunk being used as a nightstand. When Hyde lit the small lantern suspended on a chain from the ceiling, little else but a battered mirror on the wall and a book by the bed was visible. "She reads," Celia whispered to herself, surprised by this anomaly.

"I'll bring you something to change into, miss."

"Thank you, Hyde."

The lad returned with a pair of button-up breeches made of beige calico, a white linen shirt, a blue sash, stockings, and some leather shoes. "The sash'll help the pants stay up should the breeches prove too large," he said. "The shoes was the smallest I could find."

Celia picked one up and held it to the arch of her foot for size. "They'll do fine, Hyde. Thank you."

"Yes'm." He left, shutting the small door.

This was definitely—what had Gayle called it? Ah, yes, "adventure." She stripped down to her chemise and fell onto the cot in exhaustion. So far she had been abducted, sewn up a bevy of wounded strangers with a large curved needle, urinated into a pipe that passed her emission quite indelicately right out the side of the ship, and been the most sleep-deprived of her life.

She extinguished the lantern and pulled the scratchy blanket over her before she succumbed to her fatigue, briefly wondering what further "adventure" lay ahead of her.

"I don't bloody like it," Caruthers erupted. "Not one bleedin' bit. It's bad enough having a woman aboard all the time," he said with his Cockney accent. "But havin' one act as cap'n—that's just fuckin' wrong."

"Tell me," Churchill replied, eyeing the ship's bosun carefully. "Who do you trust to act as captain only until he is well enough to return? Do you think any of these blokes will step back down once the captain's recovered?"

Caruthers stopped carving a tiny nude woman with freakishly large breasts from a piece of mahogany just long enough to run his fingers through his dark, braided beard. "You're sure Cap'n will recover?"

"I am. He spoke a bit earlier today. He needs a doctor, but he's not ready to leave this world."

"And he'll not want to retire once he's healed?"

"The captain once told me he'll never retire. He'll be back at the helm, mark my words. Then we can set sail to recover his hoard, just like he promised."

Caruthers seemed to mull this over a bit, and Churchill put down his sextant and studied his face. Because the ship's majority voted pirate captains into power, he needed to make sure most of the crew would support Gayle if she was going to temporarily man the helm of *Original Sin*.

"You know he'd want her to take over, at least until we make it to the Bahamas," he said. "He wants her treated like his son, not his daughter."

"Aye, though that troubles me."

Churchill smiled through his frustration. He had expected some resistance from the crew, but had hoped that Gayle's exemplary service on *Original Sin* would make her an obvious choice. "She's competent.

And you can't say she's been bad luck, mate. She's been here nearly twelve years and we've yet to lose the ship."

"Though yesterday was pretty fuckin' close. And now we've another lass on board," Caruthers complained. "How long d'ya think it'll be before the blokes have that pretty li'l thing rogered at the rail?"

"Another good reason to leave Gayle at the helm," Churchill said softly. "If these lads touch a hair on the seamstress's head, Gayle will have their balls for breakfast."

"No doubt." Caruthers cackled, waving his knife at Churchill. "All right. We'll see how she fares. The first sign of bleedin' trouble, though, and over the side she goes."

CHAPTER THREE

Gayle?" Captain Malvern weakly turned his head, searching for his daughter.

"I'm here, Father," she answered softly, wiping his brow with a damp cloth. "How are you feeling?"

He coughed forcefully and squinted to focus on her face in the dim light. "I've had worse," he rasped. "They can't finish me."

"But they like to come bloody close, don't they?" She gently checked the bandages on his chest and abdomen. "We should be in New Providence the day after tomorrow. Smitty owes us a favor or two, I reckon. He should be able to fix you up right."

"Am I that bad off?"

"You've lost a good deal of blood, and I'm worried that you've got enough bits of musket ball left inside you to cause infection," she said.

"Thanks for sugarcoating it."

"Well, if you want the bright side, I don't think any of your organs were hit. Badly, that is."

"Christ! Do you have any more good news for me? Is my head still attached?"

"For now," she answered with a sigh. "Now drink this." She lifted his head and poured a small amount of drinking water into his mouth.

"Where's the rum?" he asked, disappointed. "I'm a man in pain, for the love of Christ."

"I used all the rum on the wounded."

"And what am I? On fuckin' holiday? Where's my bloody rum?"

"It's in your wounds, old man. Don't try me." She pulled the warm cloth from his forehead, then returned it, cooled again with water. "You are the worst bloody patient anyone could have, you know that? You're even worse than Mother was."

He winced at the memory. Holding both her parents' hands into the grave must be difficult for her. "I'm sorry, lass. Perhaps I'm too old for this life."

"Strange how when I say that, it's complete horseshit. Yet when you decide you're too old, it's an epiphany."

"And if I decide to retire, what will you do?" he asked her, concerned. "You're obviously too disagreeable to settle down with anyone."

Gayle laughed. "Like father, like daughter."

"Hardly." He chuckled weakly. "Do you think you could helm this crew? Could you manage without me?"

"I have so far. I don't know if that will change after we drop you—"

"They'll want to keep things on an even keel," he said. "I've been promisin' them a hoard they won't want to pass on. If they try and mutiny on you, let them know they'll never have a piece of the Spanish Main."

"And is the hoard truth or fiction, Father? You've talked of it as long as I can remember. If you had loot like that somewhere, why haven't you gone to claim it?"

"I know my weaknesses, lass. If I had taken it thirteen years ago and divided it up amongst the crew and retired to an island, I'd be an old beggar now. I can't keep a sovereign in my palm to beat the devil."

"This is true," Gayle said softly. "So pull through this, and we'll go claim your spoils so you can retire in style."

"Aye. Don't let me die without diggin' it up, lass."

"You have a deal, old man."

Someone knocked and entered Celia's small cabin, waking her from a sleep so sound she was completely disoriented for a minute.

"What time is it?"

"Suppertime. Miss Malvern says you need to eat." Hyde deposited something on the trunk beside her, and when he lit her lantern she saw it was a bowl of some substance with a tarnished spoon in it.

As though on cue, her stomach rumbled. "Apparently, Miss

Malvern is right," she said as she sat up while modestly continuing to cover herself with the blanket. "What is that?"

"Turtle stew."

She picked up the bowl and stirred the thick contents slowly. "I see."

"Enjoy the meat while we have it," Hyde advised. "And the vegetables we nicked from the navy ship. We was runnin' low on provisions until then, so eat hearty. It's the best we've had in weeks." With that, he departed.

After a tentative taste, Celia found the stew quite appetizing. True, it wasn't the best meal she had ever had, but it was definitely the best one in the last twenty-four hours—albeit the only one in twenty-four hours. It was warm and contained some potatoes and carrots, and the turtle meat wasn't as chewy as she had initially feared.

After finishing, she stretched, got out of bed, and put on the breeches and shirt. Hyde had been correct—the sash was a godsend. She gathered her hair up with a ribbon that rested by the bed and went out into the night on the main deck.

There, five men were seated in a circle, one of them playing a concertina and the others singing a sea chantey she had never heard before.

Down in Port Royal you'll find Mary Louise;
She's the ugly old whore
who's down by the shore,
but at least she's free of disease.

She's the favorite of many, that Mary Louise.
Her great arse is as wide
as the Indian sky,
but it's guaranteed to please.

So let's raise a tankard to Mary Louise.
Just one gold piece will pay
to have her nine ways.
'Cause she likes to come in threes.

Celia's face felt flushed, and she quietly moved off starboard to gaze over the rail at the moonlight bouncing off the vast sea. Had someone predicted her future two days ago, she would never have believed any of this. But as exciting as it was, she felt a bit like chum to the sharks.

"Well, lookee here." The menacing voice made her jump. "You look a right sea-maiden, wench."

She had to force her eyes to focus in the dense darkness, but she finally recognized Dowd, seeming slightly drunk. "Um, thank you?"

"In fact, if I didn't know better, I'd swear you were a mermaid." He lurched toward her, and she instinctively retreated until her back was up against the railing. "'Cept you ain't got no tail, do ya?" He moved toward her again. "Do ya have a tail, lassie? Lemme see."

Celia brought her arms up to push him away and braced for the impact of his hulking body, but it didn't come.

"Dowd." Gayle stood just a few yards from them. Her cutlass was drawn, but it was too dark to make out her expression. "I don't think you'll be handling any of that particular tail tonight," she said calmly.

Dowd raised his arms in surrender. "Easy, now, miss. I was havin' some harmless fun." He slowly faced her.

"Hmm. I'd have to question your understanding of both 'harmless' and 'fun.' We may need to get you a lexicon." She slowly lowered her cutlass. "Go find something else to abuse, Dowd. This one's off-limits to you."

"Savin' her for yourself, are you?" he mumbled as he skulked away.

Celia found Dowd's remark odd, but her sudden amnesty would not let her delve deeper into its mystery. "Thank you, Gayle. You have extraordinary timing."

"Most fortunate for you," she answered, sheathing her weapon. "You should probably not be out here. I'm sure Dowd isn't the only sailor who wants a handful or two of you."

"But I changed into the men's clothes, as you suggested. Surely they wouldn't want a handful of, well, of this."

Gayle smiled. "You might be surprised at how fetching you are. And you might also be surprised at how very long we have been at sea."

"Ah, I see. So am I to stay in your cabin until we return to Florida?"

"Hopefully that will not be necessary. When we dock in New Providence, the men should have some time to—"

"Indulge in some of their excesses?" Celia suggested tactfully.

"I was going to say 'buy some whores,'" Gayle clarified. "But your statement was much more elegant."

"New Providence sounds as though it will be a unique experience."

"Oh, for you it will. Don't worry. I'll keep an eye on you while we're in port. It's your engagement send-off, remember?" Gayle guided Celia back toward her quarters.

"No matter how hard I try to forget," Celia said, exhaling slowly to quiet her nerves. "Did you just say I looked fetching?" she asked, attempting to speak of happier things.

Gayle's face lit up. "That I did."

Celia spent the next two days sequestered in that tiny cabin, leaving only briefly when she found it absolutely necessary. She slept, ate what Hyde brought her, and tried to read Gayle's book about death and the afterlife, though she found it rather morbid. She counted every visible plank more than once. Therefore, a mixture of relief and trepidation filled her when, thanks to some rather robust winds, *Original Sin* finally moored at a small New Providence dock. She steeled her nerves and tried to mentally prepare herself to enter "drunk and dirty whoreville," as she now referred to it.

When Gayle appeared in the cabin doorway and salaciously asked, "Ready, miss?" Celia's stomach lurched.

"I imagine so."

"Splendid," she replied. "Take this." She handed her a small cutlass and sheath that seemed quite dangerous.

"What am I to do with this? I don't know the first thing about fighting."

Gayle nodded. "You and I realize that, but the rest of the blokes in town don't. It's there to be seen, but not to be drawn. You follow?"

"I suppose." She took the weapon and stared at it in confusion.

"It goes across your shoulder like this," Gayle instructed, draping the weapon over her.

"Are you sure I shouldn't just remain here and wait for you?" Celia suggested.

"You want to stay here on the ship with the twenty-five or so men we're leaving on board while I go into town?"

After a brief silence Celia asked, "And how do I walk with the cutlass on?"

Dowd and Abernathy were tasked with helping Captain Malvern get into town. They created a makeshift litter, and Gayle and Celia accompanied them past the dock and into a seedy-looking nearby tavern, whose conspicuously handmade sign over the door read The Bountiful Teat. They used a rear entrance, with a blanket covering Captain Malvern entirely, so it looked as though they were simply transporting some black-market goods. No one questioned them, much to Celia's surprise and profound relief.

Inside a dank back room, they met a slight, gray-haired man with spectacles and a beard that contrasted with his very blue eyes.

"Smitty," Gayle called.

"Gayle," he said, seeming surprised and glancing at the covered litter. "Who is it?"

She pulled the blanket off the captain's face. "It's Father."

"Holy Mother of God," he muttered. "Bring him over here." He motioned toward a small cot. Dowd and Abernathy deposited the captain where they were instructed, then stood back as Smitty began to examine him.

Gayle knelt beside Smitty. "He received some musket balls to the belly and chest. We tried to get them all out, but I'm not sure we succeeded. He lost a lot of blood."

"How long has it been?" Smitty asked, raising the unconscious captain's eyelids and studying the inside of them intently.

"Three days."

"And has he been conscious at all?"

"Aye," she answered. "On and off."

"And can he be left with me here? For a few days—or longer, if needed?"

"Done," Gayle said matter-of-factly. "Can you save him, Smitty?"

"I hope so, lass," he replied softly. "Go have a drink inside and give me some time to examine his wounds. I'll come find you when I know more."

Gayle kissed his cheek and stood up. "Thanks, Smitty. I'll have a drink ready for you."

Smitty winked. "Bourbon, if you please."

Gayle motioned for Celia, Dowd, and Abernathy to follow her to the front of The Bountiful Teat.

"Should I even ask how this place got its name?" Celia whispered as they entered.

"Probably not," Gayle answered, surveying the folk in the tavern guardedly.

They all settled around a rectangular table against the west wall, and after a few minutes a beautiful serving wench with chocolate-colored skin and deep emerald eyes approached.

"And what can I get—Gayle?"

Gayle looked at the woman with what Celia interpreted as feigned surprise. "Desta. How are you?" The words were pleasant enough, but she didn't sound very sincere.

"Much better now," she answered huskily, tracing Gayle's shoulder with her index finger. "It's been a long time, my love."

Celia stared unblinkingly at this very open display. She scrutinized Abernathy and Dowd, who not only didn't seem shocked, but almost indifferent, albeit slightly amused.

Gayle, though, seemed flustered indeed. "We need four rums and one bourbon."

"Whatever you desire," Desta said, and vanished.

"I wish I had women like that throwin' themselves at me," Abernathy commented to no one in particular.

"No, my friend. You just think you do," Gayle said.

When Desta returned with the tankards on a tray, everyone was silent. She laid the drinks out first to the men, then to Gayle. Finally, she eyed Celia. "And who is this?" she asked Gayle as she carelessly slung Celia's rum in front of her.

Before Gayle had a chance to respond, Celia announced her own name defiantly and locked eyes with Desta.

"Desta," Gayle broke in, "I need some sailors. We lost a lot of men and took some damage the other night."

"I might be able to find you a few recruits."

"How many and how soon?"

"Maybe a dozen, tonight."

"Good. Have them meet me here," Gayle instructed in rather hushed tones. "I'll need all you can get."

Desta nodded and disappeared again.

Celia brought the rum to her lips and drank. "By all that is hallowed," she cursed, her entire larynx ablaze. "This is rum?"

Dowd laughed, and Celia assumed he was probably recalling the other night and enjoying her discomfort. "They make it here in the backroom," he explained with a snort. "It's not for the weak of heart."

"Not a drinker?" Gayle queried, a twinkle in her eye.

"I have had wine and claret before. But nothing that burned as this does. This is like acid," she gasped.

"Shall we have Desta bring you something else?" Gayle sounded as if she was half joking, but Celia wasn't certain.

Celia set her jaw firmly. She refused to be the only one at the table unable to choke this noxious shit down. And she was certainly not ready to be a laughingstock in front of Gayle's rather antagonistic doxy. "No. I will drink this, thank you." She took another, larger sip, and when her vision blurred slightly, she merely blinked the room back into focus. She could do this, she reasoned, and hopefully it wouldn't leave her paralyzed, or brain-damaged.

Abernathy picked up his tankard and slammed the contents back in a lengthy series of swallows. He ordered another drink by rapping the bottom of the now-empty tankard lightly on the table to get the tavern keep's attention.

"Pace yourself," Gayle warned him. "We'll be here quite some time. I don't want to have to carry you back to *Original Sin* again."

"Again?" Celia asked.

"Abernathy has a bit of a problem with his legs," she explained. "Once he's passed out, they don't work anymore."

All at the table found this quite amusing, and as Celia laughed softly, she marveled at the way the inside of her nose burned, as though she were breathing fire. She mulled this over for a moment. The others would tell her if that were the case, wouldn't they? To convince herself that they certainly would, and that she need not flee from the tavern screaming madly, she nonchalantly held her fingers in front of her nostrils to make sure they were emitting no heat. To her relief, they weren't.

"So how long will we be staying here?" she asked, taking a much smaller sip of rum this time. If she didn't want this toxin to permanently blind her, she needed to slow down.

Gayle also took a swig. "We'll probably leave the captain here with Smitty, though I'm not sure for how long. We'll spend the day letting the lads unwind in town, tonight I'll pick up a few additions to the crew, and we'll head to a remote site to careen tomorrow."

"Careen?"

Abernathy, having no refill on rum yet to occupy him, explained, "We make land somewhere. Beach the ship and repair and clean her."

"We'll also need to restock provisions for the next voyage," Gayle added. "We can't stay in New Providence too long."

"Worried the authorities might catch up with you?" Celia whispered, terribly excited by all this illicitness.

"I think the lass is more worried about Desta catching up with her," Dowd said with a snort.

At that, Abernathy also began to laugh, just as Desta appeared from the kitchen— as though conjured by their words—to refill his tankard. "Thanks, lass," he muttered, obviously elated as he communed with his beloved liquid. Celia thought she could actually see the blood vessels in his nose burst as he drank.

Celia also watched Desta gaze wantonly at Gayle, clearly trying to catch her eye.

"I need to find the privy," Gayle announced, rising from the table and quickly disappearing. Desta stomped from the table in an obvious snit, heading in the opposite direction.

"What's going on with them?" Celia asked, almost without thinking.

"There's a bit of a story there," Abernathy replied, squinting his bloodshot eyes and rubbing his nose. "I think the tavern wench wants to be more than just a tumble to our girl. She must have been pining for her, waiting for *Original Sin* to come back into port."

"Aye," echoed Dowd. "Fighting's not the only thing Gayle learned from her old man, if ya get my meanin'."

"I don't think I do," Celia confessed, crinkling her brow as she tried to solve this riddle.

"The lass is as accomplished at wenchin' as any bloke on board," Dowd clarified.

"Better, I think," Abernathy added, nodding.

"I can't explain it meself, since she doesn't have the proper equipment. And I'll be damned if I know exactly what she does with all these women," Dowd said, taking a swig of rum. "But I'd pay a sovereign to watch."

"So she's quite popular with the ladies?" Celia inquired, trying to work this all out in her head. Somehow she had always pictured women who had relations with other women as mannish and big, probably because that's how Conchata Covas had been. Everyone in San Augustin had known Conchata had no real interest in men, other than adopting most of their mannerisms. The sudden notion that two very feminine and attractive women had, well, been in congress with each other intrigued her and seemed quite exotic.

"If I got but half the wenches that sidled up to her, I'd die a happy man." Dowd sighed.

Abernathy leaned toward the table and spoke in hushed tones. "I'll wager that Desta here thinks you're our girl's new bed warmer."

Dowd laughed. "Aye, you'd better watch that she's not poisoning your rum."

Celia contemplated her tankard and frowned. "How will I know the difference?"

When Gayle returned to the table, all of them were still laughing, and she immediately appeared suspicious. "I see you're all getting along," she remarked. She stared at the three of them, but none of them commented on what was so entertaining.

At that point, Smitty arrived and sat, pulling his tankard of bourbon to him and politely sipping it.

"Well?" Gayle asked. "How is he?"

"Not too bad off."

Her posture relaxed in evident relief. "No?"

"No. Poole did a fine job of patching him up."

"Poole's dead," Dowd muttered.

"'Tis a true shame," Smitty remarked, crossing himself in reverence. "But I see you've a decent doctor to take his place."

"Actually, we haven't. The seamstress here and I worked on him," Gayle explained, pointing to Celia.

"Is that so?" he asked, seeming surprised. "Well, you both did a damned fine job of it. He's quite weak, but I see no problems with his wounds that a fortnight of rest ashore can't cure."

"That's a relief," Celia commented, taking another sip of rum. She supposed it wasn't altogether a horrid concoction.

"Just the same, we need a doctor, Smitty. Any ideas?" Gayle asked.

He removed his spectacles. "I might have a notion or two. I'll discreetly look about town."

"Well, as always, Smitty, you've been a great help," Gayle said, beaming. "You don't mind watching Father?"

"Consider it done, lass. I owe you a bigger debt than this."

"We need provisions," she added.

Smitty motioned toward the barkeep. "Arrange it all with him. He won't cheat you."

Gayle assessed Abernathy and Dowd. "Can I trust you two to make sure it all gets loaded back on *Original Sin*?"

"Of course, miss," Abernathy answered. "I won't be too drunk for that until much later. We'll take care of it soon, so it won't be a problem."

Gayle laughed. "How can you argue with logic like that? Come along, Celia. We've other errands to run."

"Do we?" She stumbled slightly as she tried to rise.

"Without a doubt. There is much to be done."

Celia felt flushed, but was ready for a thrill. She had been confined for days and couldn't deny that she found the Bahamas, the salty talk — even the burn of the rum, utterly exhilarating. She was eager to see more.

CHAPTER FOUR

S o, why does Smitty say that he owes you so much?" Celia asked once she and Gayle were out in the street, on their way to the market.

"Years ago, he was the doctor aboard *Original Sin*. When he had seen all the death and dismemberment he could stomach, he told my father he wanted to be done with it all. Usually a sailor doesn't give up on the sea. Rather, the sea claims the sailor first. But Father not only encouraged him to leave the ship, he even loaned him the money to buy that tavern."

"The Bountiful Teat. He picked that name himself?"

"He said it came to him in a dream." Gayle grinned. "I told him I have dreams like that all the time. I just interpret them differently." When Celia stumbled a bit, Gayle asked, "Are you all right?"

"I'd probably be doing better if I could feel my feet."

"When did this start?"

"About halfway through that tankard. Now I can see why it's such a popular drink. I feel all warm and tingly."

Gayle laughed and lightly grasped her elbow. "I'd wager you're right, but I doubt you'll get the lads to sing the praises of feeling 'warm and tingly.'"

"What are we off to buy?" Celia stared at the vast open-air market ahead of them. She had never seen so many vendors in one place.

"Well, good seamstress, I was hoping you'd not mind helping me pick out some osnaburg to use for sails."

"I'm no expert on a fabric that coarse," Celia said, "but I'll help you as best I can."

"You are by far the most agreeable hostage I've ever taken."

"And you are a very pleasant captor. This is hardly the sea trip I had dreamt of, but I do appreciate the fact that you've kept me safe. You hear such terrible stories about pirates."

"Most aren't true, but we are a despicable lot. Don't be fooled into thinking we aren't."

Celia stopped and cocked her head to the side. "And do you ravish young women? Should I be on my guard with you?"

"That is one thing I will not steal, madam," she said in a low, husky voice. "I only take what is freely offered."

"I see."

"Come along, then. We've fabric to buy." Gayle grasped Celia's hand firmly and pulled her toward the market.

When they reached the tent of the fabric merchant, Celia shouted, "Look at this one," pulling out a bolt of gorgeous sapphire-colored silk. "And this." She fingered a plush saffron fabric next to it with a striking floral pattern. "These are incredible."

Gayle squinted apologetically at the merchant. "A bit too much rum," she explained, prompting the stocky man to laugh. "I need some osnaburg."

"I've a reasonable one over here," he said, holding up a heavy white linen. "I have a lot of call for it."

"How much?"

"Well, how much did you need? The more you buy, the less it is per bolt."

"And how many bolts can I get for this?" She produced a gold ring with a large ruby inset.

The merchant, used to haggling for objects other than currency, took the ring and examined it closely. It was exquisite, and the stone appeared flawless. "Ten."

Gayle smiled knowingly. "That ring is worth a bit more than that, old man." She glanced over at Celia. "You sell clothing, yes?"

"Yes." He was clearly disappointed in his bluffing skills.

"I need a few sets of breeches and shirts that will fit her."

He squinted over Gayle's shoulder, sizing Celia. "That can be arranged."

"And I'd like some for me as well. Something practical, yet attractive."

He sized her up with his hand on his chin. "How about some black velvet? I have a pair of breeches made of it that would suit you nicely."

"That sounds interesting," she said. He held up a few shirts and she picked the three she liked the most, then chose a few for Celia. "And I want that blue silk and that yellow stuff there."

"Done," he said, without putting pen to paper.

"Have you a boy who can transport this to my ship?"

The man spun quickly and clapped his hands twice. "Frederick."

A lad of about thirteen appeared, dirty and disheveled. "Aye?"

"I've cargo for you, lad."

Gayle whispered, "And there's a tip in it for you if it all gets there intact." She knew too well that frequently merchants instructed their own delivery boys to filch some of the items, or to simply short-ship them altogether. Frederick winked at her in tacit agreement and began to load a wheelbarrow.

"Come along, Celia," she called, ready to make the trip with Frederick back to the ship.

"Oh," she said. "I'm sorry. Did you want me to help pick out your linen?"

"You missed that part. I didn't want to break your reverie. But I managed quite well on my own."

Celia frowned. "You're not much into looking about, are you?"

"There's no need to shop when you know what you want."

They walked with purpose back to *Original Sin,* and at the dock, two crewmen helped Frederick carry the cargo on board.

"The sailcloth goes below," Gayle directed. "Put the rest in the captain's cabin." Then she gave Frederick his promised piece of eight, and his freckled face lit up as he folded his thin fingers around it.

"Do you need any help on this ship, miss?"

"Are you offering your services, Frederick? Do you wish a life at sea?"

He nodded, probably dreaming of plunder and battle.

"And what would your mother say?" Gayle asked in concern.

"I don't know where she is." He took on a soulful expression. "I haven't seen her or my brother in nearly two years."

"And your father?"

"Don't know him." The skinny boy now looked grim.

"And won't the merchant miss you?"

"Not bloody likely. Tons of lads could take my place."

Gayle considered his situation. "If you join the crew, you'll be lower than a mite on a barnacle. You'll have to clean the deck, scrape the hull—unexciting tasks."

"Aye." His red hair whipped in the wind. "Ma'am, are you the cap'n of this here ship?"

"Acting captain, aye."

"I never heard o' such a thing."

She shook her head. "Me either. Now come aboard and get to work." With that, he scrabbled up the gangway and stood gawking at the deck. "Hyde," she called.

"Aye, miss?"

"This is young Frederick, who has just joined our crew. See to it he finds a bed and some work."

"Aye, miss." Hyde motioned for Frederick to follow him.

"Nichols," she called.

A young, fair-haired sailor appeared. "Aye, ma'am?"

"Dowd and Abernathy are at Smitty's tavern. I purchased some provisions there. Make sure they actually get on board." The gangly sailor laughed, displaying a number of missing teeth. "I wouldn't be surprised if they were already half naked and dancing like Salome," she added with a wink.

"Aye." Nichols was still chuckling. "Ah, a wheelbarrow," he said when he spotted Frederick's abandoned contrivance.

"Aye, we brought that just for you," she said, slapping him on the back good-naturedly. "Grab a few of the men and head over there. Make sure you get some fruit." After he left, Gayle noticed that Celia still was a touch flushed. "Are you all right?"

"A bit woozy." She leaned on a pylon.

"And are your feet still numb?"

Celia stomped the dock loudly. "No."

"Perhaps you should stay away from rum for the rest of the voyage."

"An idea with merit," she muttered, rubbing her forehead.

"I know just the thing to sober you up."

"Hmm?"

"A visit to the bathhouse."

"Mmm, this feels lovely," Celia purred.

"I told you. Isn't your head clearer?"

"Definitely. I've never heard of a place like this." Her eyes were shut tightly and her body submerged to her neck.

"Well, they cater to those of us at sea. We don't get many baths, so when we're in port, we try to indulge as often as we can. Or at least I do."

A short, plump woman appeared in the doorway and Gayle motioned her in. She rested her tray, which held two cups, near the large bath, then scurried away.

Gayle pulled herself out of the bath and unabashedly stood there completely nude. "Ah, the coffee has arrived." She picked up a cup and offered it to Celia. "Drink this. It will do you a world of good."

Celia blinked to ensure she wasn't imagining the very wet and very naked pirate standing before her.

"Um, thank you," she stammered, awkwardly taking the cup without directly ogling Gayle's unclad form. Though she had assumed Gayle would make sexual advances toward her in the bathhouse, Gayle had paid her virtually no attention—at least not *that* type of attention.

In fact, Celia had gone out of her way to take a little extra time to disrobe and had lingered a smidgeon before slowly settling into the steaming water, just to be cruel—to show her what she couldn't have. Yet Gayle hadn't even seemed to notice her nudity. Was her naked body so freakishly misshapen that it had immediately turned Gayle's stomach, and only pity had kept her from visibly shrinking away from the horrible defect?

She sipped coffee and frowned as she mulled on this possibility.

"Is it too bitter?" Gayle asked, noting her expression.

"Hmm? Oh, no. It's fine."

Gayle ambled away bewildered and finished the other cup of coffee, then leisurely lowered herself back into the bath. Celia was still staring into space, glowering, and Gayle sighed. Perhaps she should return to The Bountiful Teat and visit Desta. Even if in some ways she was a complete lunatic, as curiously so many women she met were, at least her sexual attraction was evident. Gayle had no doubt that Desta wanted her. Spending all this time with someone so uninterested in her, and apparently not even curious enough about sex to be uncomfortable being naked with her, depressed and frustrated her.

After all, she had assured Celia that she never forced herself on any woman, which was true. But this nymph was a mystery. Her body was as gorgeous as she had imagined it to be, and her face and cerulean eyes so arresting that she could still see them clearly when she closed her own. She wanted nothing more than to traverse the warm water between them and caress and kiss her.

But Celia only sipped her coffee and scowled.

They sighed in unison.

Celia had to admit that the bath, as well as fresh clothes—which Gayle had the great foresight to bring—made her feel profoundly better. Her thoughts were no longer murky, and the ground wasn't spinning anymore. She still felt a bit out of place in breeches and a shirt, but they were actually quite comfortable.

She and Gayle strode back toward *Original Sin* saying very little. Gayle had changed into some fitted leather breeches and a pale blue, billowy cotton shirt and looked every bit the buccaneer with her leather baldric draped over her shoulder supporting her cutlass and her knee-high boots. Her strides were long and purposeful.

"Psst, pretty child."

An old gypsy woman motioned Celia over to where she sat in a wicker chair under a large mahogany tree.

"Me?" she asked.

"Aye." The rotund woman beckoned her closer. "I can tell your future."

Celia studied the woman's tanned face skeptically. "Oh, really?" She propped a hand upon her hip.

"You are a disbelieving sort," she announced with a thick accent of indiscernible origin.

Celia nodded slowly. "You might say that."

"Let me see your palm, child."

"My palm?"

"I will prove to you my gift is genuine. If you do not believe after that, it costs you nothing."

Celia extended her right palm.

The old woman lightly grasped it and scrutinized it. "You are a woman of great skill and cunning."

"I am?"

"Aye. And your beauty has brought you vast admiration from men."

Feeling rather frumpy, Celia decided to go ahead and ask. "Just from men?"

The fortune-teller seemed confused for a moment and then spied Gayle, who was approaching. "No, my child. Women admire your beauty as well."

Celia hastily pulled the other chair up and sat opposite her. "What else do you see?"

"For a piece of eight I can tell you your future."

"But I haven't any money," she explained, disappointed.

"I have," came a voice from over Celia's shoulder, where Gayle held up a silver coin. She tossed it to the fortune-teller. "Here, unleash the mystic spirits."

The woman snatched the coin from the air with astounding deftness. Before Celia could blink, she had swiftly slid it into her apron pocket and again focused on Celia's palm, tracing the lines on the skin with her index finger.

"You are lost, child," she finally volunteered. "You seek to find your way."

"Do you mean my way back home?"

"No, you seek your purpose—your center. You want more for your life than what you have been promised."

"What about my marriage? Will it be happy?"

Gayle leaned against a tree and crossed her arms. This should prove interesting, she thought.

The fortune-teller stared further at the lines of Celia's palm. "He does not love you. He never will."

Celia exhaled sharply. "Couldn't you have said that a bit more tactfully?"

"I thought you wanted to know your future. If these are things you do not wish to hear—"

"I didn't say I didn't wish to hear them," Celia said. "But I'd prefer that you word them in a way that won't make me weep. Does that cost extra?"

"You should not marry this man. You must seek your soul mate—your true love. But first you will have to endure many trials."

"What kind of trials?"

"Water, wild and fleet. A royal tempest's gale. Golden fire in twilight. A fallen woman abducted by seven sisters," she explained mysteriously.

"What the hell does all that mean?"

The fortune-teller glared. "Sometimes I get only flashes of images. I cannot always explain them fully."

"Well, you certainly had no problems explaining fully that Phillip doesn't love me."

"I can't pick what details come to me, child."

"Celia," Gayle said, greatly amused. "Can we please go, before this comes to blows?"

"That depends. Do you have any more cryptic nonsense for me?" she asked the gypsy woman.

"If you do not believe, there is nothing more I can tell you." Celia stood, seeming thoroughly disappointed. "But know this, child. Everything I've told you is true."

Gayle grinned. "And do you predict she will realize that someday?"

The fortune-teller calmly closed her eyes. "Aye, she will."

CHAPTER FIVE

Celia and Gayle rejoined the crew of *Original Sin* long enough to ensure that Nichols had overseen the unloading of all the provisions, as instructed. Gayle checked the ship's hold and had the cooper inspect and properly stow all casks of wine, water, and rum. She also had all the water casks "sweetened" with a small amount of rum and explained that without it the water would become tainted and undrinkable at sea. She referred to this as "grog."

At her command, the crew had been organizing and cleaning the areas below decks, and Celia was impressed with how orderly everything now was. Perhaps the notion of pirates being filthy, slothful villains was merely scuttlebutt, she thought.

Gayle inspected the food that was brought on board and made sure it included not only the fare that would keep u good while, but also an ample amount of fresh fruit and various types of meats. This, she said, was to keep everyone healthy. Too many stale biscuits tended to make everyone ill-tempered.

The group of crewmen who had been allowed to wreak mayhem on the town when they first docked was back on board, and the next shift had spilled into the city. They accompanied Gayle and Celia to The Bountiful Teat, though these men were more interested in seeing the bottom of a tankard and the bosom of a willing wench than in the additional crewmembers Gayle was seeking there. She entered the tavern at Celia's side and surveyed the crowd. "Hmm, it appears that Desta made good on her promise."

"What, has she sacrificed a goat to you in worship?" Celia quipped.

"She seems to have found us some new recruits. Is someone still grousing because her fiancé will never love her?" Gayle smiled fiendishly.

"Well, at least…I may have a fiancé who doesn't— Oh, sod it," Celia finally spat out in frustration, then walked over to a table and sat down in a snit.

Gayle couldn't stop laughing long enough to comment on Celia's behavior.

"Are you the captain who seeks crewmembers?" a young man with a Scottish accent asked.

"Aye," she answered brightly, scrutinizing both him and the shorter fellow who was standing behind him timidly. "And what skills do you have?"

"We are carpenters, taught by our father."

"That's a very useful occupation. Have you spent any real time at sea?"

"Aye," the young man said. "My brother and I were on the *Venture*, a sloop sunk off the coast of Rum Quay."

"Sunk by whom?"

"The *Corona d'Oro*," the brother said in disgust.

"Captain Santiago," she muttered.

"Aye," the brothers answered in unison.

"Welcome aboard, lads." She slapped the first young man lightly on the shoulder. "You're just in time for tomorrow's careening. You'll each receive a share and a half of any acquired loot." The two men looked quite pleased with this arrangement and nodded. Sailors with skills like carpentry and navigation weren't easy to find, so they warranted a larger share of any collected booty. "The ship is *Original Sin*. She's the three-masted square-rigger moored at the westernmost pier. Be on her by midnight."

"Thank ye, Cap'n. We will," the young Scotsman said, as he and his brother went to the bar.

Smitty rolled a cask of mead in from the back room and Gayle asked him quietly, "How is the old man faring?"

"Very well." He hefted the cask upright and motioned for the barman to open it. "I moved him upstairs, and he's been in and out of consciousness."

"Excellent."

He wiped the sweat off his forehead with a handkerchief. "Are you ready to meet the majority of your recruits?"

She surveyed the group of dark-skinned men in the tavern. "Maroons?"

"Aye." He poured both her and himself a tankard of freshly tapped mead. "This lot came over on an English slave ship, but somehow managed to make a break. They've been ensconced here in New Providence, waiting for a ship to come through that won't turn right around and sell them back into slavery." He took a long drink. "I assured them they could trust you."

"Do any of them speak English?"

"A few speak some broken English and will translate as best they can for the rest."

Celia sullenly watched Gayle and Smitty as they crossed the room to talk to a group of black men. She assumed they were potential recruits, but was only mildly curious.

A slightly plump, blond serving wench approached her table and deposited a glass of red wine in front of her. "From Captain Malvern," she explained. "And she requests that you drink it slowly."

Celia chuckled. "That rancorous tart." She felt better as she got an idea. "Tell me, what do you have on the menu tonight? I'm famished."

"Well, we have a lovely fish stew."

"Hmm. I want something a bit—"

"Lighter?"

"More expensive. What's the costliest thing on the menu? I'll take two."

By the time Gayle returned to the table where Celia was seated, she saw two large plates with cooked squabs, piled high with fixings. Celia was slowly dissecting a bird, while the other portion sat in front of an empty seat waiting to be consumed.

"Oh, thanks for the wine," Celia said, raising her glass in a disingenuous salute. "I've been taking small sips with my supper, as you instructed."

"Hmm, and this other platter?" She eyed a fowl with a large, two-pronged fork jutting from its thorax.

"I ordered it for you," Celia explained. "You must be half starved." She took another bite and flashed an insincere smile.

"This is quite elaborate." Gayle sat at the table and clunked her tankard of mead down.

"Well, I thought the captain should have only the best."

"And the highest priced, perhaps?"

"I was only thinking of you," she lied.

"No doubt. Me and what I might have to pay for. Very nice."

"It's quite tasty. Worth every farthing."

A small, sinewy woman, wearing men's clothing and a bandana over her black hair, stepped up to the table. "Pardon, miss," she said. "Are you Captain Malvern?"

"Aye." Gayle poked at a squab with the fork.

The woman pulled up a chair across from her and sat down. "I'm Molly McCarthy, and I've come to join your crew."

Gayle fixed her gaze on her and appraised her. "Have you?"

"Aye, Cap'n. I'm a first-rate sailor."

"On what ship have you sailed?"

Molly shifted in her chair, seeming uncomfortable. "Both the *Opal* and *Bon Vivant*."

"Those ships let a woman on board?" Gayle questioned, her mouth full of overpriced squab.

"They didn't know I was a woman."

"What?" Celia coughed, nearly choking on her wine.

"Ah." Gayle nodded. "And when they found you out, did they cast you off?"

"Aye," Molly replied. "But I was a bloody good sailor—better than most men on board."

"I believe you. You look to be made of sturdy stuff. Can you fight?"

"Like a fuckin' she-beast."

"And have you ever manned cannon?"

"A time or two."

"Well, Molly. I suppose if you are ever going to have an opportunity to sail the seas as the woman you are, it will be aboard *Original Sin*."

"I thought that was your ship in the harbor. She's a right beauty."

"Be on her by midnight. You'll get one share of any earnings." Gayle tipped back her mead and finished it off.

"Thank you, Cap'n," the young woman said as she stood. "When I heard you was here, I thought I'd found my chance."

Gayle nodded and started eating again. She flagged the serving wench down for a refill of mead as Molly left the tavern with almost a spring in her step.

"You mean to tell me that girl disguised herself as a man on those ships?" Celia finally asked, trying to keep her voice politely low.

"It happens more than you would think."

"But the crew is all living below deck together. There's no privacy at all. How would you be able to keep a secret like that?"

"I'm sure it's a challenge. But you have to take into account the will of a woman who's made up her mind. If all she wants to do is sail, she'll find a way to do it. Molly was lucky."

"How so?"

"Most women on ships are killed when they're discovered. Some believe that women are bad luck at sea. Sailors are a superstitious lot, you know. On most ships she'd have been rogered at the rail and thrown overboard. The fact that she survived two crews who discovered her fraudulence is a testament to her strength."

"Rogered at the rail?"

"Raped by everyone on board."

"What a charming lot you pirates are. Can I get some more wine, please?" she asked the wench who had arrived with a refill of mead.

"I warned you," Gayle said, taking a drink. "There are things about buccaneers that will turn your bloody stomach."

"And how do you keep your crew in check?"

"Discipline, mixed with reckless spending."

"Meaning?"

"The crew needs to know exactly what's expected. I don't bring anyone on board who's not ready to put in a solid day's work. I let them know that fighting or stealing from each other will get them keelhauled. They'd get the same if they abused you, or Molly."

Celia winced. "Do I dare ask what keelhauling is?"

"We attach a rope to you and pull you underwater along the keel of the ship. It's a very long ship, you see, and the barnacles will more than likely rip the flesh off your bones—if you don't drown while you're down there."

"Mother of God. How do you live like this? You can't truly enjoy it."

Gayle seemed to ponder this question for a moment. "Bits of it I do, I must confess. That's where the reckless spending comes in. The men are more likely to pull their weight and not be insubordinate when they know there are definite advantages to life on board."

"Like a place at the head of the queue for the rapes?"

Gayle sighed. "We haven't had any rapes on *Original Sin*. I mean advantages like good wages, gambling, drinking, and whoring when we're in port. If you never let the lads blow off steam, they'll get frustrated and wonder why they're even aboard. The trick to maintaining a good, dependable crew is keeping them content."

"Captain?" The deep male voice drew Gayle's attention and she snapped her head up.

"Aye?"

"I'm told your ship needs a doctor," the fair-haired fellow said. She surreptitiously motioned for him to sit at the table and he hastily did so.

"You're a doctor?" Gayle inquired.

"I am. Dr. Keegan, at your service." He glanced to Celia and stared at her oddly with his mouth open, then turned white and began to stutter. "Uh, you can call me James," he said to only Celia, as he eyed her in obvious distraction.

Gayle cleared her throat, calling his attention back to her immediately. "I'm Captain Malvern," she began. "This is Celia Pierce."

James looked at Celia again and seemed unable to speak.

"Um, hello," Celia said, acting uncomfortable. James smiled back but said nothing.

"James," Gayle bellowed to distract him. "Are you here for a reason or is this visit purely social?"

His face darkened. "Apologies. I am here for a very serious reason."

"You wish to join my crew as its doctor," Gayle fed him, hoping her words would spark his brain back into activity.

"I do."

Gayle frowned as she scrutinized him further. "You appear to be affluent, James. What brings you here? What are you seeking? Surely not the life of a buccaneer."

"I have traveled here from Bristol. What I seek is my sister, who was abducted by a sailor on a British vessel. I mean to get her back."

"How?" Celia asked.

"I'm here to offer you my services as your ship's surgeon. You need not even pay me. I simply ask that you help me follow this vile ruffian to Kingston, Jamaica, where he is headed with her. I am told they were here in New Providence but two days ago."

Gayle studied this tall, somewhat pale man. His blond hair was immaculately coiffed, and his clothes were stylish and costly. He looked to be in his early thirties and was not offensive to the eye, but perhaps too fragile to enjoy life on the open sea. "What ship is she on?" She took another sip of mead.

"It was called the *Pleiades*."

The name registered with Gayle immediately, and she struggled not to inhale the liquid into her lungs.

"Do you know it?" Celia asked.

"No."

"What is it, then?"

"Pleiades," Gayle repeated. "The name of the constellation also known as the Seven Sisters."

Celia looked confused, then very disturbed. "Are you serious? Is that true?"

"Aye."

"What was it the gypsy woman said exactly?" Celia asked.

"Something about a fallen woman taken by seven sisters." Gayle turned to James. "Your sister," she began hesitantly.

"Anne."

"How was she nabbed?"

James took a deep breath. "Somehow she was among a group of courtesans that this horrid cur, this Captain Red McQueen, abducted."

Gayle frowned. "I know the name. He's a British slaver." She shook her head in puzzlement. "I'm sorry, but where was your sister that she was among a group of prostitutes?"

James lowered his gaze sheepishly, focusing on the table. "A bordello," he whispered.

"Is your sister a whore?" Celia asked loudly.

"Of course not," he said defensively. "She was clearly a victim of misfortune and licentiousness."

"We're not even safe in our own whorehouses anymore," Gayle remarked wryly. "What is this world coming to?"

"I assure you," he insisted softly, peering around the room, "she was obviously duped, or there was some confusion afoot."

Celia put her chin on her hand. "So your sister merely wandered into a whorehouse?"

Gayle made eye contact with her. "I've been known to wander into whorehouses from time to time."

Celia bit her lower lip. "Hmm, good point."

"It would certainly explain it," she said with a shrug.

"Though, were she truly a fallen woman—"

"It is a remarkable coincidence."

"If that is what it is," Celia added, "did the gypsy not say that I would soon have cause to believe what she had foretold?"

James looked as if the two of them had started speaking a foreign language. His eyes darted from one woman to the other.

"Aye, she did."

"Where did you plan to travel next?" Celia queried.

"Well, if you remember correctly, I planned to take you back to your family in the Florida territory."

"And if I told you I would rather search for the missing whore?"

"Hey," shouted James, but neither Celia nor Gayle acknowledged him. "I told you, it's simply a bungle."

Gayle looked into Celia's eyes and became lost in their azure depths. "I do need a surgeon."

Celia grinned. "I would hate to live my life wondering how things would be different if I had listened to the fortune-teller."

"Especially if her other prediction is true." Gayle finally turned to James. "Welcome aboard *Original Sin*, Doctor. Once we careen, we'll head straight to Jamaica."

"Careen? How long will that take?"

"The better part of a day."

"But they already have a two-day lead."

"If we don't careen, Doctor, the ship will never travel fast enough to make up the distance," Gayle answered calmly before swallowing another mouthful of mead. "We need *Original Sin* to be as fast as possible."

She watched Celia take another sip of wine. How did this woman manage to manipulate her so thoroughly? "We'd better send that message to your father to let him know you're all right."

CHAPTER SIX

Before midnight arrived and *Original Sin* left the temptations of New Providence, Gayle stopped by to visit her father. Though she dared not let on to anyone else, she was still very worried that he might not survive, and she dreaded returning to the island to this news.

Additionally, she realized that her father's recuperation was probably the only thing keeping her crew from mutiny. If he might not command *Original Sin* again, the crew would probably kill her, as they viewed women about as highly as animals or any other possession. While she had the chance, she had to prove her abilities as both a leader and a pirate. She had to provide well for the crew and make this voyage a complete success. Her very life would depend on it.

Her father was conscious when she saw him, and though he was extremely tired, his progress encouraged her. She told him that she had acquired two carpenters and a ship surgeon, in addition to thirteen other new crewmembers. She also assured him that she would return for him after venturing to Jamaica—a round trip of at least twenty days. He had wished her luck and told her to "sleep with one eye open."

Returning downstairs, Gayle again thanked Smitty for all he had done and rejoined Celia, who had been waiting. "Did you finish the letter like I asked you?"

Celia handed her the parchment she had been working on.

"And how did you explain your absence? Or did you?" Gayle asked, perusing the note.

"Well, I'm sure Phillip told them I was abducted by pirates. So I explained that I was taking a small tour of the Caribbean and should be home in a few weeks."

Gayle laughed. "You made it sound like you were on holiday?"

"I don't want them to worry too much."

"Perhaps you can take them mementos from your travels."

"Hmm. And what would I take them from this place? Pirate vomit? Whore urine, perhaps?"

Gayle took the quill pen from the table, dipped it into the inkwell, and began to write at the bottom of the parchment in a swirly script. "You know, I hate to tell you this, but this is one of the few ports we'll actually be welcome in."

"What do you mean?"

"Most ports are not open to pirate ships." She finished scrawling her addendum and put the quill down, removing two doubloons from her coin purse. "This is one of the good ones, sweetie."

Celia was stunned. "And in the other ports?"

Gayle picked up the stick of red sealing wax and briefly held the tip over a lit candle. She then dabbed it to both doubloons and affixed them to the bottom of the missive. "In the other ports we'll need to make landfall a different way—somewhere other than the docks. We'll slip into town after dark."

Celia sighed. "I see." Gayle folded the parchment into quarters, then sealed it closed with the wax, this time pressing an image into it from the silver signet ring she wore on her left thumb. "Is that your family seal?"

Gayle handed the folded note back to Celia for her to examine. "Hardly. I nicked this ring off a Spanish privateer. There's no telling who he pinched it from before I came along. I just fancied it." The symbol pressed into the wax seal was that of a dragonfly lighting on the blade of a sword.

"Unique. What did you add?"

"I am assuming since you can read and write that your father can as well." She slipped the ring back onto her thumb.

"Aye."

"I explained that one of those doubloons was to pay the courier who delivers it. You should put your father's name on the outside."

Celia picked up the quill, loaded it with ink, and did so. "And the other doubloon?"

"To make his waiting slightly more bearable."

They left The Bountiful Teat to run their final errand while in town. Celia followed Gayle as she walked purposefully back to the docks and over to the *Juliet*—a large merchant ship that was loaded and bound for the East Florida territory. Gayle caught the eye of a young crewman, no more than fifteen, and coaxed him over to her.

She gave him two silver pieces of eight and assured him that the recipient of the dispatch would pay him another gold doubloon upon receipt. The lad's eyes went wide with greed, and he heartily agreed to act as courier, slipping the folded and sealed parchment into the front of his shirt and scurrying back up the gangplank.

When Celia awoke early the next morning, she was still in bed, but pressed firmly against the cabin wall, as the ship was listing to one side. She shook her head and marveled at her ability to sleep through something like that. Then she rose, brushed her hair, and dressed.

After she emerged from her cabin, she realized what had happened. The crewmembers had run *Original Sin* aground on a spit and were all scraping the barnacles and seaweed from the exposed port side of the hull. She cautiously maneuvered down a beam that led to the beach, then strolled through the fine sand toward the bow of the ship, studying *Original Sin's* elaborate, colorful figurehead. Clearly she represented Eve, as she held a red apple in her outstretched arms, dangling it seductively before the crew. A green serpent wound up her nude body, but stopped short of covering her ample breasts. Though her pose seemed majestic and graceful, her expression was provocative.

"Ah, good morning, Celia." Gayle regarded her warmly and nodded. "You slept well, then?"

"Seemingly. Do I smell meat cooking?"

"That you do." She motioned past the ship. "The pig on our spit has another hour or so until it's our lunch."

"Really?"

"Aye. Careening can't just be about ball-busting drudgery."

"No, of course it can't," she answered doubtfully.

Gayle led her past the shirtless, sweaty crew that toiled beneath the sun. Caruthers, the bosun, shouted commands to them while fingering his braided beard. Celia was surprised that no one else seemed to find him as menacing as she did. But then she remembered nearly all of them seemed menacing to her.

They stopped at a makeshift shelter—sailcloth thrown over the branch of a tree to create a tent. In the shade a beam supported fresh fruit and bread where Gayle sliced a large section of pineapple with a small machete and said, "Here, break your fast with this."

Celia liked its sweet juiciness. "How long will this take, all this business with the ship?" She filled a tankard with grog.

"Most of the day, unfortunately."

"But aren't they almost done? The hull looks nice and smooth from here." She took a drink.

Gayle picked up a piece of bread and tore it into mouth-sized pieces. "There's more to it than simply the scraping. The men need to replace rotten, worm-eaten planks and apply oakum, tallow, and tar. Then we roll the ship and work on the other side. That's where those Scottish boys come in handy. They have most of the new planks already cut and ready to put in."

"Blimey," Celia cursed, wiping the perspiration from her brow with the back of her hand.

Gayle appeared amused. "You've loosened up a speck, haven't you?" she said, popping bread into her mouth.

"When you are at Rome, do as they do there," Celia replied with a swig of grog.

"And when in hell?"

"Throw another log on the fire?"

"You've become the picture of acclimation." Gayle drank some grog slowly. "You know, you could actually help us a great deal today."

"I? How?"

"Our sails are in disrepair and need a practiced seamstress's touch."

"Truly, Captain? I can help?"

"We could travel much faster to find your misplaced whore. The lads aren't the best at sewing. The stronger the seams, the faster she goes."

"Done. I'll get right on it—once I've finished my meal, of course."

"Of course."

"Greetings" came a sickly sounding call from behind them. They turned to see James shambling over. "Um…ahoy, or whatever it is they say."

Gayle raised one eyebrow and scrutinized the doctor. "You don't look well."

He coughed, probably trying to suppress the reflex to retch at the smell of food. "I'm not quite adjusted to the roll of the waves," he gasped.

Celia took another bite of ripe pineapple. "You are a trifle green." She slurped softly as she bit the rind.

He gagged.

"Doctor, I'm assuming you'll pass on a bite to eat?"

He covered his mouth with his hand. "Unless you have something that will make this pass, Captain. An herb or plant, perhaps?"

"Hmm. I've heard that ginger root helps," Gayle said. "But we don't have any on board. You need to rest while we're on land, and once we sail again, stay on deck as much as you can. Going below deck will make it worse."

"How did you make it all the way from England?" Celia inquired.

"Mostly hung over the rail." He frowned at the victuals on display.

Gayle crossed her arms in front of her. "But that trip must have taken well over a month. Did it never improve, even after all that time at sea?"

He almost gagged again, then paused before he spoke. "The crew had told me it would pass sooner if I stayed below deck, though now I know this is false. They also told me to drink as much rum as I could stomach, and that wasn't helpful either. In fact, I can't remember ever vomiting so much."

"You obviously made fast friends on that ship," Gayle said, almost under her breath.

"It took me over a week to start feeling better. I must have lost a stone. My clothes are hanging on me." He tugged at the loose waist of his breeches. "I had thought all that was behind me, but I guess being on land for a day or so was enough to start the cycle again."

"Well, the more you're at sea, the sooner you'll adjust to the motion," Gayle said. "You may have a few queasy days, but by the time we get to Jamaica you'll be as hardy as the rest of the crew."

With that, James shuffled away, perhaps to find some shady area that didn't neighbor aromatic foods.

"Hmm," Celia remarked quietly once he was out of earshot. "What kind of a doctor can't treat himself?"

"He's one dandy who'll really need to prove himself, especially when we need him most. If he doesn't—"

"What?"

"If he doesn't, the lads will most likely spill his guts."

"Can't you prevent that?"

Gayle shook her head. "Doubtful. Remember, my command here is tenuous. My best chance against mutiny is to not give them a reason to kill me. If the good doctor ends up being more hindrance than help, the crew's majority, not me, may decide his fate."

"Should you tell him that? Perhaps it will give him incentive."

"More than likely it'll just make him vomit more. Let's see if he comes 'round on his own."

The careening had obviously increased morale. When the pig was roasted to perfection, the crew ate heartily, enjoying the fruits and breads that they had gone so long without. Grog and wine flowed in abundance to fight off the ravages of the Caribbean sun.

During breaks the crew amused themselves with music and dancing, and at one point—much to Celia's mortification—a farting contest, which, disturbingly, Molly won.

The crew, which labored throughout the day, seemed more relaxed after their brief time in port, yet also eager to get back to sea. They sang chanteys as they worked and told amusing stories to see who could elicit the biggest laugh.

Celia began tending to the sails, and after she showed the two crewmen who had previously been repairing them a trick or two, the men seemed genuinely impressed by her skill. She determined that the more value she brought to the crew, the more they would accept her—though she still didn't trust a single damn one of them.

When dusk had fallen, the careening was complete and the tide had finally risen high enough for *Original Sin* to depart. As the newly repaired sails inflated with the first gusts of evening wind, the ship wended south as the waxing moon ascended.

Andrew Pierce tried to concentrate on the seam that he was altering, but his mind kept wandering to his missing daughter. She had been gone for over a week, and no one had seen a trace of her after the bloodthirsty pirates had brutally abducted her.

Oh, Dr. Farquar had stated that he had fought valiantly to save her, but the man had emerged without a scratch, so Andrew doubted his story. In fact, if he hadn't heard from others that a pirate vessel had defeated the British Navy just off the coast the evening she disappeared, he would have instantly concluded that the doctor himself had done something despicable to Celia.

He felt guilty for pushing his daughter into her engagement with that great twit. If only he had listened to her when she had complained of his dry demeanor—or his lack of a chin.

Just then a young sailor entered the shop. "Are you the tailor?" he asked.

"Aye." Andrew looked over his spectacles to examine the lad.

"I've a message for you," he blurted, presenting the sealed letter clumsily.

Wary, Andrew accepted the dispatch, suddenly afraid it was a ransom note. He pulled the seal apart and unfolded the parchment, elated to see his daughter's handwriting.

Father,

I hope this missive finds you well and that you and Mother have not been overly distraught by my disappearance. I'm sure you were told of the pirates who abducted me to assist with the medical treatment of their wounded crew. At their merciful and rather benevolent treatment, I have willingly offered to stay on to assist them on a special errand. I'll be in the Caribbean Islands for a few weeks, and then I am told I will be returned completely unharmed.

My deepest love to you both,
Celia.

Beneath this message, another was written in an unfamiliar hand. And below it were two gold doubloons fastened to the parchment with sealing wax.

Please give one of these doubloons to the courier of this
letter and keep the other for yourself, as a promise of your
daughter's imminent safe return.

Andrew pulled the doubloons from the paper and used his thumbnail to scrape off the red wax. He hesitantly addressed the young man before him. "Did you see my daughter?"

The courier shrugged. "What's she look like?"

"She's got dark hair, but bright blue eyes. The top of her head comes to about my shoulder," he said, holding his hand up.

"Aye. I saw her."

"Did she seem well?" he asked hopefully.

"Aye, sir, quite well. She's quite a looker, your daughter."

"She didn't appear manhandled?"

"Not that I saw, sir." The lad looked nervously at the floor. "Do you have my payment, sir?"

He tossed a doubloon over to the young man, who snatched it greedily from the air and dashed back out into the street.

Andrew examined the remaining gold coin in his palm. He couldn't imagine what manner of pirate captain had kidnapped his only daughter. He seemed to lack the viciousness they were reputed for—to have allowed Celia to write a letter explaining her whereabouts and to have compensated him this generously. After all, this single doubloon could easily feed his family for more than a month.

What he was certain of now, however, was that the chinless doctor's story was completely false. Celia claimed that the crew had spirited her away to help them tend to their wounded. Why would they have taken her when a doctor was available?

"That weak, gutless bastard!"

He hurried upstairs to show his wife the evidence that their daughter was alive.

CHAPTER SEVEN

The first few days they headed to Jamaica were relatively uneventful. *Original Sin* continued to make decent headway due to strong gusts and the condition of the ship itself, which had never been in better shape.

Like the preceding two evenings, Gayle had asked Celia to join her in the captain's quarters for supper. After several meals below deck with the rest of the crew, Celia was more than happy to dine with someone who wasn't preoccupied with bodily functions, beheadings, or the word "fuck."

Celia had begun to look forward to the evenings she spent with Gayle, as she was able to speak openly about virtually any subject. Gayle was knowledgeable about a great many things, but she still seemed genuinely interested in whatever Celia had to say—which sadly was quite an unfamiliar feeling.

She knocked on Gayle's door.

"Come in."

Inside, Gayle was seated at her desk, with a chart before her and a compass in her hand.

"Are you busy?"

Gayle shook her head and set the implement down. "No. I evidently let the time get away from me. Please, come in," she said, rising from her chair. "Sit down."

Celia did just that, pulling up a chair at the small table and running her hand through her hair.

Gayle seemed to freeze and simply stared at her, then cleared her throat awkwardly. "I'll let Cook know we are ready for supper," she said, her voice cracking. By the time Celia turned to address her, the door had shut and she was gone.

Alone in the captain's quarters for the first time, Celia stood and slowly perused the items around her. A small bookshelf built into the wall contained such tomes as *The Seaman's Secrets* and *A Waggoner of the Spanish Main*.

"Hmph." She exhaled in disapproval because it all was decidedly dry. She drifted to where Gayle had been sitting and glanced at the chart on the desk—a beautifully colored nautical rendering of the Caribbean islands. She traced the outlines reverently and glanced at the ornate gold compass beside it and the metal dividers used for plotting distance and course.

The cabin door opened and Gayle returned, holding two tankards. She shut the door behind her deftly with her foot and extended a drink. "Here you go, *bonita*."

"Thank you." Celia took it. "We're having wine tonight?"

"Why not? We may as well indulge. We've made excellent progress so far." She brought her wine to her mouth and drank.

Celia followed in kind. "And will the meal be as celebratory as the drink?"

"Aye." Gayle looked pleased with herself.

"Ooh, and what is it?"

"Salmagundi."

"Salma-what?"

"Salmagundi," she repeated. "It's quite a treat."

"And what's in this treat?" Celia smiled broadly, showing Gayle that she was game.

Gayle didn't break the long, sultry gaze they seemed locked in. "Oh, many things. Some you may have tried before," she said in a husky voice. "Some may be new to you."

Celia suddenly felt flushed. "So how do you know I'll like it?"

"Just a feeling." She sat down across from her. "I have an instinct about these things. I'm rarely wrong." She drank her wine while still watching Celia over the rim of her tankard. "You may like it so much you want more."

Celia could do nothing in response but blink—so she did, many times. "Are we only talking about supper?" she finally managed to ask. Perhaps she wasn't as frumpy to her fiery-haired captain as she

THE SUBLIME AND SPIRITED VOYAGE OF ORIGINAL SIN

had feared, as frightening as that possibility was. She suddenly felt a mixture of confusion and elation. Maybe she hadn't thought this situation through properly.

Gayle regarded her slyly. "Of course. What did you think we were talking about?"

Celia chuckled nervously and looked at her feet. "For a moment I thought we were talking about sex."

Gayle choked on her wine.

"Are you all right?"

"Aye." She coughed. "You're not much for subtlety, are you?"

"It's not a trait I possess, I'm told. So we weren't discussing sex, then?"

Gayle bit her lower lip seductively. "Well, if you do it properly, the topic can *always* be sex—no matter what the original subject is."

"Truly?"

"Absolutely. Test me."

Celia paused to think. "What if you're talking about yellow fever?"

"Hmm, that's a tough one. Start it off and we'll see if I can manage."

"Um. Did you hear old Fanny caught the yellow fever and died yesterday?" Celia inquired in feigned sorrow.

"That's tragic," Gayle responded in a provocative tone. "You must feel bereft and in need of comfort." Her fingers lightly caressed Celia's forearm, whose skin felt like it had been set on fire.

"You really are quite good at that."

"Thank you."

"Is this how you woo women?"

"Woo?"

"Or whatever it is you do…to take them to bed."

Gayle's eyebrows arched in surprise. "You are asking me how I bed women? Well, I don't ply them with drink, if that's what you're implying. They are there of their own volition."

"I'm not saying that. But how do you know which women have such a volition?"

"They flirt with me. A wink here, a brush of a hand there, a kiss or two—"

"Have you ever lain with a man?"

Gayle scowled. "Have you?"

"No. My fiancé won't even let me call him by his proper name."

"He what?" Gayle rested her chin in her hand in amused interest.

Celia appeared self-conscious. "He insists that I call him 'Doctor' instead of Phillip. He would never agree to take liberties with me before our wedding night."

"And have you wanted him to?" Gayle was intrigued by this turn in the conversation. "Have you been overcome with lust for him and secretly ached for him to take you?"

Celia's eyes opened wide. "Good God—no." When Gayle laughed at her response, Celia's expression softened and she looked crestfallen. "That's probably not a good thing, is it?"

"If you hope to enjoy your marital relations, it's not. No."

Celia put her elbows on the table between them. "But honestly, you're the first woman I've met who said she enjoyed it—the sex, I mean. You do enjoy it, right?"

Gayle laughed wickedly. "Oh yes. Very much."

"And what about it do you like so much?"

"Would you like me to show you?"

A knock on the door disturbed the carnal tension hanging in the air, and Cook arrived with two bowls of what was possibly the most turbid, viscous stew Celia had ever seen.

"Aye, Gayle. Touch me there," Celia whispered into her beloved's ear.

Gayle's strong hand was on Celia's bare breast, and she circled the nipple deftly with her thumb as her teeth grazed the soft flesh of Celia's neck. "You taste so sweet. Give me your mouth."

Gayle gently took Celia's face and kissed her hungrily. Their tongues mingled, and their bodies began to grind together. Celia worked to unbutton Gayle's shirt, sliding her unpracticed hands beneath the fabric to feel the smooth skin there.

"I need you naked," Celia moaned, frustrated that she couldn't get Gayle's clothing off quickly enough. Their mouths met again, and Gayle's stroking tongue sent a surge through Celia like she had never felt before. This must be what desire felt like. Her whole body bristled, throbbed, and craved release.

"My love," Gayle growled in her ear. "I can wait no longer." Her hand sensually moved down Celia's belly to the exposed flesh of her thigh. "Open yourself for me."

She feverishly took Gayle's hand and resolutely pulled it between her legs.

Suddenly exhaling, Celia bolted upright in bed and looked about. She was alone in her completely dark cabin.

What a dream that had been!

She lay back down, her heart pounding, desire still rushing through her. Her palms were damp, her breathing ragged, and this salacious longing was foreign to her.

"Shit," she lamented into her pillow in mortification.

When the knock came at her door several hours later, Celia was anything but well rested. Her dream had made her sleep fitfully.

"Aye?" she called, exhausted.

The door opened and Gayle appeared, rosy-cheeked and alert. "Sorry to wake you," she began, then paused. "Very sorry indeed," she added with a frown. "But I need you on deck right away."

"What? Why?"

Gayle swept into the cabin and opened the chest beside the bed. She pulled out the dress Celia had been wearing the night she had arrived on *Original Sin* and laid it on the bed. "Put this on, quickly."

Celia squinted, still groggy. "And if I asked why again?"

"I still wouldn't answer. Celia, there's no time. Just do as I say, and meet me on deck as soon as you can."

"But—"

"You have to hurry. I'll explain later."

Celia flung back the blanket in irritation. "How does she manage to look so bloody becoming in the morning?" she cursed, rising to dress.

When she did appear on deck several minutes later, she found Gayle, also in a dress, and, peculiarly, so was Molly—though she seemed about as comfortable in it as a chicken in pantaloons. Celia saw no sign of anyone else. "Do I get to know what the hell is going on yet?"

"We're approaching a ship," Gayle explained. "The *Corona d'Oro*."

"Aren't we overdressed?"

Gayle ordered Molly to hoist the British flag, and the woman awkwardly scurried off to do so. "Here, take this." Gayle offered Celia a small flintlock pistol. "Aim for the head. You'll have only one shot."

"Are you mad? And who exactly will I be shooting at?"

"Hopefully, no one," Gayle replied matter-of-factly. "But we're about to come alongside Captain Santiago and take his bloody ship from him."

"What? Where's the rest of the crew?"

"Lying in wait. They'll emerge when the time is right."

Celia was filled with terror. "So that makes us—"

"Bait," Gayle answered. "Now take the pistol and keep it out of sight."

"Out of sight where?"

Gayle knelt down before her and lifted Celia's dress as she tied the pistol to the outside of her right thigh with a strip of linen. "Out of sight, here." She pulled the skirt back down and stood.

Celia focused on the horizon and saw the ship growing larger as they approached. "So this is how my life ends, then."

"Not at all. Trust me, Celia. I won't let harm befall you."

"She said as she strapped a pistol to my leg," Celia mocked, and rolled her eyes. "This is completely demented. Why can't we just turn around and sail away?"

"It's too late. Besides, this is what we do."

It seemed to take an eon for the ship to reach them. Unable to do anything except stare in absolute dread, Celia could finally see the faces of the crewmen on the *Corona d'Oro*.

Gayle began to wave, as though signaling the other ship for assistance. "*Socorro*," she shouted. "*Por favor*."

The Spanish crew shouted back, but Celia couldn't distinguish any of the words. Suddenly, several grappling hooks flew from the *Corona d'Oro*, and its crew pulled *Original Sin* alongside them so they could board her.

Celia felt for the pistol through the fabric of her skirt as six hungry-looking Spanish pirates swiftly surrounded her and Molly. An older sailor, dressed like a naval officer, sauntered aboard, and she assumed this was Captain Santiago.

"And what do we have here?" he asked in a thick Spanish accent.

"We were overtaken by pirates," Gayle lied. "They took all the cargo and left us here adrift."

Santiago leered obscenely, his few teeth brown and rotten. "They did not take *all* the cargo," he corrected, advancing toward her.

Celia looked nervously for the crew of *Original Sin*. Where were they? Wasn't this a perfect time for them to emerge?

"Don't make a mistake you'll regret, Captain," Gayle warned. "It may prove fatal."

Santiago laughed and continued toward her. "You have spirit," he announced. "I will truly enjoy fucking it out of you." Gayle's eyes flashed, but she didn't move. When Santiago reached her, he scrutinized her, scratching his patchy dark beard. "How long do you think it will take me to make you cry and beg for mercy, eh?"

Her chin came up defiantly. "Longer than you've got on this earth."

He laughed again and captured her left wrist. "Would you like to wager on that, *bribona*?" he goaded her, his face very close to hers. He tilted his head to menacingly sniff her hair.

"Aye, I would," she growled. Before Celia was even fully aware of what she was watching, Gayle had pulled out a dagger and jammed it hilt-deep through Santiago's chin and up through the roof of his mouth. The Spaniard's eyes grew glassy as Celia watched the life leave them. Gayle removed the blade from his head as his body fell away from her, and his blood seeped slowly onto the deck. "I win," she whispered.

Santiago's men seemed stunned by this unexpected assassination, and as one began to draw his cutlass, Gayle threw her dagger at him— hitting him squarely in the eye. He toppled backward, landing in a lifeless heap, the hilt protruding from his face.

At that moment, Gayle whistled loudly and the crew emerged, swords at the ready. Gayle drew her own cutlass from the scabbard tied to her leg beneath her petticoats and struck it against that of one of the Spaniards adeptly. Celia could only watch in horror as the pirate Gayle was fighting seized her forearm without warning, their blades locked together. Gayle kicked the Spaniard square in the groin, and as he recoiled, she kicked him again, this time in the chest. Before he could draw in breath, she ran her blade through his heart and moved on to battle another raider.

Some of the crewmen of *Original Sin* had boarded *Corona d'Oro* and the fight continued there. Celia had backed up to try and stay out of the way, and within a few chaotic minutes, no more Spaniards were left standing.

When Gayle approached her, Celia was crouched low with her arms wrapped around herself in a vain attempt to comfort herself and keep safe. Gayle extended her hand to help Celia rise, but she didn't take it.

"Are you hurt?" Gayle asked in obvious concern.

Celia shook her head and stood without aid. Rigid and in shock, she wrung her hands nervously. "How could you have done this?" she whispered. "How could you have slaughtered all these men?"

"These men who were ready to take turns raping us?" Gayle snapped, panting.

"You didn't know that before they boarded us."

"Oh, I know Santiago. I've spoken to the survivors left in his murderous wake. I've seen the scars on the wenches he has helped himself to, and I've waited for the day I could kill him."

Celia watched the dark expressions flash across Gayle's face as she spoke. This was a new side of her, and Celia felt frightened—the most frightened she had been since she arrived on board.

CHAPTER EIGHT

The crew of *Original Sin* quickly helped themselves to the cargo of *Corona d'Oro*, which proved more fruitful than Gayle had estimated. Sacks of stolen spices—sugar, pepper, clove, and cinnamon—filled the hold. And while the crew didn't generally prefer this type of goods, as they were bulky and not always easy to sell, they also discovered silks and china that would fetch a hefty sum.

Gayle found charts and navigational equipment in the captain's quarters, but even more alluring was a locked chest under the bed. She forced it open and discovered roughly 7,000 pesos and assorted gems and jewelry. A beautiful ornamental dagger with an engraved, gilded blade and a sapphire-encrusted hilt, as well as several golden rings, jeweled crosses, and necklaces all containing unusual gems. No one expected Santiago—a petty criminal renowned for his excesses as much as his vicious treatment of his own crew—to have such an expansive cache. He must have slowly accumulated these riches, probably unbeknownst to his crew, who surely would have expected their share.

They also rummaged through the ship's hold for food or medicine, but there *Corona d'Oro* came up short. After discussing the risks of manning the *Corona d'Oro* with a skeleton crew until they could sell it in port—after all, it wasn't in the most fit condition, but they hadn't had to fire a single cannon shot—they decided to commandeer it as well.

Gayle divided the cash among her crew, making sure each member got his due. The Maroons, who had recently joined them, received more money than they had ever seen, assuring them that piracy was the only way for escaped slaves to ever gain wealth.

For a crew whose morale had already been high, a fast, low-injury, lucrative acquisition made them appreciate their new captain even more. The cunning way Gayle had duped Santiago into coming on board without a weapon drawn was the stuff of legends.

Luckily, *Corona d'Oro* was swift and didn't impede *Original Sin*'s progress to Jamaica. Even with their stops, they were making remarkable time.

Churchill stood in the captain's quarters, cradling a golden volvelle as he admired its craftsmanship. "It's hard to believe Santiago possessed something this exquisite."

Gayle raised an eyebrow at her navigator. "I doubt he was using it to calculate the tides. He probably planned to have it melted down to make himself some new teeth."

"Thank God you intervened before that happened." Churchill set the valuable item back on the desk. "You've certainly started out your command all thunder and broadsides."

"Good fortune. Nothing more."

"You're too modest, Gayle. This morning's attack was brilliant."

She shook her head. "Don't take this the wrong way, but I can always count on the lechery of men. It's their Achilles' heel."

"I suppose that's fair. But let's discuss Jamaica." He strolled over to a chair and sat, facing her.

She crossed her arms. "Is this where you try to talk me into heading to a different port?"

"Well, based on our last fateful trip to Kingston—"

"I thought you'd bring that up. That was nearly two years ago."

"Pirate towns aren't like typical, law-abiding cities, you know. To be chased out is quite an achievement."

"I wasn't chased out. I left of my own choosing. Besides, I had no idea that woman's father was the governor."

"Before you declared her arse as large as the moon?"

"I said her arse was as immense and angry as a thundercloud." She chuckled softly. "Though in retrospect, she may have been able to control tidal flow with that substantial rump. The moon might have been a more precise comparison."

He laughed. "And you feel certain we'll have no issues arriving back in port?"

"I heard Governor Beeston is dead now—the unscrupulous bastard."

"This isn't all about retrieving a gaggle of whores, is it? Hoping to win their eager gratitude?" He winked.

"Hardly. I don't want a copious handful of harlots. I gave the doctor my word that I'd help him locate his sister, and that's what I mean to do."

"And you've no other impctus? You're simply compelled to be philanthropic, are you?"

"Well, obviously it secured me a ship surgeon."

"Hmm," he grumbled as he scrutinized her. "And this has nothing to do with a certain seamstress who has turned this fierce battle vessel into her bloody holiday craft?"

Gayle squinted at him. "I'll not lie to you and say she isn't comely."

"Comely?"

"Aye. She's as fair a maid as I've ever seen. And that she wished to aid the doctor in his quest may have, perchance, made the offer seem more attractive to me, 'tis true. But I've not lost grasp of my faculties, Churchill. I'd not endanger *Original Sin* or her crew for a quick tumble with any winsome lass."

"And is she just *any* winsome lass?"

"I don't wish her to be, no. But after this morning's skirmish she hasn't spoken to me. She must see me as brutal and bloodthirsty."

"If that's true, it's only because she didn't know Santiago and what a hellish cur he was."

"Perhaps, but I should have realized that battle would profoundly affect her."

"Well, she has several days to reconcile it. It's not like she can go anywhere besides the bottom of the sea. Impress her with your softer side."

"That may have merit."

"But don't let the crew catch you. If they think you're imperiling them so you can get up that wench's skirts, you'll have a mutiny on your hands faster than you can smack your bottom…or hers."

"They're too busy counting their loot to mutiny, Churchill. I'll keep an eye on them, my friend. You just get us to Kingston."

Celia had been trying to make herself scarce ever since the sudden, inexplicable attack and theft of the Spanish ship that morning. She had never seen anyone murdered, and watching people she had admired perform such a reprehensible act was rather shocking. She was still struggling to deal with the revelation.

While the late-afternoon light remained, Celia assisted James as he finished tending to anyone injured during the combat, and the last person who had requested attention was Molly.

"And did you receive any wounds?" he asked her.

"Aye." She pulled her shirt up and exposed her breasts.

He surveyed her torso. "You have an injury here?"

"Oh. No. It's on me arm."

"So why do you have your shirt up?"

"Since you've been looking at blood and the like all day, I thought you might want a glance of somethin' a bit nicer."

He looked embarrassed as he helped her pull her shirt back down. "Thanks, they are quite lovely. Now, let's see your arm."

Celia chuckled in amusement.

As Molly displayed the modest wound, she seemed to puff up with pride. "Here she is. That right bastard tried to hack my fuckin' arm clear off."

"It doesn't look too bad," James said. "Not very deep."

"Not for his lack of trying. I got my cutlass in the fucker's chest before he got too far."

Celia winced as she thought of Molly running someone through. "It's a shame so many had to die."

"And a shame so many died at Santiago's hands before Cap'n got to 'im," Molly replied as James washed the dried blood away.

"So this Santiago was a rather bad sort?" James asked.

Molly laughed. "That's like sayin' that Lucifer has a bit of a temper. He's been lurkin' about these waters for a few years now. He attacked every ship in his sights and helped himself to all their cargo. He supposedly had a letter of marque from the Spanish government that entitled him to pillage ships of any other nationality on behalf of Spain. I guess he was rogerin' all those women on behalf of Spain as well—him and his crew."

"I did hear that he was quite scurrilous," Celia said.

"He once tortured his own crewman for raping a captive before he got a shot at her. Cut him open like a mackerel and hung him still kickin' from the yardarm by his bloomin' rib cage."

James gagged slightly. "Good Lord."

"Apparently it took him a long time to die. I was more than happy to see the shitter finally get what he deserved."

Celia mulled this over. "But what of his crew? Surely they didn't all deserve to die."

Molly scoffed. "The ones that traveled with him were those who wanted to be just like him. That's why he had so few men left. He'd already killed a lot o' them, and some had run off, not wantin' to be next on the yardarm."

"I suppose no one will miss Santiago," James said as he finished bandaging Molly.

"And Cap'n was a fire-breathin' hellion to be sure. She's as brave and able as any I ever sailed with." She glanced at her newly wrapped arm. "That's a fine-lookin' bandage, Doc. Let me know if you want to tend to me other bits," she offered, standing. "I'd hate to forget how to use them." She winked at James, then sauntered away.

"She's certainly…unique," James said with a frown.

"Unique yet common at the same time. Quite peculiar."

"Quite. So, might you join me this evening for supper, Celia?"

"I appreciate the offer," she explained, looking awkwardly at the deck. "But I've had a rather trying day. I think I'll skip supper and simply go to sleep."

His face fell. "Ah, I see. Well, perhaps tomorrow night?"

"I don't know."

"It's just that we really haven't had much chance to become familiar." His eyes widened. "Not familiar in a…familiar way," he muddled nervously. The words seemed to flow from him like the rushing tide—without pause and with no dam on the horizon. "I certainly wouldn't be asking you to bed me—not that I wouldn't be interested in bedding you, obviously. You're a terribly attractive woman, and bedding you might very well be the highlight of an otherwise dull and pedantic existence. Though I certainly don't want to give you the impression that I have sat and pondered overly what bedding you might be like—though admittedly it is not abhorrent to me in the least."

Celia blinked twice and studied this frazzled man, but said nothing.

"Should I stop speaking?" he finally asked weakly.

"Please."

"I do apologize. I so want to say the right things, and for some reason—"

She held up her open hand. "That's fine. I'll see you later, James."

He nodded vigorously, as though in the throes of a seizure, and kept nodding as she left.

Having nowhere else to go, she headed to her cabin. She was surprised to see the door open and to observe Frederick—the lad they had recruited from the fabric merchant—stacking several bolts of cloth on her bed.

"What's all this, Frederick?"

He seemed startled. "Cap'n asked that I deliver this to you so you can make whate'er you please."

"And was this all filched from Santiago's ship?" she asked gravely.

"This green one was. But these two the Cap'n purchased for you in New Providence."

Celia scrutinized the cloth, then remembered commenting on how much she liked the pieces. How thoughtful of Gayle to have taken note and bought them for her. "So I'm to make anything I please?" she clarified, fingering the fine silk appreciatively.

"Aye."

"Thank you, Frederick. And please tell the captain the same."

"Aye, miss." He shut the door behind him.

She sat on the edge of the bed and ran her hands over the fabrics. They were some of the most exquisite she had ever seen. She rarely got an opportunity to work with such amazing materials. Closing her eyes, she tried to think of what she wanted to create, trying to block out the image of a brown-toothed Spaniard bleeding to death.

CHAPTER NINE

Gayle found the next few days at sea rather frustrating. Though *Original Sin* wasn't a large ship, somehow Celia had found ways to avoid her. They hadn't dined together since the skirmish with Santiago, and during any exchange between them Celia had been brief, cordial, and utterly aloof.

Gayle glanced back down to her chart of the islands. If these strong winds continued throughout the day and into the evening, they would be in Kingston by tomorrow afternoon. She wasn't certain Celia would even care to travel back to Florida with her on *Original Sin*, as she was suddenly so disaffected—all but teeming with disgust for Gayle and her piratical practices. Celia hadn't even thanked her directly for the expensive fabrics.

She sighed. She wouldn't have a chance to show Celia her "softer side," as Churchill had called it, if they were never in the same bloody room.

She exhaled loudly and sat up. She was running out of time with Celia, and she needed to be assertive before her opportunity passed.

Inside her cabin, as Celia busily sewed the beautifully patterned green silk, she attempted to focus, but again her mind wandered. She had been very disconcerted over the last few days.

What had begun with a single, albeit very disturbing erotic dream had now progressed into something bordering on preoccupation, involuntary though it was. True, seeing Gayle in battle had horrified her, but something about the sight of her in such command and with such physicality had apparently stirred her and made her dream even more frequently.

She was now having several a night, and little varied except trivial things like their location—sometimes in a lavish bedroom, sometimes on a beach amid the rushing waves, and sometimes, most peculiarly, on the back of a great sea turtle. What on earth might that represent? When the dreams first began, she thought she could simply roll over and drift calmly back into slumber. But overwrought, when she did at last nod off, another sexual encounter with Gayle spun her right back up.

Embarrassed and afraid her expression would somehow lay bare these troubled thoughts, she couldn't even make eye contact with Gayle.

She momentarily wondered if Gayle had paid the gypsy woman to put a curse on her, perhaps a curse of lusting. She laughed at herself. She really needed to get more sleep.

Even her sewing—what she had focused her attention on for the last three days—was ultimately for Gayle. When Celia had brushed her hand over the fine embossed emerald silk, she immediately envisioned it on Gayle as a lush vest, her fiery garnet hair tumbling over her shoulders in contrast. Compelled to create the garment, she had worked on it almost constantly, though she did wonder how she would actually bestow it upon her. She winced and hoped they wouldn't need any fittings, as those might prove awkward.

She flushed when she suddenly remembered Gayle pulling up her dress and strapping the pistol to her thigh. Now that she wasn't panicked, she found the contact extremely sensual.

"Damn, damn, damn," she muttered, trying to force her thoughts back to the seam she was basting. Dear Lord, what must she do to get this lasciviousness out of her mind? Must she simply go to Gayle's quarters and pounce upon her, acting on the desire to finally exorcize it?

She imagined that experience for a moment. Rising and striding to Gayle's cabin, entering without knocking. Gayle would be startled, of course, but she would simply walk inside and bolt the door. She would say nothing, unless it was something provocative like "I need your hands on me," or perhaps "Captain, I have something I need hoisted."

She scowled. On second thought, that scenario wasn't nearly as sexy as she had initially imagined it to be.

A knock at the door brought her back to reality, and she tossed the vest into a dark corner. "Come in." She was surprised to see Gayle enter. Her stomach sank, and she was certain she was blushing.

"Are you busy?" Gayle asked.

"Hardly. I have naught but time here."

"Might I have a word with you?"

Celia fixed her eyes on the floor, avoiding her gaze. "If you wish."

"You have seemed a bit under the weather of late," Gayle began softly, sitting beside Celia on the bed.

Celia abruptly stood. "Have I?"

"Aye. You spend little time on deck, and you have supped neither with me nor with the men. Are you well?"

"I wish I knew."

"Well, I thought perhaps a hot bath might aid you."

"A hot—"

"Bath," she repeated.

Celia panicked. "And where would I take this bath?"

"Well, this cabin is obviously too small. And it would certainly not be appropriate for you to engage in a bath out on deck where the crew takes theirs."

"Absolutely not."

"So I thought I would offer the use of my quarters. It will afford you privacy, but enough room to manage."

Celia closed her eyes. Hadn't one of her dreams taken place in a bathtub? "Shit."

"Pardon?" Gayle sounded perplexed.

"I said 'quit,'" she quickly lied. "Quit worrying about me. I'm fine. You needn't exert the effort."

"'Tis no effort, Celia," she said, as she stood to face her. "Your demeanor concerns me. I want you to be well and happy."

Celia's resolve melted at this heartfelt admission. And Gayle looked so deeply into her eyes that, unnerved, Celia nearly forgot to continue breathing. "That's quite nice of you."

Gayle smiled slightly. "I do have my occasional nice moments. It might do you well to take advantage of them when they come along."

"I wouldn't want to burden you."

Gayle's expression softened into what Celia determined was either tenderness, desire, or perhaps complete amusement. Damn that she couldn't read her better.

"'Tis certainly no burden. I have missed our suppers together."

Celia's mouth opened but nothing came out of it. She closed it and then opened it again. "As have I," she conceded softly.

"Then it is settled. Come to my quarters shortly with a fresh change of clothes and I will ensure you have a relaxing bath. When you are finished and refreshed, we will dine."

Celia studied Gayle's face and found she liked the amiable expression there. She then noticed Gayle's hands, which rested lightly on her hips. They were strong and capable-looking. For a moment, a flash of what Celia had dreamt those hands had done to her filled her mind. She blinked the thought away in irritation.

"Fine," she finally sputtered.

"Splendid." Gayle clapped eagerly. "I'll have Cook begin heating the water." She turned and left the room.

Celia sat on the edge of the bed and put her forehead in her hands. "Shit," she said again.

When Celia knocked on Gayle's cabin door, she was startled at how quickly it opened.

"Excellent timing," Gayle said, motioning for her to enter. "The bath is mostly filled and the water quite warm."

Celia shuffled in and examined the large oval metal tub, its steam rising lazily. She set down the clothes she held and stood uneasily. "I'm sure it will be lovely," she remarked, trying to fill the awkward silence.

"Aye. Hyde just has to bring one more load of hot water."

Celia examined Gayle, who was wearing a blousy tan shirt and black velvet breeches that fit her very well. "You appear somewhat refreshed yourself."

"Aye. I indulged myself earlier this morning. It's a panacea of no equal."

"Well, sea life does seem a bit filthy."

"It can be. I usually have the crew at least wash the day before we make port. Sometimes I need to twist their arms a bit, if you get my meaning. Nothing's as upsetting as the smell of a ripened, unwashed arse. And out of consideration to whores everywhere, I try to send my lads into town as fresh as possible."

"How thoughtful of you."

"I do try."

"And do you give them the same courtesy?" Celia waited for Gayle's response with interest.

"I'm not really much of a whoremonger. I don't know what some of the lads have been telling you—"

"They are impressed with your 'wenching' abilities, I believe is how they referred to them. They apparently feel that you spend as much time fondling breasts as you do breathing."

Gayle looked uncomfortable and for a moment said nothing. She crossed her arms and then bit her thumbnail sheepishly. "They are prone to exaggeration," she finally said.

"Hopefully. As I've seen you take quite a few breaths since I entered your quarters. You would have a great deal of fondling to do tonight to catch up, were that the case."

"True. And since you and Molly are the only women on board, I'll obviously have to have more than one go at both of you." Celia could only stare in response to the comment. Gayle cleared her throat repeatedly. "At any rate, wenching and whoring are two different things, you know."

"You're not going to tell me that the wenches pay *you*, are you?"

Gayle laughed. "No, but I may use that tale the next time I boast to the crew. You don't mind, do you?"

"Not at all. Feel free to embellish it even further if you please."

"That may be difficult, but I'll mull on it."

Hyde knocked and entered with another large pot of hot water, which he dumped into the bath. And at Gayle's nod of thanks, he departed silently.

"Well…" Celia began stiffly.

"Ah, right." Gayle moved toward the door as if to leave, then turned around. "Oh, I have this soap I got in Cuba. It smells of flowers." She picked up a gray brick of the substance from the table and handed it to Celia.

"Thank you," she whispered, pulling her hand anxiously away from Gayle's when their fingers touched.

"You are most welcome," she said with a hint of desire.

Celia gazed at the floor again. "And how long will I have before you return?"

"However long you wish. If it would please you, I could stay and keep you company."

"No, thank you. I shouldn't monopolize your time so. I'll be done soon, and I'll come and find you."

"As you wish." Her eyes searched Celia's before she left the cabin.

Celia dashed to the door and bolted it, then leaned wearily against it. She should never have agreed to this bath, she admitted to herself. Though it had sounded absolutely heavenly, and nothing of a sexual nature had happened, she was tremendously anxious about the whole thing. Every time she looked at Gayle, the captain seemed to be eyeing her as though she were a fresh melon, ripe and succulent.

She sighed and moved to the bath, putting her hand in the water to determine the temperature. As she stripped her clothing off, she contemplated what would happen if she were to let things progress. She didn't need to be the next notch on Gayle's baldric. It was clear that Gayle had been with so many women that they had ceased to even register as memories beyond a casual thought of "I remember old what's-her-name. She was a pleasant way to pass the time."

She slowly lowered herself into the bath and used the soap to scent the warm water. After several minutes of focused scrubbing, she sank beneath the water to soak her hair. She emerged, brushed her wet hair away from her face, and leaned back, closing her eyes.

This really did feel marvelous. She exhaled loudly. She supposed she had forgotten what a strong-willed woman she was. As intrigued with the notion of how carnal relations with Gayle might be, ultimately she had no desire to be the next nameless tart in a long line of wenches—a line no doubt peppered liberally with some whores who had to have been paid.

She herself was simply too traditional. She wanted a spouse, not a lover—and not a female lover at that. Perhaps she had been simply swept up in the whole buccaneer way of life. That was probably what had caused her to lose her head.

She began to pay great attention to the washing of her feet. No doubt, the fact that Gayle had treated her with the type of attention she had sought from Phillip since they had met had affected her.

Celia thought back on her meeting with Phillip. It had been at a small affair held by the Ortegas, and she had worn a low-cut, burgundy dress she had created especially for the occasion. Phillip's jaw had dropped so low at her entrance that she had seen it unhinge from across the room. They had spoken briefly that evening, though she hadn't been terribly interested in what he had to say, she recalled. He had talked mostly about himself. She should have recognized that as a sign of not only how utterly self-absorbed he was, but also that she wouldn't be able to share Phillip's fascination with himself.

She sighed again and dunked her head back under the water.

CHAPTER TEN

Celia finally drew herself from the bathtub with great unwillingness, though she wasted no time drying and dressing. She didn't want Gayle to return to her quarters while she was unclothed. As she ran the towel over her hair, she inventoried her resolve again. Yes, she was certain she could resist Gayle's rather abundant charm.

She unlocked the cabin door and strode confidently out onto the main deck. Twilight was settling in the humid air, and the ship's concertina player was again regaling the crew with lively music. She glanced about and saw Gayle speaking to Churchill and Abernathy, her arms crossed with poise and purpose, her red hair blowing madly behind her.

Celia swallowed loudly as the familiar queasiness in her stomach returned. "Shit," she uttered softly, like a hymn, at the revelation that resistance perhaps wouldn't be as simple as she had hoped.

Gayle turned and smiled warmly at her.

"Shit," Celia repeated quietly.

"Feeling better?" Gayle called as she approached her.

"Aye, thank you."

Gayle brushed a stray tendril of Celia's damp hair out of her face. "I'm simply glad it helped. You're welcome to a bath whenever you please."

"I appreciate that."

Gayle took a step back and surveyed Celia's fresh clothes. "These fit nicely," she commented with an appreciative tone.

Celia glanced at her pale yellow shirt and beige breeches and explained, "I altered them slightly to fit better."

"Most impressive. And have you begun sewing anything with the fabrics I sent you?"

"Actually, I have." She motioned for Gayle to follow her to her cabin, where she retrieved the green silk vest she had been working on and handed it to Gayle. "What do you think?"

Gayle held the garment out. "This is beautiful."

"Try it on."

"This is for me?"

"Aye."

Gayle seemed taken aback but, after a brief hesitation, slipped the garment on. "How does it look?" she asked as she buttoned it.

Celia smoothed the fabric over Gayle's shoulders in what was initially a purely professional attempt to gauge the fit, but rapidly became a rather discomfited moment of unexpected intimacy. "It looks"—she drew her hands back self-consciously but couldn't control the fact that her voice had dropped in pitch and taken on a breathy quality—"absolutely gorgeous."

Gayle's gaze became sensual, and she turned around and showed her back. "How's the fit here?"

Celia inspected the garment and noted how roomy it was through the back and waist. She tugged at the sides. "It could come in slightly. But would you still have enough room to draw your weapon and properly sunder your foes?"

Gayle turned to face her. "Hmm. I think so. After all, I do want my best features suitably showcased." She assessed her own bosom, to which the vest conformed snugly. "Will this do?"

Celia tried not to look at Gayle's breasts, but under the circumstances, she was unable to avoid it. "I think so," she answered nervously.

"It's flattering, then?"

"I would say so."

"And why did you choose to make me something, when you had all that fabric that you fancied at your disposal?"

Celia glanced away. "For some reason when I saw this silk, I thought it suited you perfectly." She looked into Gayle's eyes again. "And it does."

Gayle moved toward her. "Let's eat."

☠

When Celia awoke to the sounds of knocking, she was in her cabin splayed across the bed—still completely clothed, shoes and all. Her head pounded, and she rubbed her forehead as she tried to sit up.

The knock returned—a heavy clatter like the gods themselves were warring. She managed a weak "Who is it?" though the words seemed to splinter in her head like thousands of tiny spears ripping through her brain.

Gayle's face appeared in the doorway. "'Tis the captain, madam," she replied jovially. She frowned and then entered. "Do you remember who *you* are?"

Celia shut her eyes as tight as she could, but still the painful light filtered in. "A woman who can scarcely focus, much less stand," she grumbled. "Tell me, how did I get this way?"

"I am sorry to report that the wine did you in, good woman."

"The wine?"

"Aye. Perhaps if you cast your mind back to supper last night, you'll recall my recommendation that finishing that second bottle by yourself might prove costly." She knelt by the bed and beamed maddeningly.

Celia groaned. That did seem familiar, but felt like a dream—and she had been having those in such plentiful numbers lately that she was not currently able to completely distinguish them from reality. "That was you?"

"It was."

"Were we on a large sea turtle at any point?" Celia asked, still uncertain what had been a dream.

Gayle appeared confused. "Not once."

"Ah, well," Celia said with a heavy sigh. "The wine was very tasty," she recollected, struggling to swing her feet over the side of the bed.

"One of my favorites," Gayle agreed with a nod.

Celia rested her throbbing head in her hands, then raked her fingers through her hair. "And did I come back to the cabin on my own?"

"I helped a bit."

"A bit?"

"Well, your feet had stopped working, if you recall," Gayle explained casually. "When I let go of you, you kept falling over." She sat down next to her on the bed.

"I do remember lying face-down on the deck at one point, now that you mention it." She turned toward Gayle. "But there was no large sea turtle? You're certain?"

"Very certain."

"So you helped me back to bed." Celia couldn't keep a slight inflection of indictment out of her tone.

"Aye."

"And did you…" She couldn't actually say the words.

"Did I what?"

"Did we…" She jumbled her fingers chaotically together in some sort of peculiar, yet demonstrative hand gesture.

"Milk an animal of some kind?" Gayle apparently wasn't very good at this game.

"No, no," Celia barked in frustration. "Did we…have relations? You and I," she clarified when Gayle looked perplexed.

"Ah, you mean, did we have a tumble last night?" She seemed quite pleased with herself.

"We did?" Celia put her head back in her hands as she processed this information. "Was I enjoyable at all?" she asked, muffling her question with her palms.

Gayle laughed. "You were extremely enjoyable. But we did not have a tumble."

Celia looked at her, surprised. "We didn't?"

"Sadly, no."

"Did I fight off your indecent advances?"

Gayle shook her head. "Now, you mustn't tell anyone this, as I have a reputation to consider. But I did not attempt to bed you, even though you were completely in your cups."

Celia squinted at her in distaste. "I suppose I'm too hideous for you to lust after, is that it? My rump too wide?"

Gayle chuckled, moving a stray lock of Celia's hair with her index finger. "Your rump is absolutely perfect, and there is nothing hideous about you, love, except this headache of yours from too much drink. You're bloody gorgeous."

"You think so?" Celia attempted a feeble smile.

"I'm utterly certain of it. Even totally askew, as you are now."

"Oh." She stopped short of thanking her for the compliment, because that last part seemed to have somehow negated it. "But…" she added, starting the sentence for Gayle.

"But…" Gayle repeated. "I want you to be wholly coherent when I touch you." She leaned close to Celia's ear. "I want you to want it even more than I do—without two bottles of wine in you." She kissed Celia's cheek softly and stood. "Now, are you ready to join the living?"

Celia, unable to respond to Gayle's admission, nodded dumbly.

"Good. Meet me on deck."

"You don't plan to dress me up as rape bait for another approaching ship, do you? I'm really not well enough today to manage."

"No, we're nearing Jamaica."

"We are? How much time has passed?" Celia tried to stand, but immediately sat back down.

"It's late afternoon, I'm afraid. I had hoped you would stir on your own before now, but obviously that wine does more for you than simply taste good."

"Apologies," she muttered.

"None needed. I'll have Hyde bring you a drink that should make you feel a bit more yourself. We'll be stopping in Port Royal soon, and we'll go ashore there briefly if you're up to it."

After Gayle left the cabin, Celia flung herself back on the bed, too pained to be either embarrassed or aroused, and wondered how to make the ship stop spinning.

Hyde brought Celia a drink he referred to as "bumboo." Though it smelled so strongly of rum she didn't think she could get it down, once she finally tasted it, she liked it and the fact that it made her head throb much less.

Night had fallen when she ventured out to the main deck. "Hello," she said, joining Gayle at the rail as she gazed at Jamaica. "Did I miss anything?"

"Isn't Port Royal beautiful?" Gayle asked wistfully.

Celia saw the flickering firelight in the various buildings and heard lively music drift over on the wind amid the sounds of cicadas and croaking frogs. Fireflies seemed to glint in every direction, and the sound of water lapping against the moored ship almost hypnotized her. "Aye," she answered, awed.

"You should have seen it before the disaster."

"Disaster?"

"Aye, it devastated the place. There was a great tremor, a quake. Then a tidal wave rolled in and buried thousands of people where they stood. Buildings sank into the ocean. 'Twas a ghastly tragedy."

"When was that?" It must have struck this serene tropical Eden many years back, Celia assumed.

"Ten or so years ago." She sighed deeply. "Christ, I miss it."

"What are we doing here? Didn't James say his sister was taken to Kingston?"

"Most of the island's commerce has moved to Kingston, now that Port Royal is crippled. But I need to sell *Corona d'Oro* here and get some information. Do you feel like coming with me?"

Celia nodded. "That bumboo made me feel a little better."

"I assumed that you must, since you're fully upright."

"What's in that drink, anyway?"

"Sugar, nutmeg, and 'the hair of the dog that bit you,'" Gayle answered cryptically.

"The what?"

"To get over too much drink, you need to engage in even more."

"How peculiar."

"But don't drink any liquor while we're in port."

"You can be over-bitten by the dog, I assume?"

Gayle laughed. "Aye, and you just might lose a limb."

Celia again donned a cutlass, at Gayle's prompting, and the two joined Abernathy, who as usual was ready for a drink, and Caruthers, who still made Celia somewhat nervous. They walked through the docks toward a rather seedy-looking tavern and gambling hall on the edge of the island called The Sign of Bacchus.

"Why do you need to sell the *Corona d'Oro*?" Celia asked softly as they trudged along. "Why not keep it and amass a fleet?"

"A few reasons," Gayle replied. "First, I don't have enough crew to properly man her. She's a large vessel, and I've barely enough men to sail my own ship. Also, I'm worried that her reputation is too notorious in these parts. Everyone in the Caribbean despised Santiago as a brutal rotter. I don't need people engaging me because they have a score to settle with him."

"That makes sense."

"And I don't want a fleet. The more men you have, the more attention you call to yourself, and the more ways you have to divide your loot. After a certain point, you would have to actually sack entire townships to earn enough wealth to keep everyone happy."

"So you don't have grand dreams of vast riches? You don't plan to retire someday soon to your own island somewhere, ridiculously wealthy?"

Gayle slowly responded. "I *would* like to retire one day and not want for anything, but I don't need vast riches. Obviously I wouldn't turn down being ridiculously wealthy, but that's not my goal."

"What is your goal?"

"To be happy—nothing more. I don't need to be famous, or infamous, for that matter."

At the tavern Celia surveyed the surroundings and realized what a palatial and inviting drinkery The Bountiful Teat had really been. She even pined for it momentarily. This place was much darker and decidedly more sinister. It smelled of an amalgam of mildew, urine, and at least one other key ingredient—decaying flesh, perhaps?

"Abernathy," Gayle asked discreetly, "what's the name of the bloke who runs this fine place?"

"Deadeye Magee."

"Is he sightless?" Gayle asked.

"No. Not completely, but he can supposedly make anyone blind with just one drink—some concoction he brews himself. He calls it Satan's Foul Seed."

"That sounds scrumptious," Celia commented sarcastically to herself.

"Have you tried it yet, Abernathy?" Caruthers asked.

"Aye. And while things blurred a bit, I'm still drawing breath."

"Well, if anyone can stomach it, Abernathy, it's you," Gayle commented. "You could swallow flaming lamp oil and still think the barman diluted it."

Caruthers laughed so hard he snorted like a pig.

"There Deadeye is," Abernathy said, pointing to a stout, dirty man behind the bar with a cloudy eye that didn't move with the other. "I'll tell him you wish to speak to him."

"Bring back a bottle of rum," Gayle said. She paused and looked at Celia. "And a bottle of water."

Abernathy turned up his nose at the mention of water, but he nodded acceptance and shuffled over to address Deadeye Magee. Celia sat with the other two at a squalid table in a very dimly lit corner.

After an awkward silence, Celia turned to Gayle and asked, "At some point last night, did I stand on a chair and crow like a rooster?"

Gayle grinned. "Now that you mention it, I believe you did."

"Christ. Don't you think that would have been courteous to mention?"

"Mention?"

"Aye. Something along the lines of 'by the way, last night you were pretending to be farm animals.' Like that."

"It seemed more polite not to. Kinder somehow."

Before Celia could respond, Abernathy returned with a bottle of rum, a bottle of water, and four glasses. Gayle filled a glass with water and set it in front of Celia with a wink. "Here you go," she said. "Make tonight farm-animal free."

Celia glared at her as the rest of them poured rum into their glasses, clinked them in celebration, and started to drink.

Deadeye Magee soon pulled a chair noisily up to their table and sat down, his girth making the chair creak tiredly. "You wanted to see me, girly?" he rumbled at Gayle, his voice deep and gurgly.

"Aye. I heard you have a bounty out for the pirate Santiago."

He squinted his good eye at her, then spat something dark on the floor, much to Celia's disgust. She downed some water to keep from staring at him and grimacing in revulsion.

"I might," he wheezed. "What's it to ye?"

"Easy money."

Deadeye Magee's laugh was throaty and obnoxious. "You think you can rid the seas of a brawny bastard like that? A little slip of a bitch like you?"

Gayle's face showed no emotion. "Aye."

He continued to jeer, wiping the tears from his eyes. He laughed deafeningly, but as he began to move his arm back to his side he seemed caught off guard by the dagger that now firmly held his shirt sleeve to the tabletop. Gayle winked at him.

"Now look here," he began forcefully.

"Shut your cake hole, old man. I'm here to collect the reward."

His eyebrows arched. "On what proof?"

"I have two things to show you. The first is moored not far from the docks."

"I don't follow."

"It's the *Corona d'Oro*. I'm told you might be interested in purchasing her."

He spat on the floor again. "You're fuckin' serious."

"I am. We took her unscathed."

"Well," Magee seemed to mull on this for a moment, "if what you say is true, I'll give you six thousand gold for her."

"Nine thousand. She's an impressive vessel."

"Seventy-five hundred," he countered, trying unsuccessfully to remove the dagger from his sleeve.

"Nine thousand," she repeated. "It's not negotiable."

He scrutinized her with his lone, functional eye. "If you can prove to me that stinkin' freebooter is dead, you have a deal—nine thousand total for the reward and the ship." Still he struggled to pull out the dagger, but couldn't. "But I'm not convinced yet."

Gayle removed the weapon with one deft movement of her wrist and began to clean her fingernails casually with the blade's tip, leaving it visible during their conversation. "That's when we come to the other thing I have to show you."

She nodded at Caruthers, who produced a golden snuffbox and sat it on the table before Magee. He ran his hands over the etched gold, which had Santiago's name ostentatiously engraved into the lid. "'Tis a beauty, sure," he grumbled. "But anyone could have—"

"Open it," Caruthers commanded.

Magee cautiously did so, and the real proof lay inside—Santiago's signet ring, still encircling his severed finger. He cackled brazenly, displaying a mouth full of brown nubs that Celia acknowledged was exactly how she had expected his teeth to look. Magee pulled the finger out in delight, and Celia gasped and flinched, startled at the spectacle. Magee kissed the fingertip in triumph. "You have yourself a deal, girly."

"Good," she replied calmly. "I need one more thing from you."

"What's that?"

"Some information. I'm told a slaver by the name of Captain Red McQueen came through here not too long ago. His ship's called the *Pleiades*." Magee seemed too elated with his newly acquired appendage to focus on what Gayle was saying, and he didn't respond. "This bloke may have brought his own whores to town," she added.

"Ah," he finally said. "I know the fella you speak of. He was through here but two days ago, and he did have a pack o' whores with him—on his ship, no less." He obviously expected Gayle and Celia to share his outrage, then realized these women were probably from a ship as well, apparently oblivious to their damage to good seafaring men and their vessels. He dropped that subject.

"Did he say where he was headed?" Celia asked.

"I didn't see or talk to the sailor, but I heard tell he's holed up over in Kingston waiting for his next load of slaves to haul back to England. He's taken over The Seven Spirits Inn, from what I'm told."

"Taken it over?" Abernathy asked.

"Aye. He's payin' the owner a tidy sum for all the rooms and the right to come and go as he pleases. He's moved his whores into the rooms to service his crew, they say."

"I understand," Gayle mumbled, finally sheathing her dagger. She glanced at Celia, Abernathy, and Caruthers. "Seven Spirits it is, then."

CHAPTER ELEVEN

T ain't fuckin' right," the grimy little man spat. "Those ruddy bastards have been at those whores for a good day and a half." He shuffled back to patrol the other side of the main deck of the *Pleiades*, but continued to rant. "We ain't had so much as a quick feel."

"Hold your wretched tongue," his shipmate replied. "Cap'n Red said he'd send men to relieve us, and he will. I'm sick of your bloody whining."

The shorter guard spun around quickly. "Whining? I just want what's bloody well due me. You don't think we've been left high and dry here, while the officers roger those whores all the livelong day? You're dafter than I thought, mate."

The taller, trimmer guard glared at him in disgust. "And you've no bloody discipline. If you'd leave your cullions alone for a fuckin' minute, mate, maybe you could forget about those whores long enough to do your bloody job."

"Sod off." He ambled along the deck "It's not right to go without like this," he muttered. "Goes against bloody nature, it does."

There was a loud splash and he whirled around, snapping his head from side to side.

"Mate?" he called hesitantly. "You there?" He hurried back to where his argumentative colleague had stood just a few seconds prior. "Hello? Where are ya, you fucker?"

His brow furrowed and he turned again to glance behind him, and in so doing, he moved his body directly onto the extended blade of Molly's very sharp cutlass.

"Lose something?"

His face contorted after she drove the steel completely through his chest and out the other side between his shoulder blades.

He didn't speak, and after he gave a last violent shudder she removed her weapon from him by placing her foot on his abdomen and pushing against him as hard as she could. The inertia sent his lifeless body over the rail and it landed gracelessly in the water.

She caught the eye of both Nichols and Dowd, and the latter motioned that they should head below deck. They did so silently, listening for signs of both the crew's whereabouts and their number.

Molly held up her hands to signal the rest of them to stay back and then slowly descended the steps below deck, holding her cutlass securely. A dozen or so pirates sat around a table, most so drunk they couldn't even hold their heads up fully.

A few turned toward her as she stopped at the foot of the stairs and stared at them.

"What's this, now?" one of them said. "Looks like we got ourselves a slut for the takin', fellas."

Another stood and ogled her hungrily. "Bring that sweet cunny over here, darlin'."

Molly slowly broke into a menacing smile. "Why don't you come take it?"

James lay across his bunk trying to read *A Field Guide to Tropical Diseases*, but his heart simply wasn't in it. Normally, the description of swelling limbs filled with vile fluids would thrill him, but today he kept thinking about his sister Anne.

What if the captain and her crew were too late?

What if she had been sexually defiled?

What if Celia and the captain had been right and Anne really was in that whorehouse because she was seeking a doxy herself?

All of those options made him wince, and he didn't know which of the three he liked least.

He tried to force his mind back to where it belonged and read aloud about pus. The passage did little to settle him.

A knock came from his cabin door.

"Aye?" he asked as he opened it.

Before him stood Celia, with a small trunk in her hands. "This is for you," she explained, offering him the chest.

"Here, let me take that." He set it on his bunk. "What is it?"

Celia stepped over the threshold. "Medical supplies that the captain obtained in port."

"Ah, good show," he said stiffly. He popped the latch. Inside were bottles of powders, assorted salves, and bandages. "She's quite thoughtful, our captain." He began to remove the bandages and roll them individually.

Celia picked one up also, wanting to assist him. "Let's hope they won't be needed tonight," she muttered softly.

"Is the captain a foolish woman? You know her better than I. Does she take unnecessary risks?"

"I haven't known her to be foolish." Celia clenched her jaw. "After all, she's never pretended to be a rooster, or something of that nature."

James frowned. "A what?"

"And even if she had, it certainly wouldn't have been necessary to tell her about it afterward. No. Just let it come back in small embarrassing snippets, right?"

He cleared his throat nervously. "I'm afraid I don't know what you're on about."

She was instantly self-conscious. "I'm sorry. I'm sure you're very worried about your sister."

"I am."

"You probably wish you had been able to join the battle party," she observed, continuing to roll bandages.

"Good heavens, no. That's no place for me, I'm afraid. I'd very likely run myself through with my own sword."

"How very troublesome."

"Quite." He glanced at her work with the bandages. "You are rather good at that, you know."

"I've done this before. My fiancé is a doctor."

"The devil, you say. Where is this fiancé of yours?"

"Back in Florida, gutless poltroon that he is."

"Do not malign the gutless, miss," he quipped. "We are not all a bad lot."

"You cannot be completely gutless, Doctor. After all, you dropped everything to come find your sister. Now look at you—a surgeon aboard a pirate vessel. You're waist deep in romance and adventure."

He quickly surveyed his quarters in distaste. "Hmm. Quite."

"Not really your cup of tea, is it?"

He shook his head, digging deeper into the contents of the trunk and sorting through the medicines. "I'm completely miserable." He appraised her. "This type of existence seems to agree with you more than it does with me."

"Oddly enough, I believe it does. This is the most excitement I've ever had. If you strung together all the moments before I boarded this ship that I thought were exciting, their sum total would be but an instant—like a lightning flash."

"But too much lightning can kill you. A life of security and predictability should not be diminished."

"Nor should it be overstated," she added pointedly.

He squinted at her as though unable to figure her out. "You are peculiarly refreshing, miss. Have you perhaps reconsidered dining with me?"

"I would not be able to eat tonight, I fear." She dropped her eyes. "Not until the battle party returns and everyone is out of harm's way."

He nodded somberly. "I do pray Anne is unscathed and the captain is able to commission her safe return."

"She seems a very cunning and daring woman, our captain. I am certain your sister is in the very best of hands, Doctor."

She again bit back her fear that something ghastly might happen to Gayle and she would be miles away here on the ship—powerless to help her.

Gayle finished her quiet surveillance of The Seven Spirits Inn and returned to the small group of crewmen waiting in the distance under the cover of large shrubs. She motioned to Abernathy, pointing at the guard outside the front door of the inn.

"There's that fat bloke," she whispered, "and another at the back door. The rest of them must be inside."

"That doesn't sound too tricky," Abernathy whispered back.

"You got a ladder?" She checked to make sure the guard hadn't discovered their presence, but he still seemed oblivious to them.

"Aye."

"Then be ready, my good man. Watch, and learn." She emerged from the shrubbery dressed in a fine lilac gown, then pulled the already plunging bustline down even farther, to enable her voluptuous breasts an apt and notable presentation.

She sauntered up to the fleshy guard at the front door, who was busily digging in one of his nostrils with his pinky. She tried to blink this vile vision from her eyes, but it wouldn't disappear.

When he finally noticed her, he removed his finger and ogled her lecherously. "Well, ain't you a lovely li'l slice of finger pie."

"I might be," she answered in a husky voice. "I need a man, something fierce."

"I got what ya need, dearie," he murmured, lunging for her.

"I'll just bet you do," she sidestepped him, "but not out here." She bored a hole into his eyes with her steamy gaze, grabbed the hand that had not been digging in his nose, and pulled him toward her. "Come with me."

He was astonished that a sex-starved nymph had dropped from the heavens right where he stood. And he had thought only mermaids answered wishes like this.

Suddenly, they were so far from the inn he could see no light at all. He reached out to grab the beauty by the waist and was disappointed that not only did she somehow evade him, but that in the very next instant a thunderous sound crashed and his head seemed to split open.

As the ground rushed to meet him, he completely lost consciousness.

Inside The Seven Spirits Inn, Captain Red McQueen—a large brute of a man—sat at a table, drinking rum straight from the bottle. His name obviously referred to his hair color, and he sported a thick orange mustache and beard that contained small souvenirs from the last several meals he had enjoyed.

His linen shirt, brightly stained from numerous random spills, hung loosely from his torso as he listened to a fiddle player, clapping to the rapid beat of the music.

Next to him sat Anne Keegan, bored with this revelry. Going into that whorehouse had been the worst mistake of her life. What she had hoped would be an opportunity to pass some pleasurable time with a lovely and willing courtesan had turned into many horrid and degrading weeks of abduction and sexual exhibitionism.

When the captain's men had burst into the brothel where she had stopped, they had simply assumed that she was also a whore. Luckily, she had been able thus far to avoid actually having sex with any of the crewmembers by informing the captain that she preferred the company of women. Now anytime the captain directed, she had to have sex with one of the whores—and he got to watch.

She supposed this wasn't a completely unbearable situation, as it was certainly better than being raped or killed, but it wasn't exactly gratifying. In fact, the captain made so much noise and carried on so lewdly while he watched, she found it increasingly difficult to pretend he wasn't in the room—which made it a challenge for her to arrive at her happy moment. Nonetheless, she somehow always managed.

Captain McQueen took another swig from his bottle of rum, then belched loudly. "Dance, lassie," he instructed Anne, motioning with the bottle.

"I'm not much of a dancer," she lied.

He set the bottle down and clapped to the fiddle music again. "You think I give a wicked shit? Dance."

"I would think you would want to observe someone more skilled."

"What I want to see, if you must know," he explained with a slight slur, "is your bloody tits properly jostled. So go on. Get up and shake 'em, or I'll cut the fuckin' things off and shake 'em myself."

Anne frowned and looked about self-consciously at several other crewmen in the inn. "Can I just shake them for you here at the table?"

The captain seemed as though he might contemplate this offer, when in strode a beautiful redheaded woman in a low-cut lilac gown. She glanced about the room, and when her eyes settled on McQueen, the corners of her mouth rose slightly.

"Great jumpin' Jesus," he called, clearly pleased with her countenance, yet puzzled by her arrival. "Who are you, lassie?"

Gayle seductively strolled over to his table and stopped, instantly certain that the petite blonde next to him was James's sister—so strongly did she resemble him. "The name is Gayle," she said provocatively. "And who are you?"

"The hell with who I am," he spat, rising to his feet. "Who let you in here?"

"I told that nice fellow outside the door that I was meeting my beloved here, and he let me come right inside and wait. He said something about getting a drink. Are you having a party?"

McQueen stared lewdly, obviously thinking that his guard had procured him another pretty girl to fill to the brim with his seed. "Aye, and a fine party it is," he declared. "Come and have a seat here with me while we wait for your beloved."

Gayle feigned delight as she did so.

"Want a taste?" He waved his rum under her nose.

"Might I get my own?"

He laughed drunkenly and waved to the man at the bar, who appeared only moments later with a new bottle of rum and a glass. Gayle pulled the cork out with her teeth and poured herself a shot, downing it quickly to steel her nerves. She nodded toward the blonde and smiled. "And is this your lovely wife?" she asked McQueen.

The woman looked horrified and McQueen laughed. "No bloody chance o' that."

Gayle rested her chin on her hand and poured herself another drink. "And why is that?"

"She likes rogerin' women even more than I do," he proclaimed, drinking another few swallows of his spirits.

Gayle was amused. "Is that because she fancies ladies a bit too much? Or because you don't fancy them enough?"

Now the blonde laughed and McQueen scowled. "What the fuck does that mean? I'm all man, sweetie." He thumped his chest to convey the requisite virility.

"So I see." Gayle peeked again at the woman, who was studying her lustily. She should have bet money on this one, she mused. Her sexual orientation was like an ancient riddle Gayle had deciphered.

Question: When is a woman in a whorehouse not a whore?

Answer: When she's bedding a whore.

"And what are we celebrating?" Gayle watched the blonde's eyes fixed on her arresting bustline.

"Your arrival. I'm Anne," she said in a throaty timbre.

Gayle met her suggestive gaze, and it scorched her. She refilled Anne's glass with rum from her bottle. "Then have a drink on me."

As McQueen watched her and Anne, Gayle knew that, even as tipsy as he was, he could feel the sexual pulse that coursed through them like lightning. He was probably wondering why the blonde didn't see the power and the glory of the magnificent cock, as the rest of these whores did.

Anne drank the rum in one gulp, then held out the glass to Gayle for a refill.

"Aren't you worried you'll get sotted?" Gayle refilled Anne's glass anyhow.

"I have no problem holding my liquor."

"One of the few bloody things she'll hold willingly," McQueen groused. He picked up a long clay pipe on the table and turned it over, lightly rapping it against his palm to shake the old ash free.

Gayle chuckled at the inebriated man's obvious disdain. "Here, let me do that for you." She took the pipe from him and scooped up a wad of tobacco that lay on the table. Expertly, she loaded the pipe and stood, heading to the fireplace at the far end of the room. She grasped a long wick from beside the fire and lit the tobacco in the pipe, drawing in the smoke and alternately expelling it. Tossing the wick casually into the fireplace, she returned to the table and sat. She inhaled one last breath of smoke, then opened her mouth to form a circle and blew a large smoke ring into the air.

"Here you go, man with no name," she uttered in her husky voice, offering him back the pipe.

McQueen sat speechless and could only accept the pipe and gape at it as if wondering why it had never before pleased him in this way.

"Such skills you have." Anne seemed equally impressed. "Might you teach me that?"

"It would be my absolute pleasure," Gayle replied with a smoldering stare. Getting this woman upstairs would prove easier than she had planned.

"Oh, I can assure you it will," Anne added with a lusty wink.

Gayle was almost surprised by this woman's brazen sauciness and decided to see how far she could encourage it. "It's all in the way you hold your mouth, you see. You have to imagine you have a full, ripe plum in it."

"But we have no plums," Anne whispered, leaning closer. "What might I use in its stead?"

"Hmm. Quite a dilemma." Gayle lightly traced her lower lip with her index finger. "I'm sure we can find something about that size and shape that will accommodate our needs."

"Just a fuckin' minute," McQueen finally shouted. Gayle and Anne each snapped her head around to watch his sudden outburst. "I'm a goddamned captain." He slurred his words. "And if anyone eats any plums here, I'm the one who'll do it."

Gayle sighed. Why had she let herself imagine anything about this endeavor would be easy? Clearly the easiest thing in the room was Anne. "A captain?" she asked, trying to sound impressed. "How very manly."

Anne glowered in reproach.

"Aye," he answered, drawing in deeply from the pipe. The smoke came from his nose in white wisps. "And as the captain, what I say bloody well goes."

Gayle squinted as she assessed him. "Captain, you set me atwitter with your firm dominance."

He appeared quite pleased with himself. "Right," he said, standing. "Let's start eating those plums." He grasped her wrist and jerked her to her feet.

"But what about my beloved?" she asked innocently. "He'll be here any minute."

"He'll just have to wait his bloomin' turn, won't he?" He pulled her toward the stairs.

Gayle didn't struggle, but took the opportunity to count the number of crewmen in the inn. Eleven were in the main hall, and she estimated about a dozen bedrooms would potentially hold more.

McQueen reached the top of the stairs and pushed her into the first upstairs room. He immediately groped her ass, and she shoved him backward toward the bed, afraid he might feel her weapon through her gown.

"You're a plucky bitch," he observed, almost admiringly, as he wiped his mouth with the back of his hand.

She smiled. "And you are very astute." She shut the door and sauntered toward him. When she reached him, she grabbed his soiled shirt with both hands and ripped the fabric at the front, exposing his chest and abdomen—both covered with coarse orange hair.

He laughed malevolently and moved to grope her again, but she seized his wrists. "You'll get what you want in due time, Captain," she cooed, challenging him with her gaze. "Lean back and let me touch you. I'll take you to heaven."

He relaxed and sat on the bed, and Gayle pushed him onto his back seductively as she reached under her skirt behind her for the hilt of her dagger. She crawled astride him, moving her left hand over his exposed chest. When her face neared his, he wriggled as though he teemed with lust.

She stopped, their mouths only inches apart. "Are you ready for heaven?" she asked, letting her left hand continue down his body to his waist.

"Aye, bring it."

Before McQueen realized Gayle's plans, she had sliced his throat so deeply with the dagger in her right hand that his vocal cords were severed. "You've been a right bastard, McQueen," she whispered venomously, their faces still very close. "You may have to give up heaven and settle for hell."

His eyes were wide with pain and shock. He began to flail, and she moved off him and stood. In a moment he quit moving. She wiped the blood from her dagger on the bed linens and resheathed the weapon against her thigh.

Then she darted over to the open window and searched for the fifteen men who awaited her signal. Responding to her waving, they rapidly moved the ladder to the window and climbed into the room one at a time.

"Damn," Abernathy said, as he approached the bed. "He's a right mess."

"He looked no better when he was alive," she explained quietly. She outlined how many men were in the main hall. "Three ladies, including our Miss Keegan, are down there as well."

Gleeson, a tan, muscular buccaneer with long blond hair and a thick beard, sounded enthusiastic for a fight. "So the rest are upstairs somewhere?" He clutched his sword tight.

"Aye," she answered. "No doubt enjoying the other whores."

Abernathy's expression was serious. "Well, if we burst into the other bedrooms first, they'll make enough noise to alert those downstairs."

"True. Ten of you will come with me downstairs. We'll launch an attack on the main hall and surprise them. The rest of you fan out upstairs. If anyone emerges, finish him." She stopped, but had a sudden afterthought. "And nobody harms a whore, understand?"

They all nodded, apparently too excited about the impending battle to be disappointed that they couldn't rape at will.

"Who has my cutlass?" She extended her hand.

CHAPTER TWELVE

Annoyed, Anne sat slinging back rum faster than was prudent. What had happened?

That extraordinary redhead had entered. What was her name again?

Gayle, that's right.

She was absolutely ravishing, and even more captivating. She certainly seemed very different from the women Anne had known in England. If only she were not upstairs now rutting with that filthy swine.

She sighed, saddened at this most recent example of her theory— that the best women always seemed to prefer the company of men

Suddenly, a loud boom erupted upstairs. By the time she turned to see what had caused it, several pirate types armed and apparently crazed with bloodlust—leapt over the upstairs railing and landed behind her, swords drawn.

Anne screamed, which only seemed to prompt even more mayhem. McQueen's men quickly rose, drew weapons, and began to fight their attackers. Someone flipped a table over and its contents flew against the wall, the sounds of shattered glass filling the room like pealing bells.

She shrieked again and covered her ears as she backed into a corner to try to escape the mêlée.

A hand unexpectedly covered her mouth, which prevented her from uttering any more loud sounds.

"Shh," someone murmured into her ear. Able to turn her head just enough, she could make out that both the voice and the hand silencing her belonged to the redhead. She pulled sharply away.

"You," she said, again unable to remember the woman's name.

"You called the whole bloody fleet with your screams," the redhead hissed. "If you want to live through this rescue, Anne, you need to shut your gorgeous gob."

A short, wiry member of McQueen's crew advanced on the strange woman, who countered his cutlass deftly. Anne stepped back another few feet as the redhead took on this quick swordsman and matched him strike for strike. When he thrust his blade at her midsection, she spun away, grabbing his wrist tight, then struck it with her keen-edged weapon.

Both his sword and his hand dropped to the floor with a clatter. He cried out in pain and grabbed his bleeding stump with his remaining hand. His shrieking would have continued, if Gayle—yes, that was her name—hadn't chosen to run her blade through his chest. With a quick, upward jerk, she silenced him and he fell motionless onto the floorboards.

"By all that's holy," Anne shouted.

Another foe ran toward Gayle at full speed, and with remarkable dexterity and timing, she dropped her shoulder and elbow into his abdomen—leveraging his body weight and sending him sailing over her head. Once he lay on his back, her cutlass quickly found his heart and he was dead before he knew what had happened.

Before Gayle had fully withdrawn her blade from the body, a loud crack filled the air as the thick leg of a wooden chair connected with her head—sending her to the ground. Warm blood stung her left eye, and she fought valiantly not to succumb to unconsciousness. Completely disoriented, she glanced about for her sword, which was still protruding from someone's chest several yards away.

"Damn!"

Seeing no other nearby weapon to draw, she reached for her dagger. The man who had thrown the chair now stood before her, sweaty and imposing. Gayle wiped some of the blood out of her eye and drew the dagger with her other hand.

"Come on, then," she taunted, making her attacker laugh.

"I want to savor killing you," he said slowly.

She tried to clear her head enough to gauge the distance to him if she were to throw her dagger. Sadly, with one eye so irritated, she was afraid her aim would fail her—and a missed shot would leave her with no weapon at all.

"I'm sorry I can't oblige you," she answered weakly.

He opened his mouth to respond, but before he uttered a sound, the blade of a cutlass emerged through the center of his chest. His face froze, and blood trickled from the corner of his mouth as he sputtered, then collapsed.

Abernathy stood tall, holding the hilt of the weapon that had saved her.

"Thanks, mate," she said, trying to stand.

"No worries." He assisted her to her feet. "If I save you another fifteen times, we'll be close to even, I reckon."

Gayle surveyed the room. All of the enemies down here were dead or unconscious. She directed her men to settle a scuffle upstairs, and four men dashed back up, ready to strike.

"You're an earsplitting one, aren't you?" Gayle asked Anne as she retrieved her weapon.

Anne assessed the redhead now. She was bent at the waist, cutlass again in hand, trying to catch her breath. Her head was still bleeding, and blood flowed down her face, her jaw, and farther still down her neck. She still wore the same lilac gown, which was now stained crimson, though most of the blood wasn't her own.

"Who are you?" Anne was awestruck.

"Captain Gayle Malvern. I'm here to rescue you."

The crew that had remained on *Original Sin* was elated when the captain's battle party returned to the ship. Celia had not been prepared for how bedraggled they would be—especially Gayle. Abernathy was helping her walk, and she wore a blood-soaked, makeshift bandage around her head.

As they staggered on deck, Celia ran to her. "Gayle, are you all right? You look like hell."

Gayle chuckled. "Thanks. I suppose I am a bit out of trim."

James emerged from below deck ready to give aid, but when a small blonde boarded the deck of *Original Sin*, he ran up to her and hugged her—twirling her around in the air joyously.

"Anne. Thank God, you're safe."

"James?" She seemed confused. "How did you get here?"

"I followed you all the way from Bristol. I signed on to the crew of this ship in return for rescuing you." He finally put her down.

"You signed on with Captain Malvern?"

"I did."

She smiled. "Thank you."

He then darted over to Gayle. "Hell's bells, Captain." He examined the gash in her head.

She shook her head wearily. "You need to tend to Gleeson first. He's losing a good deal of blood."

James nodded, but didn't rush off to see Gleeson until he gave Celia some instructions. "Take the captain to her cabin and clean her up. If the head wound keeps bleeding, come get me straightaway. Otherwise, give her some rum and put her to bed."

Celia agreed and encircled Gayle's waist, leading her back to her quarters. She paused as several prostitutes stepped on board. "You brought the whores back with you?"

"Temporarily. They're not here for me," she told Celia when she raised an eyebrow. "They asked to come, and I thought they would be good for morale."

Celia began to guide her again toward the captain's quarters. "Morale on this ship is fine and you know it," she muttered.

"Fine, perhaps, but not outstanding. It can always be better."

They walked through the cabin door, and Celia pushed Gayle toward the bed. "You and your bloody doxies. I'll be right back. Get comfortable."

Gayle removed her bloodstained gown and stripped down to nothing. She climbed under the blanket, pulling it up to her waist, and sat propped up, her back against the wall.

"Here we—" Celia stopped speaking as she entered and her eyes locked on Gayle's bare breasts. "Um…you…" The door shut behind her.

"You said to get comfortable. That dress was binding."

Celia merely blinked several times, quickly.

"What's that you've got?"

"Ah, yes. I brought some water and a sponge to clean you up." She didn't move any closer, but merely stood there gaping.

"Are you trying to will it over here with your mind?"

"Oh, sorry." Celia moved hesitantly, looking very uncomfortable.

"Is it still bleeding?" Gayle touched her head softly.

Celia finally sat on the edge of the bed. "Let me see." She dropped the sponge into the water and wrung it out, then began to wash some of the blood off gingerly. "This isn't too bad."

"Shit." Gayle jerked her head away. "That stung."

"Sorry. I'll try to be gentler." She resumed her efforts. "I see you located James's sister."

"Aye, she's quite a handful."

Celia stopped what she was doing. "Is that a good thing? Being a handful?"

"No, *getting* a handful is a good thing. *Being* a handful isn't."

"Ah. I see. A subtlety that changes things significantly."

"Verily."

"And did you discover why she was in a brothel in the first place?"

"She was sampling the wares, so to speak."

"Was she now? Our good doctor may find that news somewhat disquieting."

Gayle laughed. "I imagine he just might."

"What hit you—a brick?" She rinsed out the sponge and wet it again.

"A chair, I think. Whatever it was, it flew."

"And you caught it with your head?"

"More like it caught me."

"Are you dizzy?" Celia asked.

"Slightly, and my vision is a bit blurred." Gayle pointed to a bottle of rum on her desk. "Do you mind handing me that, sweetie?"

Celia retrieved it. "Shall I get you a glass?"

Gayle scoffed and put her lips to the neck of the bottle. "Would you like some?"

"I'd hate to mimic more barnyard animals," she replied as she removed the remaining dried blood from the side of Gayle's face.

Already taking another medicinal swig, Gayle nearly inhaled the rum into her nose when she began to laugh. She sputtered and choked.

Celia patted her on the back. "I'd like to apologize and say you didn't deserve that. But I can't, because you do."

Gayle scrutinized her with one eye closed. "You are a sweet vexation, Celia Pierce."

She chuckled. "Not a handful?"

Gayle moved toward her slightly. "Not you."

They sat for over a minute, their faces only inches apart. They looked longingly at each other, but Gayle didn't have the nerve to move closer.

A knock at the door broke their silent reverie.

Gayle pulled the blanket up to cover her breasts. "Enter."

As Dowd hurried in and strode to the side of the bed, Celia busily rinsed the blood from the sponge.

"Cap'n," he said. "The *Pleiades* is ours."

"Excellent. Did any of the men want to join us?"

"No, but I did learn that their cargo arrives in the morning—just before dawn."

"Black ivory?"

"Aye."

"Then we should have a party on board to claim this cargo."

Dowd appeared pleased. "Consider it done. How many men, Cap'n?"

She thought for a moment. "Take ten, since we've no idea how many men they will have transporting it."

"Aye, aye." He nodded, then turned and left.

Gayle reached back for the rum and helped herself to another large gulp.

"Black ivory?" Celia asked, evaluating Gayle's wound a final time.

"Slaves. McQueen deals in slaves, and a new group will be delivered before first light. Very fortuitous timing."

"Why fortuitous?"

She took another swig. "Because by late tomorrow, everyone will probably know McQueen is dead."

"And then they wouldn't bring the cargo. Did you kill McQueen?"

"Would it bother you if I did?"

"I'm not sure. I might feel better if I knew you at least had some regret about it."

"It's hard to feel regret when the man had so little good about him. He bought and sold people for a living."

"Perhaps he was a devoted husband."

"He kidnapped a pack of whores for his own amusement and took them to another country."

"A man of temperance?"

"He had a bottle of laudanum in his pocket when we searched him."

"He was kind to animals?"

Gayle laughed. "No doubt. He hated people and treated them like shit, but monkeys he probably loved."

"Why are all these people so bloody awful?"

"I told you there were things about buccaneers that would turn your stomach. McQueen is a prime example, I'm sorry to say."

"Well, I'd say you look a damn sight better." Celia finally set the sponge and bowl of water aside.

"It's stopped bleeding?"

"I believe so." She paused awkwardly. "Is that the only wound you sustained?"

The question hung in the palpably silent air.

"I'm not sure."

Celia rolled her eyes. "You don't have a cramp that needs to be massaged out, do you?"

"You've heard that one, have you?"

"Deception is beneath you."

"If only you were, as well."

"Is this you at your seductive best, Captain?" She seemed amused. "Is this the point where the wenches tumble blithely into your bed?"

Gayle sighed. "Apparently not."

Celia helped Gayle recline, then pulled the blanket over her. "Don't underestimate the power of sincerity, Gayle."

"Sincerity?" She felt somewhat groggy.

"Some ladies want to know they're more than just a lap-clap. They don't want to hear the same declarations that won some other wench the night before."

"And some ladies won't believe anything you say, no matter how much you mean it."

"Shh. Close your eyes. You need to sleep."

"Aye." Her fatigue was rapidly taking over.

Celia brushed her fingertips lightly over Gayle's swollen temple.

"Are you staying a while?" Gayle asked, without opening her eyes.

"I might."

"Because I do love to flirt with you. It cheers me."

"Then it seems the least that I can do."

"The very least. Please let me know when you're ready to do more."

Celia stayed in the captain's quarters until Gayle fell asleep, which took very little time. Clearly she was drained from battle, and the blow to her head had done little for her vigor.

As Celia opened the cabin door, she was startled by a small figure lurking just outside it. As she shut the door and her eyes adjusted to the darkness, she recognized Anne.

"Ah, am I too late?"

"Too late?"

"Has the captain already found a companion for the night?"

"I'm sorry," Celia stammered. "Are you saying you're here to—?"

"Tend to some unfinished business."

Celia furrowed her brow in irritation. "Not tonight, you won't."

"What do you mean?"

"Exactly what I said." Celia tried to keep from raising her voice and waking Gayle. "Ask your bloody brother to find you a place to sleep, and sod off."

"Are you completely mad?"

"No, but apparently you're deaf. Gayle's been injured and she's sleeping now. You'll need to find someone else to mount tonight, you bloody gadfly."

With that, Celia returned to the captain's quarters and shut the door. She stood silently, waiting for the sound of Anne's departing footsteps, and after an extended moment, it finally came.

Celia wasn't sure what had upset her so much that she became totally unhinged, but she decided it was probably something quite logical and completely appropriate and pushed the thought aside.

Gayle lay on her right side in bed sleeping soundly, her chest slowly rising and falling.

Celia sighed and climbed in next to her. She didn't trust that shrew Anne to stay away all night. After all, someone needed to make sure the captain was safe and resting comfortably. She owed it to the entire crew, didn't she?

She turned on her side to face Gayle's back, then awkwardly tried to stretch out without brushing against her.

Gayle suddenly rolled over, facing Celia, and her right arm intimately moved over Celia's waist, but she didn't awaken.

Celia lay uneasily studying Gayle's striking and now placid features that, at present, were extremely near. She tried to force herself to relax and close her eyes.

CHAPTER THIRTEEN

When Celia's eyes fluttered open, she was momentarily disoriented. Behind her sat Gayle, dressed and seated at her desk, drinking a steaming tankard of tea.

"Good morning, Celia. Did you sleep well?"

Celia ran her hand through her mussed hair in bewilderment. "I suppose so."

"I imagine you did, since you're still completely clothed— damn the luck." She took another sip of tea. "Would you care for breakfast?"

"I would." She swung her legs over the edge of the bed and stretched. "Clearly you're feeling better. Aren't you the least bit interested why I slept here last night?"

One corner of Gayle's mouth rose playfully. "If it's any reason other than that you simply couldn't bear to be away from my side, then no. I'm not interested."

"Are you aware that James's sister came here to see you?"

"Really? Why?"

"Apparently she felt you and she have some sexual chemistry. I believe she meant to bed you." She rubbed her eyes sleepily.

"And you stayed here with me to thwart her?"

"Well, you needed your rest. Besides," she stood and faced Gayle, "you certainly wouldn't have been at your best—head wound and all. Would you want to send that girl back to Bristol thinking you were an inept fumbler?"

"Inept fumbler?" she asked, rising.

"Surely you have a reputation of some kind to promote. Had I not intervened, all of England might soon have heard that you were all thumbs, so to speak." She coughed nervously and stared at the floor, fidgeting.

Gayle chuckled. "That reason may be even better than the one I was deluding myself with. I'd say you owe me."

"Pardon?"

"You owe me," she repeated, holding up her index finger and stepping closer. "One night of torrid, passionate, hungry sex." She waited for a response, her finger still erect in the air.

Celia raised a saucy eyebrow. "I'll see if Anne's still willing, then."

"Sweetie, Anne is nothing but willing. That may be the solitary word on her tombstone when her life is snuffed."

"It's good to see that you fancy the intellectual types."

"I thought we were speaking about the types who fancy me."

"Yes, the blond and lusty type, it appears. I'm sure you'll have no problem arranging your night of sex." She said the last word as though it were something extremely distasteful.

"As much as it saddens me, we have other, more pressing things to attend to, Celia."

"Do we?"

"Aye. We're back in Port Royal. We need to make a quick stop and then take our leave in a brace of shakes."

"What's happened?"

"Only what we planned to happen. Dowd and some of the men went to the *Pleiades* and waited for the slavers to arrive with their cargo."

"How many did they have?"

"About a hundred." Gayle crossed her arms. "Once we dispatched the traffickers we gave the slaves the option of either signing on to *Original Sin* or going free and trying to find their way back to the Ivory Coast."

"Did any sign on?"

"Twenty-four did. The rest disappeared into the night with their families, or were hoping to return to their families. The poor, bloody bastards."

"So we're sailing back into Port Royal to—"

"Sell the *Pleiades* and all the jewelry we've acquired. There's a shop in town run by a fellow who'll buy the loot we're carrying, which makes it much easier to split among the crew."

Celia nodded.

Gayle cleared her throat. "So, are you interested in coming along?"

"To fence your plundered spoils? How can I refuse?"

"If only you were this eager in regard to my first offer."

By the time Celia had readied herself, Gayle had already sold the *Pleiades* to Deadeye Magee for a very healthy sum—as, sadly, fully fitted slave ships were worth a great deal more than simple sloops or merchant ships.

It was still very early in the day, though, when she and Celia entered a seedy place in Port Royal called The Queen's Lavaliere. It was amazingly filthy, considering the fact that the stock was nothing but jewelry and gemstones.

The proprietor of the shop, a short, elderly man, sported the red, blotchy complexion of a raging alcoholic.

"Good day, fine ladies," he said, seeming to sense from Celia's and Gayle's odd yet tailored clothing that they might possess ample purses.

"To you as well, sir," Gayle said, striding to the counter, a substantial leather satchel slung over her shoulder. "I've been told that you have a fair eye and will give a proper price for gold jewelry."

In actuality, Gayle had heard nothing of the sort and knew that statement to be utterly false. This little man was known to be as crooked as a ram's horn, and it took someone who knew what they had and what it was worth to beat him at his own game—just the kind of challenge that Gayle relished.

His rosy, gnomish face crinkled in delight. "You have heard correctly, my dear." He shuffled over to where she stood at the counter.

"I have acquired a number of fine items," she said, opening her satchel.

The gnome's eyes lit up. Gayle could smell the aroma of rum on him and was glad she was here early in the day, as she envisioned him to be a wee, angry monkey of a drunk. She eyed him suspiciously.

She produced several jeweled items from Santiago's stash and set them on the counter. The shopkeeper picked up the sapphire-encrusted dagger and withdrew it from the bejeweled scabbard, examining the blade.

"'Tis a pity this is so flawed."

"Flawed, is it?" Gayle asked. "Show me where."

He pointed to one of the larger stones. "Here. This jewel has a blemish, inside."

She studied the stone closely. "That must be the drink talking, little man. That sapphire is perfect. Every jewel on this is perfect."

"What?" He seemed stunned by her recrimination.

"I have no problem putting this 'flawed' merchandise back in my satchel and disappearing from this shop forever, my soused friend."

"Bah. I didn't say the flaw was a large one." He retrieved the dagger and assessed it again.

Celia slowly perused the wares on the other side of the shop and tried not to touch anything, as several layers of grime covered it all. Behind her the little shopkeeper was making an offer of some kind, to which Gayle firmly replied, "Bollocks, old man." She tried to ignore them both.

So much had happened in the last two weeks—she felt like a completely different person. The thought of returning to Florida to marry Phillip seemed totally foreign now.

Perhaps the gypsy woman had been right after all. Phillip had never really been the one for her—she supposed she had known it all along. She'd tried to convince herself otherwise to make her lot in life seem more palatable, but she wouldn't be able to abide such delusions now.

What had the fortune-teller said was her fate? Something about water, which, given the past two weeks, truly was a given. Practically every moment had been on or near water.

Then she had said something about a tempest—"a royal tempest's gale." Lord only knew what "golden fire in twilight" referred to. And if Anne was the woman abducted by the seven sisters, then the rest of her fortune might be just as painfully inadequate. She sighed.

"Look, you vinegar-pisser," Gayle was saying—the bitter words commanding Celia's attention—"I'll not be bamboozled."

"You are abusive, woman," the elf shouted back.

Suddenly, an item in one of the cases seized Celia's interest. She wiped some of the scum away from the glass case to get a better view of the ring inside.

It was magnificent—a gold band with a stone the likes of which she'd never seen. It sparkled with blue, green, and red.

"Something catch your eye, Celia?"

Gayle was suddenly beside her. She had been so rapt in this bauble that she hadn't even heard her approach. "That ring's exquisite," she whispered, pointing to it.

"Aye, that's a beauty."

The goblin appeared to remove the ring for closer perusal. Celia pointed out which one she wished to see, and when he withdrew it, the stone caught the light brilliantly.

"What is this gem?" Celia slipped the ring onto her finger and marveled at how well it fit.

"It's an opal," he answered reverently. "That one is a twilight fire opal, as it looks like fire, ocean, and sky are inside the stone."

"It's lovely." She admired it on her hand, holding it in a beam of sunlight, then caught herself. "What did you call this again?"

"A twilight fire opal."

"On a gold band," Celia added.

Gayle didn't seem to understand and shook her head curiously.

"A golden fire in twilight," she clarified.

Gayle's eyes widened in recognition. "Well, trice me. And what ungodly sum are you charging for it, old man?"

His eyes twinkled. "Well, this ring does two things for the wearer," he explained dramatically. "It protects from disease, especially blindness. The opal is said to keep your eyes clear and bright."

"And the second?" Celia asked.

"It's an aphrodisiac."

"We'll take it," Gayle blurted.

Celia supposed that she could have resisted more when Gayle offered to buy her the opal ring, but she did feel strangely drawn to it. And apparently, buying the item had helped the negotiation process with the shopkeeper. Gayle managed to unload all her precious items, netting them an astounding 7,500 gold doubloons.

"'Tis a pity we can't stay in town longer and spend some of this money," Gayle said as they strolled from The Queen's Lavaliere.

"I had no idea piracy was so lucrative." A gust of wind blew her hair wildly.

"In ordinary circumstances, it's not. You must be a good-luck charm."

"I doubt I'm the cause," Celia said humbly, stopping at a merchant's fruit stand and lifting a ripe mango to smell. "Perhaps it was that gypsy fortune-teller. Maybe it wasn't my fortune she saw. Maybe it was yours."

"It was your palm she studied, not mine. Besides, two of her predictions have come true. What else was there?"

"Ah, a 'royal tempest's gale.'" She put one mango down and picked up another, testing its firmness. "Perhaps she meant you."

Gayle stared off to the south. "Hmm…I don't like the look of those clouds."

"Aye," the fruit merchant replied politely. "Storm's a-brewin'."

Another gust of wind hit them, and Celia asked the merchant how much the mangoes were.

"Three for a penny," he answered toothlessly.

"Maybe next time." Gayle took Celia by her hand. "We need to get back to the ship."

"Why the rush? Still worried about what happens when they find McQueen and his crew?"

"No, we have a newer, fresher concern." Gayle pulled Celia briskly through the marketplace.

"Bloody hell." Celia sighed in exasperation. "What's happening now?"

Gayle stopped and faced her. "Look at the clouds over my shoulder."

"Gray, and pleasantly billowy."

"And the wind?"

Celia paused. "Rather blustery."

"Now stop and listen. Do you hear the birds? The frogs? The cicadas?"

"No. How very odd."

"Are you ready for the rest of your fortune to be realized?"

Celia saw nothing but solemnity in Gayle's expression. "A royal tempest's gale?" she asked weakly.

"We're in bloody Port Royal, after all." She jerked Celia back into motion and they hurried toward the docks.

Celia processed that statement as she allowed Gayle to weave her through obstacles. "Shit," she mumbled, viewing the storm clouds in a new and alarming way.

CHAPTER FOURTEEN

"Cap'n," Dowd screamed. The wind and rain whipped him so strongly Gayle could barely hear him. "We're making no headway."

"Aye. I was afraid of that. She just won't wear it," she yelled. *Original Sin* was almost totally unable to maneuver in the storm.

"Can we ride it out, you think?" he shouted, clearly fearful.

Gayle wiped the rain from her eyes. She had tried to outrace the storm, and that tactic had clearly failed. If she was to truly try to weather it, she needed to decide now—while it was still possible to climb the rigging and secure the sails without anyone being swept overboard.

"Aye," she finally answered. "Furl the sails and drop the anchor. We'll ride it hawse-fallen and hope the masts don't get spent."

"Aye aye, Cap'n," Dowd called, scurrying off to pass her orders to the crew as quickly as possible.

"And we'll hope we don't get spent either," she added to herself.

Below deck, Celia was becoming nervous. Gayle had practically sprinted back to *Original Sin* once she saw the storm rolling in, had all but lobbed the whores back onto the dock, and had departed in great haste. As the ship rocked violently, its wood creaking in dissent, she sat on the edge of her bed in virtual darkness, as no one was allowed to have a lit flame aboard while the seas were so rough.

She sighed.

She had left her door propped open so that faint light from other parts of the ship provided something for her slowly adjusting eyes to focus on. Above deck, powerful gusts blew, and the scrambling crewmen shouted as they battled to keep the ship afloat. She worried for Gayle and wondered about her safety up there, as this wasn't fit weather for anyone to be in.

Celia fidgeted nervously with her hands and fretted about their fate. "Bloody fortune-teller," she muttered.

She thought she heard a scream from above deck and jerked her head up, but she was uncertain if it was another vicious gust of wind shrieking through. The ship lurched suddenly starboard and, thrown off balance, she had to steady herself with both hands or be thrown backward.

They could perish in this tempest, she supposed, but she wasn't really afraid to die—though she regretted not doing certain things. She had wanted to accomplish so much in her life and had thought she'd have so much time. Now she realized that before she'd boarded this ship she hadn't really been living—merely going through the motions of a life.

She again heard what could have been a scream, but this time it sounded more clearly like a woman. Suddenly concerned that something had happened to Gayle, she stood and stumbled to the passageway, listening for any sign that might ease her mind.

Another shriek came, louder this time, but briefer and seemingly closer. She decided that whoever it was, it certainly wasn't Gayle. She crossed her arms and waited curiously.

The ship suddenly lurched to the windward side, prompting another shrill cry. Now the source of the caterwauling was unmistakable— Anne, who was stumbling toward her, trying to steady herself with her arms extended sideways to brace her against the passageway walls. An aftward lurch produced another screech as she struggled to stay on her feet.

"What are you doing?" Celia was nonplussed by this woman's irrepressible panic.

Anne leaped and screeched again, obviously startled by Celia in the darkened doorway.

"Od's bodkins," Celia exclaimed. "What's gotten into you?"

"We're all going to die, every bloody one of us!"

"Calm down, for Christ's sake. It's just a little squall. It'll pass in no time."

"Every time we get thrown one direction or another, I know we're going to roll over. And every time, the bloody sea's teasing me."

"Exactly," Celia said, trying to use her best let's-calm-down-the-loony voice. She put her hand on Anne's back and ushered her into her quarters. "Come in and sit. You'll feel better if you do."

Anne moved slowly into the cabin, taking tiny steps. "It's so dark in here."

"It's soothing," Celia lied. "Like having your eyes closed without having to go to all the trouble of actually closing them."

When the ship pitched violently, both women hit the aft wall of the cabin. Anne began to wail again, this time ostensibly without end. She only stopped long enough to draw enough breath to start again.

"Stop it," Celia shouted, grabbing her by the wrists. "Stop it, I said." She shook her slightly, hoping to jerk her back to her senses.

When that rather direct approach failed, Celia did the first thing that crossed her mind. She slapped Anne sharply across the face.

Her screaming ceased.

"You bitch," Anne growled, and struck Celia back as hard as she could.

Celia couldn't believe this woman had slapped her, and fury suddenly coursed through her. "Bloody harpy." She struck Anne again and grabbed her by the forearms.

They struggled wildly, working against both each other and the motion of the ship as it tossed violently on the waves. Anne screamed again as they struggled, prompting Celia to shout, "Oh, shut the hell up, you tedious shrew."

Abruptly, the ship heaved leeward again just as Celia pushed Anne in the same direction, and the two of them lost their balance and flew against the wall, landing hard across the bed. Anne's head struck a thick wooden beam of the cabin wall, and Celia slammed against her.

Anne's eyes were now closed, her face peaceful and her mouth open.

"Anne?" She placed her hand in front of Anne's nose and mouth and felt air moving in and out. That was a good sign. She saw and felt no blood, though she did detect a small bump on her temple, which would no doubt be a large, unsightly knot by morning. She sighed in relief.

"If only I'd done that sooner." She stood and swung Anne's legs onto the bed so that her body rested fully across it. "Bitch."

"Is everything all right in here?" Gayle stood in the doorway, completely drenched but looking concerned. "I thought I heard screaming."

Celia froze for a moment guiltily. "Shh," she finally whispered, putting her index finger to her lips. "Anne's asleep."

Gayle seemed completely perplexed, since she had clearly heard heated cursing mere seconds earlier. "Asleep?"

"Aye. We mustn't wake her. The storm's got her knackered." Celia shambled to meet Gayle in the doorway in an obvious and shameful attempt to feign sneaking.

"And she's in your bed why?" Gayle asked in hushed tones, gamely playing along with this excruciatingly evident ruse.

"Fatigue simply took her." She gestured with her upright hand toppling over to one side like a newly felled tree. "She literally dropped off to sleep."

"And you didn't...help her find sleep?" Gayle asked in disbelief, checking Anne for signs of life.

"Of course I helped her. I'm a good Christian." The corners of Celia's mouth rose ever so slightly.

Gayle spied the bump on Anne's head, then turned back to Celia. "And how are you?"

"Quite well, thank you. How are you?"

She was charmed by Celia's completely unexpected and bright response. The woman seemed to have no fear whatsoever. "I've certainly been better. You might as well come with me. We wouldn't want to wake Anne."

"No, I imagine she'll be quite cross when she wakes. She's not really a morning person, you see," Celia explained.

They left, shutting Celia's door behind them, and struggled to Gayle's quarters, the ship still being tossed wildly as they entered. The windows on the aft of the ship provided more natural light in this room.

"Hell's bells, Gayle. You're completely soaked. You look a right mess."

"You do love to tell me that," Gayle replied as she rummaged through her trunk for a dry change of clothes. "You may not have noticed, but it's raining."

Celia closed the door behind her and latched it. "Really? I thought I heard something outside. Are we still trying to sail our way out of the storm?"

"No, we've secured the sails and dropped the anchor."

"Why?"

"We've little hope of doing anything other than riding it out now. With any luck we traveled fast enough that we're on the outskirts of the storm, and it's not bearing down on us."

Celia walked slowly toward her. "Are you terribly worried? Surely you've faced storms at sea before."

"Aye, but this is a particularly nasty one. It's blowing marlinspikes up on deck. By guess and by God, she's a hurricane."

"Oh."

Gayle turned to her in concern, suddenly questioning if she should have been so candid. "Are you worried? Have you been through a hurricane before?"

"Aye, Florida gets its share. But I've never experienced one on a ship in the middle of the ocean."

"We'll be fine. *Original Sin* has weathered many a storm, mark my words."

Celia stepped toward her and scrutinized her. Her wet hair was plastered down her back, and small droplets of rain still clung to her face and fell from her clothes to form shallow puddles beneath her. Celia placed her hand gently on Gayle's cheek, brushing her cheekbone softly with her thumb.

Gayle was unable to speak, amazed at this unforeseen show of tenderness.

"Gayle." Her hand now slowly traced Gayle's jawline.

She stared into Celia's crystal blue eyes, stunned by what she saw in them. "Aye?"

"Before I die, I need to touch you."

CHAPTER FIFTEEN

Pardon?" Gayle was completely astounded that Celia seemed to be making a sexual advance toward her, and that she was taking this rather inopportune time to do so.

The ship continued to sway as Celia's hand moved downward to trace the buttons on the front of Gayle's sopping-wet shirt. "I know I probably sound completely mad," Celia said, her eye contact sultry and intense. "But I can't stop thinking about you—what it would feel like to be with you."

"You can't?"

She shook her head seductively while biting her lower lip. "My desire consumes me," she added in almost a whisper. "I want you so very badly."

Gayle needed no more time to contemplate this situation. She crushed her mouth against Celia's with an immense hunger and moved her hands smoothly along Celia's back as their tongues touched and entwined.

The ship, thrown windward, propelled them against the door, but they didn't stop kissing or slow their frenzied exploration of each other.

Celia grasped Gayle's sodden shirt with both hands and yanked it open, propelling buttons everywhere. "I'll sew them all back on later," she promised hastily before she started kissing Gayle's exposed neck, all the while still struggling to remove the shirt.

"Sod 'em," Gayle blurted, flinging her shirt behind her and pulling Celia to her again with zeal. She began to unbutton Celia's shirt with her right hand while she moved her left down Celia's lower back to cup her firm backside. "Christ," she murmured into Celia's ear. "You feel so good, love."

Celia shook as though chilled and moaned before she continued her ravenous attack on Gayle's lips with her own.

Once Gayle had completely unbuttoned Celia's shirt, she slid her hand around Celia's waist and up her back, the smooth skin making her throb. With her other hand she made contact with Celia's right breast and gasped.

"You're so beautiful, Celia." She moved down to unbutton Celia's breeches. "I need to feel you."

"Aye, feel me. Feel my want of you."

Before Gayle could do so, a sudden lurching of the ship sent them hurtling leeward, and though they struggled to stay upright they didn't let go of each other. Gayle pushed Celia so she sat on the bed, then removed Celia's shoes and breeches. She then took off what remained of her own wet clothes and moved toward her, tenderly leaning Celia against the mattress—their mouths locked and their tongues eagerly exploring.

She rolled Celia onto her back and began to impatiently kiss her way down Celia's body.

"You're so bloody good at that," Celia whispered as Gayle interrupted her journey south to lovingly taste Celia's right breast and gently nibble it. Celia's back arched and she placed her hand behind Gayle's head, her fingertips mimicking the movements of Gayle's mouth.

Celia's body was on fire—just as in her dreams, only tenfold. She had never known she was capable of feeling this way, but as much as she loved the sensations, she needed release—a magnificent frustration, of sorts.

"God, Gayle. Please touch me."

Obligingly Gayle did so, without taking her mouth from Celia's breast, and her fingers slid easily across Celia's slick sex.

Celia cried out softly at the first sensation and closed her eyes as Gayle repeated the motion. Everything felt so damn good that she thought she would burst from sheer bliss.

She ran her hands along Gayle's naked back, scraping her fingernails inadvertently across her skin. Gayle returned her mouth to

Celia's, and their tongues tangled excitedly while Gayle continued to stroke her.

Gayle's nude body over hers inflamed her, and she couldn't get enough of the taste of her lips. She began to grind against Gayle's hand, and her legs opened wider.

"Do you feel it building, dear?" Gayle whispered. Celia could only nod as she closed her eyes, her body surging with need. "I can feel your hunger. You're aching, aren't you?"

Celia answered with a loud moan, so Gayle concentrated on Celia's clitoris, her mouth moving back down to one of her full breasts. The motion of her tongue on Celia's nipple mirrored the motion of her fingertips, which Celia liked tremendously.

"Christ," Celia called, as something within the depths of her soul began to slowly intensify. "God damn," she added, her hips grinding erotically. A stirring slowly moved through her, amplifying in exquisite torture. She cried out as it continued to build until her sight and hearing temporarily ceased to function. Then she cried out again as the release finally took her, surging through her veins like lava.

Gayle repositioned herself and rested her forehead against Celia's. "All right?"

Celia was breathing heavily and nodded. "No wonder you like sex so much. It's bloody brilliant."

Gayle laughed, stopping only to kiss Celia. She let her hands roam over her lover's flushed, luscious skin. "You become quite religious in bed."

"What?"

"You do a lot of conversing with the Lord. Calling out to him, and the like."

"Truly?"

"Aye," she answered, kissing Celia's neck seductively. "I'd have preferred to hear my own name on your lips, but I suppose I can't complain."

"Mmm. You're making me want you all over again."

"Well, you'll not have me again until you've…had me, if you catch my meaning." Gayle moved her hand intimately down the curve of Celia's waist and lingered there.

"I don't want to disappoint you." Celia kissed her deeply. "I'm afraid I'm completely hopeless. I don't know how to touch you like that."

"There's nothing hopeless about you. You're a passionate, sexual woman, Celia. I saw how you arched your back and ground your hips against me."

"You say the most extraordinarily perfect things sometimes," she said as their eyes locked.

Gayle took Celia's hand as she rolled onto her back and pulled it gently between her legs. "I want you to feel my need for you, to know how hungry you make me." Celia gasped at the remarkable wetness there. "Do you feel how ready I am for your touch? How you make me burn? You always have."

"Tell me what to do."

"I need you, here," Gayle answered, placing Celia's hand precisely where she wanted it. "Stroke me, love."

Celia complied, and the feel of her lover's arousal was powerfully provocative. Gayle kept her hand on top of Celia's, and Celia watched as Gayle's body began to writhe in pleasure. Remembering how incredible she had felt in the same position, she kissed Gayle's breast and traced the nipple sensuously with her tongue.

Gayle moaned and thrust her breast eagerly toward her, clearly wanting Celia to somehow take all of it into her mouth. "My love," she said, pulling Celia's hand away.

"What is it?"

"I need your mouth on me. Your beautifully skilled mouth."

Celia was caught off guard by the request, but the thought of making love to Gayle and potentially bringing her the same type of ecstasy she had just experienced kept her from hesitating. She moved down Gayle's trembling body and began to kiss her muscular inner thighs.

"Please, my love. I can't wait any longer."

Celia charitably did as she was asked and began to kiss Gayle's vulva, noticing how her tongue sent tiny tremors through her body. Slowly, she became more confident as her lover's hips began to rock against her mouth. Celia loved both her seductive movements and her passionate taste.

Little by little she began to tease Gayle, purposely moving her tongue from where she could tell Gayle wanted it to be. Then, just as quickly, she would return it to that spot and linger there, making Gayle breathe heavily and moan.

Gayle's hand rested lightly on Celia's head, then she shuddered and cried out. Celia curled her lips in delight at her newfound sexual power. She moved back up the mattress, and when Gayle captured her mouth Celia relished the taste of her lover's lips.

"Was that my doing?" she asked playfully, sitting astride Gayle.

"Every last bit of it." Her hands trailed reverently down Celia's throat between her breasts and to her stomach. "Did you enjoy it?"

"Every last bit of it."

"Since the storm hasn't killed us yet, I'd like to keep making love to you until that happens, if that's all right." Gayle ran her hands over Celia's backside appreciatively.

Celia leaned close and they kissed. "I'm yours for the taking."

Several hours later Gayle and Celia finally realized that the storm was abating. They had relished every moment of each other's insatiable ardor, and other than take a few brief catnaps, they had done nothing but make love.

Gayle lay on her side, her body spooning Celia's as she languidly appreciated the feel of her perfect bottom against her stomach. She let her fingers travel to her lover's right hand and lightly traced the opal ring on Celia's finger. "This was the best bloody money I ever spent."

"You undervalue your natural charisma." Celia ran her thumb along Gayle's palm.

"Something I've never before been accused of. I should rise."

"But I'm not done with you yet," Celia growled, turning over to face her.

"As appealing as that sounds, I don't know that I'll be able to accommodate you further without at least several hours' rest."

"Then why are you caressing my bottom?"

Gayle laughed lustily. "Because it's bloody magnificent. I can't seem to leave it alone. I'm drawn to it like a moth to a flame."

"I'm happy that it pleases you."

"'Tis merely one thing about you that does. There are so very many more."

Celia's blue eyes twinkled. "You needn't try so hard, you know. You've already gotten me into bed."

"And I hope I can keep you here," Gayle said, rising.

"Not if you're getting up, you can't."

"But the rain has almost stopped. I need to go take stock of the weather damage." She pulled on a fresh pair of breeches—the black velvet ones she had purchased in New Providence.

Celia eyed her appreciatively as she dressed. "And how bad might it be?"

"Well, if the masts are spent, we'll have the devil to pay and no hot pitch."

"Spent?"

"Broken off." She put on a royal blue shirt and began to button it. "If the masts did not withstand the winds, we'll have no way to unfurl our sails and control our course. We'll merely drift with the tide until we run aground, our supplies exhausted, and we starve, or we get captured."

"Oh." Celia frowned.

"Sorry you asked?"

"Completely."

Gayle bent down and kissed her deeply. "You are bloody adorable, you know that?"

"And I have a magnificent bottom."

"Verily." They kissed again, and Gayle was serious for a moment. "Now I need you to do me a favor, *amor*." She continued dressing.

The Spanish endearment lit Celia's face. "Anything."

"Get dressed and go check on Anne to ensure she's not dead. I'd hate to have gone through all that derring-do to rescue her just so you could snuff her."

"What if when she sees me, she attacks?"

Gayle winked, opening the door to leave. "Just trounce her again."

Celia peered into her own cabin with trepidation, somewhat surprised to see the room empty. Unsure of where Anne would have gone, she decided to search James's cabin. There was no telling what

Anne had told her brother, she thought as she ambled to his quarters with a pronounced lack of motivation. Perhaps she had made accusations that someone had pummeled her in some dramatic fashion, or maybe even beaten her with a mallet.

When she arrived at James's cabin, the door was slightly ajar, and with a renewed burst of courage she pushed it open. "Doctor, have you seen your sis—?"

Celia unwillingly focused on the sight before her. There stood James—his breeches around his ankles and his pasty ass on full display—mounting Molly, whose rather dirty feet were acrobatically resting on his shoulders.

"God's teeth!" She was so stunned she was unable to move.

"Celia."

James gasped and started to pick his trousers up, prompting Molly to shout, "Hey."

"Apologies. Forget I was here. Carry on," Celia finally stammered, backing away and climbing to the deck, mortified.

The rain had almost totally stopped, and she could see the sun behind a few clouds. Around her, many crewmen scurried about assessing the state of the ship and unfurling the sails. She was relieved that all three masts were intact.

"Celia," someone called from behind her. Turning, she saw James awkwardly holding his bunched breeches up at his waist. "Celia, wait." He shambled over hurriedly, unable to move fluidly with his pants unbuttoned. "Let me explain."

She winced, then tried to politely feign congeniality, though still embarrassed by the scene she had interrupted. "There's no need, Doctor," she said, opening her hands before her. "I should have knocked."

"The fault is mine, miss. I was acting as a common cad. I am not typically so very base."

"James, I am not here to judge you. You must do as your will dictates. I am only sorry I interrupted…that," she said, choosing the last word when nothing better came to her.

James looked panicked. "You misapprehend, miss."

"Do I?" She was bewildered that she could have simply mistaken innocent behavior for something otherwise, but since the notion intrigued her she decided to give him the opportunity to try and convince her. Across the deck, Gayle approached them, appearing interested.

"Aye." He cleared his throat. "She came in for treatment of a malady."

"And were you checking her internal temperature?" Celia asked in amusement. "Did she have a fever?"

James's face turned red and he fumbled for something to say. "She said she had something she wished me to examine."

"And you were merely being thorough," Celia said as Gayle stopped beside them. "If only all doctors shared your dedication."

"Is everything all right?" Gayle surveyed her ship's doctor standing on deck holding his unfastened breeches up and put her hand protectively on the small of Celia's back.

"Aye." Celia seemed derisive. "James was just explaining one of his medical-examination methods. It's quite innovative."

Gayle studied the doctor's completely sheepish expression and his state of partial undress and raised an eyebrow. "How so?"

"Apparently, he can ascertain illness with his member."

"I never said that," he stated. "It wasn't like that, I assure you."

Gayle was starting to become uncomfortable with the direction of this conversation. Instinctively, she pulled Celia to her and wrapped her arm around her waist. "And who, pray tell, was he attempting to examine? You?"

"Not at all. He was simply clarifying what I walked in on. It was strictly therapeutic in nature."

"And it involved his member?"

"Aye, it was in someone, but purely in the name of medicine, apparently."

"You're putting words in my mouth," he insisted. "It did start out as an examination but simply became something more."

"And this was completely consensual?" Gayle inquired suspiciously.

"Absolutely."

"Good," she replied. "Then I'd prefer to hear no more. You should go below and make yourself presentable, Doctor. You'll more than likely have some minor wounds to tend to shortly. I'm sure not all of the crew came through the tempest wholly unscathed."

He nodded, but seemed so completely thunderstruck that he couldn't move. His level of shock apparently tripled as Gayle leaned toward Celia, whispered something to her, then provocatively nibbled her ear. Celia's eyes closed in what appeared to be rapture, and she seemed utterly impassioned.

"Ah" was all he mustered in response. As Gayle gently fondled the round ass of the woman he obviously loved, he said "Ah" again and nodded frenetically. "I'll just go, then." He stared at them again, and they both looked back expectantly. "Right. Off I go, then." He turned and headed back below deck.

"Who was his member in, anyway?" Gayle asked after he vanished.

"Molly."

"What an odd match."

"I could have gone the rest of my life without seeing that, I'll have you know. I may have to stare at the sun to burn the image from my eyes."

"Well, before you blind yourself, I need a favor."

Celia's voice dropped an octave in desire. "What kind of favor?"

"Some of our sails were loosened and shredded in the storm—"

"And you need someone to sew some proper new ones?"

"Precisely," Gayle replied warmly.

"Consider it done. Other than that, how did the ship fare?"

"Not too badly, though we'll need to head to the nearest port for some repairs before we can sail any great distance."

Celia nodded. "I didn't find Anne."

"I saw her a short time ago wandering on deck. She seemed fine."

"Fine, as in not completely bone-sucking insane?"

Gayle beamed. "Well, more like fine for someone with a huge purple knot on her head."

The closest port was Saint-Domingue, and though it wasn't Gayle's favorite location—it did not boast the gamut of imports and exports that New Providence or Kingston had, for in those ports you could find anything you wanted, for a price—she was nonetheless pleased to find a fairly remote area to repair *Original Sin*.

The two new carpenters worked resolutely to get the ship trim and proper to sail again, and Gayle ensured more roasted meat and fresh fruits were on hand, and copious amounts of grog for the swigging.

Celia and Gayle traveled a fair distance on foot to reach a town that actually had a tavern. Prior to embarking on this journey, Celia had not spent much time in taverns, and now she understood why. This most recent establishment, a dilapidated and tiny structure called La Malediction du Diable, was by far the least desirable of the lot. Somehow each pub they managed to enter was exponentially more filthy and depressing than the previous one. Celia could scarcely imagine any place more revolting than La Malediction du Diable, as it was stale, dim, and dank inside, rather like a primordial cave, but it would have to do.

"What does the name mean?" she asked Gayle, trying not to touch anything as they entered and approached the bar.

"The devil's curse." Gayle stepped over a tanned, weathered man who lay prone on the floor, singing loudly in French.

"What a perfect description. They read my mind."

"Aye. It could do with some curtains," Gayle said, waving down the barman.

"Oui?" the dark-skinned, broad-shouldered native asked.

Celia marveled as Gayle and the barman began a lengthy conversation in French, of which she was able to interpret only occasional syllables. The barman seemed very interested in whatever Gayle was saying, and ultimately he nodded and left.

"Where's he going?" Celia inquired quietly.

"To see what provisions he has in the back to sell us."

"I didn't know you spoke French."

"Un peu," she answered smugly.

"Conceit is so unattractive."

"Well, how can you command someone to surrender if you don't speak their language?"

"I suppose that has a certain logic."

The barman reemerged then, and he and Gayle discussed something else at length. She finally withdrew some coins and paid him, then motioned for Celia to head back outside with her.

"His son will follow us to the ship to deliver the goods."

Sure enough, a boy of thirteen or so met them around back with a wheelbarrow filled with smoked meats, and they began the long walk back to the ship.

"So, I guess we need to decide our next destination," Gayle finally said, somewhat hesitantly.

"Meaning?"

"Meaning that we can either head back to New Providence to pick up Father…" Gayle swallowed as though the conversation was uncomfortable for her. "Or we can go back to the Florida Territories and take you to your family."

"And which would you prefer, Gayle?"

"Obviously, I'd rather you stay a bit longer. Which would you prefer?"

"And what happens once your father rejoins the crew?"

Gayle was silent for a moment. "I suppose he'll become captain again."

Celia shook her head. "Pity. You cut a fine figure of a captain."

Gayle's face lit up at the compliment as they continued up the dirt path. "Well, perhaps when he finally swallows the anchor and retires from the sea I'll have another chance to command my own vessel. Or if Father's stashed hoard is still where he left it, with my share of the loot I'll be able to buy myself the grandest ship ever built. Or perhaps purchase my own island."

"He has a hoard?"

"Aye, he's talked of it the whole time I've sailed with him. He was a crewman on a sloop that took a Spanish merchant vessel one clear morn and lost nearly all of its crew in the process. This resulted in a great many spoils and very few people to split them amongst."

"Typically not what would be considered a hardship."

"He loved the sea so much that instead of quietly retiring with his wealth, he took enough of the booty to buy *Original Sin* and stashed the rest somewhere in the Caribbean."

"Where?"

"He's never told me—or anyone, for that matter. He's not what you would call a trusting soul."

Celia chuckled. "After getting to know what buccaneers are like, I can't say as I blame him."

"Verily."

They marched on silently for a spell.

"So," Celia said, "I suppose someone here in Saint-Domingue could take another message back to my father, don't you think?"

Gayle looked quite pleased. "I have no doubt."

CHAPTER SIXTEEN

Nearly four weeks after his daughter's abduction, Andrew Pierce was becoming increasingly agitated and found it difficult to sleep at night. His wife Lucita had tried to help him relax— to convince him that their daughter's letter was a sign that she would be back soon, as healthy as she was when they last saw her.

He was filled with a profound growing doubt, however. The more the days wore on without any further contact from Celia, the more anxious he became.

When the scrawny seaman entered the tailor shop late in the day on that humid June afternoon, Andrew dared to hope that he might carry another missive penned by Celia.

"Can I help ye?" he asked expectantly.

"I have a letter for the tailor." He offered him the parchment in his hand.

Andrew eagerly snatched the dispatch and examined the seal on the back. It was the same dragonfly symbol that had been pressed into the last one. He quickly tore the parchment open and began to read.

Father,

I wish so much that I could talk to you and Mother about the amazing things I've seen in the last few weeks. I've witnessed deadly duels at sea, the despicable misery of the slave trade, and a perilous hurricane. Never have I dreamt that such vim and excitement existed. Before now I lived my life passively—allowing things to simply happen to me. Now,

I am in the thick of it, and everything that has preceded this venture pales in comparison. In a few days we leave Saint-Domingue and set sail for New Providence. I'll write you again at the next chance I get.

My deepest love to you and Mother,
Celia

This time, secured to the bottom of the letter, were five gold doubloons. He pried one off and held it out to the courier.

"Is this what you were promised, lad?"

"Aye."

"Then you'll have it, but I need to know a few things first."

The young sailor glared. "What things?"

"Who engaged you to deliver this?"

"A lady. A right pretty one at that."

Andrew narrowed his eyes. "What did she look like?"

"She had dark hair. And eyes blue—like the ocean."

"Was she with anyone?"

"Aye, with the cap'n of *Original Sin*."

"*Original Sin?*" He scrutinized the floor as he processed this information.

"Aye, quite a trim and proper square rigger, one of the nicest I've seen. It looks to have a crew made up largely of liberated slaves." He paused and laughed to himself. "A rather varied crew, you might say."

"And this dark-haired lady, did she seem well? Happy?" he asked, thinking only of his daughter.

"Aye, most happy, and right chummy with her cap'n, if you ask me."

Andrew was appalled. "Chummy?"

The seaman snorted in crude amusement. "I'd wager her depths have been plumbed, if ye get my meanin'."

Andrew grabbed the lad by his shirt and pulled him sinisterly close. "That lass is my daughter, you black-mouthed galoot."

The messenger's face registered instant remorse and a fair amount of fear. "Apologies, sir. I only meant that..." He clearly fumbled for a lie. "Her beauty goes deeper than her looks." He seemed somewhat satisfied with himself for being able to come up with anything at all.

Andrew glared at him angrily, unsure whether to indulge his powerful desire to disembowel this man. He took the doubloon in his hand and pressed it into the sailor's forehead firmly with his thumb. After several seconds, he let go and the coin stayed affixed there. "Take your bloody wage and get out of my sight. If I see you again, I'll spill your guts onto the ground."

The cowering seaman grabbed the gold from his forehead, leaving its impression embedded lightly into his skin, then darted out the door into the street, where he quickly disappeared from view.

Andrew stood motionless for a moment in the middle of his shop. "I'll not bloody have it."

Phillip Farquar stared at himself in the mirror before him. He combed his unruly eyebrows with his pinky finger and sighed, rather pleased with his results. How dashing he was.

True, his betrothed had more than likely been raped and cannibalized by murderous pirates, and he was terribly saddened that he would never be able to press his face between her melon-like breasts and thrum his lips together happily—such a waste of a wonderful figure. He sighed again.

Well, he would have to secure himself a new fiancée at the supper party hosted by the Ramírez family. He glanced at his black attire again and turned to the side to assess the exact slope of his posterior. What a shame that decorum prevented him from wearing anything bolder than this dreary color. Only by feigning that he was in mourning could he attend functions at all, though, fortunately for him, Celia had not yet become his wife, or he would have to perpetuate this charade even longer. He would simply have to make the best of it.

With any luck, the butcher's daughter would be there—a lovely little dark-skinned slice of pulchritude ripe for the picking. He imagined mounting her and closed his eyes to enjoy the fantasy.

A loud knock on the door jarred him from the butcher's daughter and her plump thighs. "Bloody consumptive quibblers." He stalked to the front door and opened it. "Pierce!"

Andrew Pierce eyed the fop angrily. "Going somewhere, Doctor?"

Phillip's eyes shifted nervously to the right, but he said nothing.

"Out to meet women, perhaps?" Andrew said darkly as he stepped over the threshold, shoving Phillip backward. "Has your fiancée's abduction already slipped your mind?"

"Of course not, sir," he stammered. "But I feel the need to be in the company of others, to console my broken spirit."

"Well, let us see what else of yours may be broken before the sun has set this evening."

Phillip blanched. "Are you mad, sir?"

"Not mad. Determined. You bloody well gave my daughter to the pirates, didn't you?"

"What? How can you accuse me of such a deed?" Phillip blustered.

"She has been corresponding with me, you great, addled blackguard."

"She's alive?" The instant he uttered the words he regretted them and contorted his face, biting his lower lip.

"I knew you had figured her for dead." Andrew drew a dagger that had been sheathed and cached in the small of his back. "You knew those ruddy pirates had only come for medical help, and you let them take her instead of yourself, didn't you?"

Phillip began to panic. Andrew appeared crazed and was brandishing a weapon that he clearly looked as though he meant to use. He was definitely going to have to get better locks for his front door. "I meant to save her," he shouted, lifting his hands protectively in front of his chest, palms exposed. "But they…they were so fast."

"Fast to take a seamstress over a surgeon? Not bloody likely."

"But 'tis true. I swear it."

"Well, you'll have your chance to save her now," Andrew announced. All Phillip could do was whimper slightly. "And then you can court all the bloody tarts you want. You're not good enough for Celia, or anyone with a heartbeat. You'll never have her now."

"You're raving like a lunatic, sir."

"Perhaps I am. It doesn't matter. You're coming with me to make this right."

"Coming? Where?"

"Down to the tavern," he growled, the dagger now pointed at Phillip's throat. "And bring every farthing you've got."

After Andrew dragged Phillip into The Three Sheets Tavern, Phillip felt horribly out of place. The sun had now set, so a number of criminal-looking miscreants were already sitting about slugging back rum.

"Why are we here?" Phillip whispered, still wearing his elaborately embroidered black overcoat. Everyone in the place stared at him, and he could sense them appraising his personal items and sizing him up for a good trouncing.

"To save my daughter, you worthless bastard." Andrew peered about the dark, fire-lit room. "He looks promising." He pointed to a dirty, swarthy man in the corner with long, dark hair trussed in a braid.

"Promising for what? An evisceration?" Phillip was starting to feel nauseous.

Andrew stared at him sinisterly. "Exactly." He grabbed him by the elbow and shoved him over to the tavern dweller's table, angled himself in his line of sight, and nodded. "Might we have a word with you?"

The mysterious man said nothing, but motioned for them to sit. He had a dark mustache that trailed to the edge of his jawline. But what commanded attention was a scar that cut a swath from just below his left eye, across his left cheek to his upper lip, then disappeared into his mustache and emerged on the other side across his right cheek.

He did not look like a kindly man.

Andrew sat down, appearing somehow pleased by just how nefarious this stranger seemed. And when Phillip insisted on standing, he pointed to an empty chair at the table. "Sit, you foppish poltroon."

Rapidly, Phillip did so. "Um, greetings. Allow me to introduce—"

"Shut your gob," Andrew barked. "We're not here to learn names, if you get my meaning."

The man with the scar squinted. "What's your business?" He spoke with a slight, yet indistinct accent.

"We seek someone to liberate my daughter from the horde of pirates that kidnapped her."

"Which pirates?"

"I'm told the ship is named *Original Sin*." Andrew glanced about in what Phillip assumed was an attempt to ensure no one was eavesdropping.

"Ah," the man with the scar replied. "Madman Malvern's crew. He once ate out another man's throat for singing an unsavory chantey."

"Mother of God," Andrew blurted. "Is he truly a madman?"

The man with the scar took a swig of rum. "Compared to some, he is judicious and wise."

Phillip was completely appalled and kept glancing at the tavern door to plan his escape. "Pierce," he whispered, "this is madness."

Andrew appeared oblivious to the danger of being in this wretched environment. "I need someone who will take on this Madman Malvern and return my daughter to me safely."

"She sails on board the ship?" the stranger asked incredulously.

"For the last few weeks," he answered. "I'm told he has despoiled her."

The man with the scar stood and headed to the bar. Phillip looked imploringly again at Andrew. "He's not interested. We should leave."

The man then returned with a fresh bottle of rum and two more tankards. He sat and poured the rum, offering the liquor to his guests. "Drink," he commanded them. Andrew took the pewter mug and emptied it, whereas Phillip held his in trepidation.

"Drink," Andrew rumbled, causing Phillip to throw the libation into his mouth and cringe as the liquid burned a path down his larynx.

"I am Fuks," the man said, offering no insight into his ethnicity.

"Beg pardon?" Phillip asked.

Instead of repeating the name, Fuks stared at Phillip appraisingly. "This lass is your daughter," he said, motioning to Andrew. "But who is she to you? Your sister?"

Andrew scoffed. "This cobbling oaf could never be the fruit of my loins."

"Hmm. So who is she to you?"

"Well…" Phillip eyed the door again hopefully.

"He is her fiancé," Andrew answered sharply. "Who let the pirates carry her away without lifting a bloody finger to stop them."

"So you have no bollocks." Fuks took another sip of his rum.

"But—"

"Not even the stub of one," Andrew said with a nod. "But he's only here for one reason."

"Oh?"

Andrew motioned with his head to Phillip. "Put it up, you de-balled mook."

Phillip slowly placed his swollen coin purse on the table and sighed in utter misery.

"And how much is she worth, then?" Fuks asked.

"Upon her safe return, five hundred gold," Andrew answered softly.

Fuks whistled. "Do you know where they are?"

"On their way to New Providence from Saint-Domingue."

"Hmm. And when did they leave?"

"The missive from Saint-Domingue arrived just today," Andrew answered. "It stated they were not departing for a few days."

Fuks finished his rum and slammed the tankard on the table dramatically. "Then there is time. You have a deal."

Phillip's stomach lurched. "Shit."

CHAPTER SEVENTEEN

F aster, my love," Celia moaned as she ground her posterior against Gayle's pelvis and Gayle's soft breasts pressed against her back.

Gayle sat behind her in the bathtub, one hand caressing Celia's left breast and the other urging her to climax. Her teeth lightly grazed Celia's shoulder and neck as Celia surrendered to the throes of her yearning.

Celia ran her hands along her lover's thighs as waves of pleasure racked her body and she cried out softly. After several tremors, she relaxed again and slumped against Gayle, sending warm water streaming over the edges of the tub.

Gayle kissed her shoulder and held her close.

"You know," Celia said, "that just keeps getting better."

"Mmm."

"Will each time be better than the last? How long can that continue?"

"Wouldn't you love to find out?" Gayle's provocative tone was a catalyst for goose bumps.

Celia turned over to kiss her. "Is that an offer?" she asked, when their mouths finally broke apart.

Gayle stared at her. "It is."

They kissed again, sending more water over the side of the tub, but not caring in the slightest.

"Land to," came a faint cry from above them. "New Providence off the starboard side."

"So we'll continue this later?" Celia asked in a husky tone.

"You bet your bewitching arse we will."

By the time *Original Sin* made landfall in New Providence, night had fallen and the amber Caribbean moon was lazily ascending. Gayle was anxious to see her father again and learn what progress he had made in the few weeks he had remained behind, recuperating.

Gayle, Celia, Dowd, Abernathy, and Churchill trooped ashore to The Bountiful Teat, eager for a fresh drink and a visit with Captain Malvern the elder.

"I'm sure he's better for this rest," Churchill said as they trod through the dimly lit docks.

"Aye," added Abernathy. "He's a salty old bastard. He'll outlive us all."

Gayle chose to remain quiet on their journey over, and Celia wordlessly held her hand as they walked.

When they entered The Bountiful Teat, Gayle was elated to see her father seated at the bar, a tankard in his hand. He seemed gaunt and significantly aged, but if he was drinking, he was certainly improved.

"What manner of landlubber is this I see?" she asked loudly.

Malvern smiled. "You didn't forget me, then."

"No matter how hard I tried." As Gayle hugged him, she could tell he was stiff and awkward. "How fare ye, old man?"

"Fair to middlin'." He groaned as he rose. The rest of the group had secured a larger table in the center of the tavern, and he slowly joined them there. Gayle steadied him as Smitty appeared from the back room.

"Gayle. There's a sight for sore eyes."

She kissed Smitty lightly on the lips. "Things go well, I see."

"Aye, I've a charmed life. Rum, miss?"

"How well you know me, Smitty." She felt a relief and ease that she had not experienced since her father had been wounded. "Enough for the table, and for yourself, of course. Join us."

"It's good to see you all." Malvern sat back down stiffly and his eyes steadied on Celia. "You…didn't you help tend to my wounds?"

She nodded silently.

"Has she joined the crew?" he asked Gayle.

"In a manner of speaking."

"I've joined the captain," Celia said, with a seductive expression.

Malvern's eyebrow cocked in surprise. "What an excellent predilection for the ladies my daughter has. You are quite easy on the eyes, sweetness." He regarded Gayle appreciatively. "Have you let all this captain business go to your head, lass? Is she part of your plunder?"

Gayle shook her head as Smitty arrived with a tray full of drinks. "She's here to fulfill a gypsy's fortune, quite by choice."

He winked at Celia. "Well, good luck taming her. She's a bit of a stormy petrel."

"She's brought us some rather good luck of late," Abernathy said, grabbing the tankard placed before him.

Gayle laughed and then watched her father reach for his rum with his left hand. Suspiciously, she appraised his right arm. He wasn't moving it at all. "So how are you feeling, Father?"

"Better."

"Well enough to take command of *Original Sin*?"

Malvern set the drink down and rubbed his bristly gray beard with his left hand. "I think my sailing days have ended, lass. It's time to swallow the anchor, I'm thinkin'."

"Why is that?" Churchill asked.

"Because he's not left-handed," Gayle interjected, taking a swig of rum.

Malvern chuckled. "I never could get anything by you, lass."

"Can you move it at all?" she asked in concern.

He looked down at it. "A bit. I can't hold anything. My fist won't close. It makes for a rather useless swordsman, I'm afraid."

"Perhaps you just need to practice," Dowd said.

Malvern shook his head. "This is my chance to get out alive, mates. God himself damaged my arm—to save my bloody life. I'm inclined to listen to him."

"What'll you do?" Abernathy asked.

"It's time to dig up the hoard and retire to the islands…get myself a good woman."

Gayle was intrigued. "So we're off to find your stash, old man?"

"You are. I'm staying here."

"Why?" Churchill queried. "Don't you want to command *Original Sin* one last time?"

Malvern's expression grew dark. "I don't think I'm meant to, mate. I have these cursed dreams…every night." He took a long swig of spirits. "Something's telling me to stay put, to belay here."

Gayle had never seen her father so weak and daunted before. She wasn't sure what his dreams had shown him, but he was a superstitious, unwavering man, so she didn't see any point in arguing. "You're a trusting soul, Father. How do you know we won't take your riches and keep them all for ourselves?" She asked the question playfully, but she genuinely wanted an answer.

"You'll all get a share. And you'll get the ship, of course. I just need enough to live on here. Enough to keep me in my boots with kill-devil, and in the company of a winsome wench or two." He swallowed more rum. "Preferably both at the same time if I can manage it."

"Then you shall have it," Gayle said. "So where is this hoard of yours?"

A smile crept slowly over his face. "Closer than you'd think."

Off in the dim glow of a small bonfire, many yards away from The Bountiful Teat, Captain Fuks, smoking a clay pipe, leaned against a tree. He strained to focus as someone approached. He hoped it was his quartermaster, but reached for the hilt of his cutlass just in case.

"Crenshaw?" he asked suspiciously.

"Aye, Captain Fuks," came the whispered reply.

Crenshaw—a tall, strapping fellow—stood before him with a woman, though he could not make out her face in the dark.

"And who would this be?"

"Desta," she said. "I was told there was a doubloon in it for me to come here and answer your questions."

Fuks did not try to hide his disdain. "And what's to keep me from slashin' your fuckin' throat right now, you simple bitch?"

"The pistol I have pointed at your bloody gut, you rancid bastard."

He squinted to make it out. The pale moonlight did seem to glint off something she held there. "Well done, Crenshaw," he spat. "You didn't disarm her first? I would expect a cabin boy to know better, and much more so a fucking quartermaster."

"I didn't think I'd need to, Captain. She's just a tavern wench."

Desta took a step back, assuring that neither man was out of her line of vision, then slowly took their weapons, tossing them several feet away. She scrutinized the man with the disfiguring scar on his face. "Where is the money you spoke of?"

Fuks nodded to Crenshaw, who produced a gold coin from his pocket. He held it up before her and she took it with her left hand, still firmly gripping the pistol with her right. Satisfied, she spoke again. "What did you want to know?"

"Some of the patrons in the tavern you work at," Fuks said. "I'm seeking a wench who may be among them."

"A particular wench?"

"Aye. A young beauty by the name o' Pierce. I'm told she's been of late on the arm of a certain pirate captain."

"Which captain?"

"Malvern."

Desta grimaced as she realized it was Gayle they sought. And the wench this man wanted must be the brunette who was with her, the one fawning over her in a most bothersome manner. "I know of whom you speak," she finally said.

Fuks sneered, his golden tooth visible even in the dim light. "And what does she look like?"

"Dark-haired, blue-eyed—the kind of woman who'd boldly take those that don't belong to her."

Fuks appeared surprised. "Surely the cap'n can't be rogerin' you as well."

Irritated, she pointed the gun directly at his head. "What else do you want to know?"

"What else can you tell me?"

She felt smug. "I know that the crew is off on the morrow to retrieve a buried hoard. They speak of its riches like it has no equal."

"A hoard, eh?"

"Aye. From the Spanish Main, no less. They say it's nearby, in fact."

Fuks looked at Crenshaw, his interest obviously piqued. "Well, we may just have collared two treasures for the price o' one."

Crenshaw laughed nefariously.

As much as Desta wanted to squeeze the trigger and finish this ugly bastard, she needed to tend to her wounded pride first. Gayle would be very sorry that she had chosen to ignore her and instead spend her time with that strumpet—very sorry indeed.

CHAPTER EIGHTEEN

At Madman Malvern's direction, Gayle drew up a map. True to his word, the location where he had buried his hoard was quite close to New Providence—in fact only a day or so away in the Berry Islands.

This cluster of small, mostly uninhabited islands was a vast collection of natural quays and beaches…and the perfect place to bury treasure, as those unfamiliar with this unsettled land would find it confusing and labyrinthine.

The hoard supposedly lay ripe for the picking beneath the white sands of a place called Deadlight Quay, which *Original Sin* made out for early the next morning, before dawn. The weather was bright and breezy, and the ship raced through the water.

In the doctor's quarters, Anne sat dejectedly nursing a tankard of grog.

"So how long are you staying on board?" she asked James, who was wiping down his medical implements.

"I'm not sure. I'm hardly what one would consider a sea dog. Most of the time I'm spewing over the side, but I told them I'd stay on if they recovered you from McQueen."

"Quite unexpectedly thoughtful of you," she said, sipping her drink.

"It would only be proper of me to remain until they can find another doctor."

"And you are nothing if not proper, James."

"Hmm, speaking of proper," he said, facing her, "you never have explained to me what you were doing in that house of ill repute."

"If you must know, I was there seeking company."

"Company?" His eyebrows raised in interest. "Company of a sexual nature?"

"Well, I did get my shilling's worth, if that's what you're asking."

"By God's great forelocks. And when were you going to tell me of this…this inclination of yours?"

Anne shrugged. "It isn't really your concern."

"Not my concern? Have you gone completely mad?" He shook his head. "I should have listened to Celia when she suggested you had such proclivities. She was right about you all along."

"Celia?" Anne saw the same fire in his eyes as she suspected burned in hers at that moment. "And what did that bellicose shrew have to say about me?"

"Don't speak of her like that. She's a beautiful angel and I adore her."

Anne was stunned for a moment, then laughed.

"What?"

"You do realize she's the captain's doxy, don't you, brother dear?" Her words were still liberally mixed with chortles. James looked bewildered. "Your wondrous bloody angel has the same 'proclivities' that I have."

"Well, I did suspect there was something between those two."

"There is little between them, if you get my meaning. Celia is the only thing that has kept me out of the captain's bed, you thickheaded prig."

He seemed unable to speak.

Anne laughed again at his reaction. "Did you really think she was pining for your glorious member?"

"You've been trying to seduce the captain?"

She could not suppress a grin. "Well, look at her. Wouldn't you?"

"No."

"Ah, so you prefer the dark-haired, shapely type?"

"I suppose I do."

"But Gayle is bloody magnificent. That gorgeous red hair and sense of danger. What a woman."

"Celia's body is more to my liking. She has a breathtaking bosom."

Anne nodded. "Noted, but Gayle's is more athletic. She cuts a fine figure, she does—swinging from a chandelier with a cutlass in her hand and a dagger in her teeth."

"I can't believe we're having this conversation."

"How about this? I'll help you win Celia if you help me win Gayle."

"I don't know."

"Mark my words, James. If you and I cooperate, we'll both get what we want."

He gazed at her in resignation. "You've a deal, sister."

Far behind *Original Sin*, just within the view of a first-rate spyglass, lurked the *Belladonna*—a fast, trim sloop purposely trailing them. Captain Fuks stood on the deck watching his prey eagerly and pleased that Malvern's crew seemed too focused on the loot they were bound to recover to notice him lagging in the distance.

"The winds aid us greatly," Crenshaw commented as he studied the chart in his hand. "They seem to be headed for the Berry Islands. If the treasure lies there, traveling at this speed they'll land by nightfall."

Andrew Pierce shuffled up to the two men, obviously irritated. "Why do you put off apprehending them? Surely a swift vessel such as this could easily close on them. You aren't even trying."

Fuks sneered at his passenger. "Look, old man. I agreed to bring you along so you could be certain no harm befalls your daughter. Though from the chatter I've heard, I think you're a bit late for that."

"You…what?" Andrew's eyes flashed with rage.

Fuks went on without skipping a beat. "But I didn't agree to involve you in my plans and let you question my orders. It would bode best for you to head back to your hammock before I set you to scutwork."

"Look here, you bloody maggot." Andrew's face turned red.

"Crenshaw," Fuks said, peering again through his spyglass calmly. "Take our inhospitable guest below and see that he is silenced."

Crenshaw grabbed Andrew by the throat.

"If you think I'm bloody paying you after this—"

"You will pay us, you great halfwit," Fuks stated menacingly, without tearing his attention away from *Original Sin*. "One way or the other."

As Fuks laughed, Crenshaw pulled Andrew below deck.

Even though the sun had almost entirely set by the time *Original Sin* reached Deadlight Quay, Gayle decided to lead a party ashore anyway, darkness be damned. She was accompanied by Molly, Nichols, Dowd, Sully—a small, dark-complected gunner's mate—and Caruthers, and they took the map, several lanterns, and many shovels.

Celia had asked Gayle if this quest couldn't wait until morning when they could see properly, and Gayle had simply answered, "Fortune waits for none," and kissed her heartily.

Excited, they rowed a small skiff past the shallow coral reefs that kept *Original Sin* from docking any closer to land. As they reached the white sands of Deadlight Quay and pulled their boat aground, the last glimmer of daylight had faded and what seemed like a billion stars surrounded them.

"Nichols," Gayle asked eagerly, "what does the map say?"

The gap-toothed fellow was little more than a boy, but he had proved to be dependable. Though now she trusted him with such undemanding tasks as overseeing the unloading of cargo, someday he might make a fine quartermaster, she mused. After all, he had done surprisingly well with Molly and Dowd when they cleaned up the *Pleiades*.

The gangly young man squinted at the map by the light of his lantern. "We should head east until we see a large dead tree," he finally answered.

Gayle drew her pistol warily as the group headed off where Nichols had directed. This quay seemed completely uninhabited, with little vegetation. After several minutes, they reached a tall charred tree, which had obviously been hit by lightning.

"That must be it, aye?" Dowd shone the light of his lantern on the tree and studied it more closely.

"One could assume," Gayle said. "Now what?"

"We head southeast and will eventually come across a group of small caves," Nichols added, facing that direction. The wind was now blowing forcefully against them.

The party adjusted the hoods on their lanterns to prevent the flames being blown out and trudged southeast. After traveling nearly two miles, they spotted the caves and breathed a collective sigh.

"According to this," Nichols explained, studying the map closely, "we need to find a cave opening so small that we'll have to crawl to enter it. That's where we need to be."

Gayle and her party scoured the cave formations eagerly, the adrenaline building as she and the others anticipated the feel of the exquisite hoard within their shaky grasp.

"Here," Sully shouted. Gayle led the charge to where he stood as he shone his lantern light on the cave near his small, bare feet. True enough, he had discovered a cave with an opening no larger than two feet in diameter. To enter it, one would need to be on his hands and knees.

"In we go," Gayle ordered, and each person dropped to their knees to carefully enter the cave one after the other. Inside, the cave was larger than it had seemed from the beach. All six were able to stand comfortably, though there wouldn't have been room for many more.

"There should be a diamond carved on the wall," Nichols said. "The mark of where to dig."

All shone their lanterns on the cave walls and began to slowly search for the symbol.

"Got it," Molly called with satisfaction. Gayle moved to where Molly stood and, true enough, a small diamond shape was scrawled there.

"My good crew," Gayle said happily. "It's time to start digging."

By the wee hours of the morning, they had completely exhumed the hoard—and what a hoard it was. Madman Malvern hadn't exaggerated when he had spoken of its vast wealth and some of the pieces' inestimable artistry. Euphoric, Gayle stood with her exhausted crew, transfixed by the wondrous gold.

They unearthed one large chest filled with doubloons, loose gems of assorted colors and sizes, and jewelry and small hand weapons of such adornment that no one had ever seen their equal. The other chest was filled with art objects that seemed profoundly valuable—rolled paintings, bejeweled plates of solid gold, and figurines—religious and otherwise. This truly was a treasure trove of vast riches.

Dowd pulled the first chest outside of the cave as Nichols and Sully pushed from the other side. In no time, they had both coffers, and as they exited the cave one at a time, Gayle heard a sound behind her. Before she could draw her flintlock pistol, a malevolent voice shouted.

"Leave it." Crenshaw had already drawn his own pistol. Behind him stood five henchmen, swords in hand. "All of you out," he directed. "Move."

Once all six crewmembers stood outside the cave, Crenshaw scrutinized them one at a time. "It's about bloody time you finished digging this shit up. Do you know how many hours we've been waiting for you? Bloody laggards."

"Who the hell are you?" Gayle snapped.

Crenshaw menacingly appraised her. "Your captor, sweetie," he cooed, inching toward her. "You're quite a juicy slice."

"Touch the captain and I'll break your bleedin' legs," Dowd murmured.

Crenshaw arched his eyebrows. "Captain? This young, supple bitch is your captain?"

"Aye," Gayle answered. "But I'm not too supple to slit your gullet in a fair fight."

Crenshaw laughed at her challenge, both unable and unwilling to conceal his profound amusement. "You...wish to fight me?"

"Nay. I wish to kill you. The fighting will simply get the job done."

He was puzzled at her defiance, yet found her bravado and beauty such a striking combination that he couldn't tear his eyes from her. He would give her the fight she was seeking, but he wouldn't kill her right away. He would first experience the bliss of being inside her. What a glorious feeling that must be, he mused. Then he could kill her. "How can I decline such a polite threat?"

"Just let me draw my cutlass."

Crenshaw passed his cocked pistol to one of his accomplices and drew his own sword. He gestured to the female captain to arm herself as well, and she wasted no time in doing so.

"Do let your shabby-lookin' crew know that if any of them move to help you, they'll get a bullet in their skull," Crenshaw added, as he started to move toward her.

The defiant woman's teeth flashed as she held her cutlass confidently. "And you might want to mention to your scab-ridden cronies that if they attempt to intercede in this fight they'll lose an appendage. Though we'll leave it a surprise which bits get severed. I do so like surprises."

Suddenly they collided, their blades clashing loudly amidst the starry sky and distant dirge of crashing waves.

Gayle lunged aggressively, emitting a hostile grunt as Crenshaw dodged her. She took some small satisfaction in the sound of his heavy breathing. "Am I not the weak, simple tart you took me for?"

He grimaced and lunged at her. She spun away and attacked again, slicing into his shoulder, eliciting the sound of tearing fabric coupled with his gasp of pain. A deep, guttural growl rumbled from him, and he flew at her. "Do not vex me, impudent whore. You will not like the way you die."

Deftly, Gayle deflected his blow, ducking and then leaping back up in attack. With each ensuing strike she advanced, putting him on the defensive and getting the upper hand. "But who is bleeding, you addled bastard? It surely isn't me." Her provocations were clearly affecting him strongly, and as his eyes flew open in fury at her words, her blade cut his cheek, drawing blood from his jaw and earlobe.

He screamed in explosive rage, and Gayle took advantage of his momentary outburst to attack again, this time targeting his abdomen. Crenshaw seemed insane with outrage, and every successful blow Gayle landed only seemed to feed it more. His shirt began to show bloodstains, whereas Gayle was untouched.

Suddenly, a shot rang out and she crumpled to the ground as everything went dark.

CHAPTER NINETEEN

Though Celia lay in bed, she was simply pretending to pursue sleep. She had no real intention of dozing—not until Gayle returned from her late-night treasure hunt.

The fact that so many hours had passed worried her, though she wasn't really certain what she was anxious about. Gayle's crew wouldn't turn on her after they unearthed the hoard, would they? Celia squinted at the burning lantern hanging beside the bed as she tried to imagine such a scenario. It was hard to envision. The men seemed to genuinely respect and care for Gayle, didn't they?

Suddenly a loud commotion began on deck. Already mostly dressed, she threw on some boots and darted topside to investigate.

Once there, she was horrified to see the crew pass Gayle over the rail, completely unconscious and covered in blood. They laid her gingerly on the deck as James knelt beside her and examined her wounds.

Celia glanced to Dowd, who stood beside her, appearing beaten and exhausted. "What happened?"

"Thieves," he rasped, breathing heavily and wiping his sandy face with the back of his hand. "Somehow the bastards knew we were there to recover a hoard. When the cap'n commenced slicin' up their leader, they shot her, then turned on us and took the treasure."

"By the Blessed Virgin!" She knelt next to James, who had ripped open Gayle's shirt to get at her wound. "How is she?"

"I'd say lucky." He stood. "Take her to my quarters where I can start removing some of this shot."

Gleeson, a very muscular lad, bent and lifted Gayle as though she weighed nothing and hurriedly carried her below deck.

"Is anyone else injured?" James asked Dowd. "Is she the worst off?"

Dowd spat on the deck. "Hardly. Caruthers and Nichols are dead."

"No," came an anguished plea from the crew that had begun to gather there.

"Aye, lads," Dowd said. "And the thieves have taken Molly. They'll make her pay for all our sins, I'd wager. Thank God they left Sully alive too, as I'd never have been able to get Cap'n all the way back on me own."

This grizzled, stocky man no longer resembled the drunken bastard who had tried to take liberties with Celia when she had first boarded *Original Sin*. He now looked like a man who had taken a thrashing for Gayle, then carried her unconscious body miles for medical treatment. Without hesitating, Celia kissed his sandy cheek and thanked him.

Less than an hour after Gayle returned to *Original Sin*, she was awake and in a good deal of pain. James had removed from her left shoulder all the shot fragments from the flintlock pistol that he could find, and had sewn up her multiple wounds.

Celia had stayed by her side for the duration and assisted him with the procedure.

"That should do it," he said, finishing the last of his sutures and dropping his medical implements into a shallow pail of water. "How does it feel?"

Gayle grimaced. "Like my bloody arm is on fire."

"Good. That means you still have blood flow. Let's get you bandaged up."

Celia took Gayle's hand and held it tight.

Gayle smiled weakly. "You always see me at my best."

"This wasn't exactly how I had imagined getting your shirt off," Celia said. "But I suppose it'll have to do."

James awkwardly cleared his throat as he applied the bandage, as though to remind them that he was still in the room.

"Tell me, how is the rest of the crew?" Gayle asked.

"Sully and Dowd have some nasty bruises and gashes." Celia hoped to put off giving her the bad news as long as possible. "They're the two who dragged you back to the ship."

"Good men," Gayle commented absently. "What of the rest?"

Celia glanced at James in discomfort, but neither spoke.

"What happened?" Gayle squeezed Celia's hand.

"I'm afraid Caruthers and Nichols didn't make it back, my love."

Gayle was obviously horrified. "And Molly?"

"The thieves took her."

"Bastards," James hissed. "Who are they?"

Gayle struggled to sit up, though she was clearly in a good deal of pain. "And how did they know about our mission?"

"Could one of the crew have had a drink too many and disclosed it to someone at the tavern?" Celia asked.

"Or someone overheard us." Gayle stood, pulling her torn shirt closed to cover her bare breasts. "We head back to New Providence. No one helps themselves to my crew and gets to live."

"Here it is, Cap'n." Crenshaw coughed as he directed the heavy coffer of gold he placed before Fuks on the deck of the *Belladonna*.

"You look a damn sight, Crenshaw," Fuks croaked, surprised to see his senior officer covered in what appeared to be his own blood. "Did you fight Malvern himself?"

Crenshaw clearly bristled at the inquiry. "Aye." The five crewmen who had made the journey with him began to chortle. "Silence," he screamed, as though he'd become completely unhinged. "I've acquired all the treasure with which you tasked me, Captain."

With that he bent and opened the first chest, and the rest of the crew gasped. Fuks marched forward to take a closer look at the gleaming gold and gems and nodded. "Excellent, Crenshaw. And the girl?"

Crenshaw snapped his fingers and someone pushed Molly forward before Fuks. Her mouth was gagged and her wrists and ankles were tied. "She's quite a fighter, that one. Not like any seamstress I've met."

"Jones," Fuks called. "Bring the tailor out here to reunite with his daughter."

Jones threw Andrew onto the deck, where he landed squarely on his ass, to the delighted guffaws of the crew.

"There you are, sir," Fuks said. "Just as we promised."

Andrew quizzically examined first the chest of spoils, and then the bound and gagged girl standing before him. "Whatever do you mean?"

"Your daughter, you great oaf," Crenshaw shouted. "At no small cost to my men. She bites."

"But that is not my daughter."

Crenshaw grasped Andrew by the hair, pulling his head up and staring daggers at him. "What do you mean she isn't your daughter? Of course she is. She's the dark-haired doxy of Captain Malvern."

"Nay. My daughter is taller and fuller than this girl, and she has eyes the color of the sea."

"Shit," Crenshaw said under his breath. "Malvern must have a whole harem of courtesans. We filched the wrong brunette."

Fuks strolled over to Molly and removed the gag from her mouth. "Who are you, maiden?"

Molly promptly spat in Fuks's face. "I'm Molly McCarthy, you ugly whoreson."

"Neptune's cullions," Fuks screamed, wiping the saliva from his face. "You're an insolent cunt."

"Do you know my daughter?" Andrew asked her, still cowering on the deck. "Celia Pierce?"

Molly paused. "Aye, the seamstress—the cap'n's lady."

"Is she well?" Andrew asked, hopefully.

"Aye. I'd gladly trade places with her right now."

"Exactly how many women are on this ship of yours?" Fuks asked.

"The seamstress, the doctor's sister, the cap'n, and me."

"The captain is a woman?" Fuks shouted. Agog, he turned to Crenshaw. "A woman maimed you this badly?"

Crenshaw glared back at him. "Aye, but she didn't live to tell of it."

"Hmph," Fuks muttered. He shifted his attention back to Andrew. "Well, sir. You've got two options. You can pay us what you promised, take this lass that we nabbed for ye, and treat her as you would your loving daughter; or you can head over the rail."

"What? But that wasn't our agreement."

"Aye, but that was before I had a bloody fortune at my feet. Now your five hundred gold looks like shit to me."

"You villainous snake."

"That's it," Fuks said. "Over the rail he goes. Give my greetings to Davy Jones."

As much as Celia wanted to talk Gayle out of simply changing her clothes and setting out on a journey of retribution, she couldn't set aside the thought of Molly at the hands of murderous thieves. She helped Gayle dress, marveled at her shoulder's dark bruising and swelling, and as the sun began to rise she stood nearby while Gayle addressed the crew of *Original Sin* up on deck.

She released her anger, and her fiery words riled the rest of the crew and forged them into a cohesive army like never before.

"So we find the bloody bastards that killed our brothers and kidnapped our sister and helped themselves to my father's fortune," she concluded.

The crew all cheered, prompting Gayle to shout, "Then man your stations. We return to New Providence to find the scum and run them through!"

CHAPTER TWENTY

Celia entered Gayle's quarters holding two warm tankards of tea. Gayle didn't even look up from her charts as she sat at her desk, busily plotting her course.

"Here, love," Celia said, setting the tea before Gayle. "Drink this. It will fortify you."

Gayle's gaze darted to the tankard but she didn't touch it. "Many thanks."

"Are you all right?"

"I fear not." She sighed. "I've been deluding myself these many weeks, thinking myself a fit and proper captain. Thanks to me, crewmen have died, been kidnapped and no doubt accosted, and my father's long-coveted wealth has been lost forever. I have to return to him with naught but regret and tell him I am a failure."

"You are no failure," Celia said, turning Gayle's chin to look deeply into her mahogany eyes. "You are the most amazing woman I have ever met. You are strong, yet compassionate—swift, yet canny and shrewd. You are all that I had thought I was foolish enough to aspire to."

"But I couldn't save Nichols or Caruthers, Molly may be enduring defilement a thousand different ways as we speak, and I am no closer to emancipating her—should she still be drawing breath. What if we are sailing completely in the wrong direction?" She raked her hand through her crimson hair.

Celia took her chin and kissed her softly on the lips—not an act of passion, but of reverence. "I, and every soul on this ship, know you to be a wise and capable captain. This crew would knowingly follow you to the ends of the earth if you commanded it. Do not doubt yourself, love, for no one else does."

Gayle wrapped her arm around Celia and pulled her close. "I do thank God for you," she muttered softly.

"Who you should really thank is Churchill," she commented. "He's the one who picked me out." She sat on Gayle's lap and continued to hold her.

"He does have very good taste."

"I'm glad I've passed muster."

"All hands to," someone called from outside. They both scrambled to their feet and rushed out on deck.

Hyde stood barefooted, his legs interlaced in the rigging of the ship, pointing over the starboard side of the bow. "A body, Cap'n," he shouted. "There's a body a-floatin' in the water!"

Gayle rushed to the starboard railing and stared at what Hyde had seen—a man draped over a barrel, floating with the tide. "Heave to and drop the anchor, lads," she called. "He looks to be alive. Summon the doctor."

Gleeson and Diego—a first-rate Spanish gunner—climbed the netting over the side and fished the waterlogged man out of the ocean. After tying a rope around his chest, they hoisted him up over the rails to other members of the crew.

"Father," Celia cried, running up to him.

"Celia? Is it finally you, dear?"

"Aye, Father," she replied. "What happened? Why are you floating around the Caribbean?" She began to untie the rope that encircled him.

"I could ask the same of you," he said weakly.

James then arrived and examined their new passenger. "He appears to have spent but a few hours in the water," he declared. "Can you stand, old man?"

"Aye. Though I am hardly old." Andrew struggled to get to his feet, and Celia moved quickly to his side to support him.

"Now isn't the time to go into it all, Father," she said. "Let's get you to the doctor's quarters."

"Father?" James repeated. Gayle simply shrugged and followed them all below deck.

"Father, I wrote you how I've come to be here. You did get my letters, didn't you?"

"Aye," he murmured. "I can't believe 'tis really you, girl."

"Did you come in search of me?" she asked hopefully as she led him through the doorway of James's quarters.

All Andrew could do was nod.

James entered with a ladle of drinking water. "Here, have some of this."

Andrew swallowed it eagerly and sat on the cot breathing heavily and completely soaked.

"Are you wounded anywhere, old...er...man?" James asked awkwardly.

"I don't believe so."

Gayle instructed Frederick to get Andrew a dry change of clothing, and the lad sprinted off to do so. She then bade everyone leave except for herself, James, Celia, and her father, shutting the door behind them.

Celia sat beside her father and hugged him. "How did you end up in the ocean, Father?"

Andrew took a deep breath. "I had hired a ship's crew to find you in New Providence, as your last letter said that's where you'd be. The blackguards threw me overboard after stealing a king's ransom from some other poor blighters. The reward I offered is a paltry pittance to them now, it seems."

"And what ship would that be?" asked Gayle. "What ship stole this 'king's ransom' and then sent you by the board?"

Andrew blinked several times. "The *Belladonna*, sailed by one Captain Fuks."

James glanced at Gayle. "Have you heard of this...Fuks?"

Gayle shook her head. "I'd remember a name like that. Where did you meet him?"

"In a tavern in Florida. He agreed to help me rescue my daughter from pirates in exchange for five hundred gold pieces."

"But you came with him?" Gayle asked.

"Aye, as I dare not trust a mercenary with my only daughter. But they returned with some other lass. Molly someone or other."

"Trice me," Gayle exclaimed. "You saw Molly?"

"Aye," Andrew answered tiredly. "A real vinegar-pisser, that lass."

"That's definitely her," James said.

"Do you know where they were headed?" Gayle asked.

He shook his head. "But they come from a pirate haven in Baracoa, Cuba. Mayhap they are headed back there to sell their booty."

"Mayhap," Gayle repeated softly. "And Molly? How does she fare?"

"I know not. Though she was bound, it would take a braver man than I to engage her."

"That's my girl," James said.

A knock at the door proved to be Frederick, arriving with a set of dry clothing. Gayle took the garments and handed them to Andrew. "Here you are. Change into these and you'll feel a world better."

"My thanks," he uttered. "But now I must find the hard-hearted cur who has despoiled my daughter."

"Pardon?" asked Celia, whose stomach lurched.

"The courier who brought your last missive said you had taken up with the captain of this vessel, Celia. Is that true? Has a ruthless reprobate stolen your chastity?"

Celia was very uneasy and awkwardly fumbled for an answer. "Stolen is such a harsh word, Father."

Andrew leapt to his feet. "I'll run the scoundrel through!"

"You would think a doubloon would be enough to buy a little discretion," Gayle mumbled to James. "What is this world coming to?"

"Easy, Mr. Pierce," James interjected, pushing the weary man back into a sitting position. "There's no need to run anyone through."

"Tell me I'm misinformed, Celia," he bade her. "Assure me you're as unsullied as the first days of spring."

She grasped his hands reassuringly and gazed into his eyes. "Would you settle for some time in midsummer?" she asked optimistically. "Perhaps July or August?"

"Ahh," Andrew bellowed, jumping to his feet again. "I'll cut out the mongrel's heart and eat it!"

"June," Celia amended. "I meant more like June."

James again stepped forward to placate Andrew.

"You're wholly tactless, aren't you?" Gayle whispered as she leaned near Celia's shoulder.

"Show me where your captain is," Andrew demanded. "I'll show him a thing or two at the tip of a blade."

"Sir," Gayle said. "I am the captain of this vessel."

Andrew fell completely silent and stood agog, unmoving.

"Captain Gayle Malvern," she introduced herself calmly. "Your daughter was good enough to help us tend to our wounded and mend our sails. No one has accosted or manhandled her in any way since she boarded this ship. It was I who sent you the doubloons attached to her missives, and it is I who beg your forgiveness now for the callous and desperate way in which she was spirited away into the night."

"Well said," Celia whispered back.

"So 'tis true," Andrew finally rasped. "Your Molly said the captain was a woman, and so she is. I thought it was just the rantings of a fearful trollop."

"Please, sir," Gayle continued. "Change into something dry. You and your daughter have a good deal of catching up to do. In the meantime I'll arrange something for you to eat. For now, I must take my leave as we need to mark a course for Baracoa."

Gayle turned and left the room, leaving a rather tense and baffling atmosphere behind amidst Celia, her judgmental father, and the ill-at-ease doctor.

As Andrew reclined on a cot in the doctor's quarters, he continued to pore over all that had happened to him in the past month. How had he lost control of his family? How had everything gone awry so suddenly?

After a knock at the door a petite, blond girl entered holding a bowl of some type of food.

"Beg your pardon, sir," she said politely. "I've brought you a morsel to eat."

Andrew was unable to offer thanks, so he sat up and simply nodded at her. She carried the steaming bowl to him and presented it.

"What is this?" he asked softly, not recognizing the smell.

"Boucan stew," she answered modestly. "It's actually quite good."

He tasted a small spoonful and found it somewhat on the salty side, but definitely edible. "And who are you?" he asked finally, in afterthought.

"Anne Keegan—the doctor's sister."

"Blimey, there are thirty lasses on this ship if there's one," he said, slurping up another spoonful.

"The captain agreed to take my brother to Jamaica for a small fee so he could rescue me from a slaver who had abducted me," she explained. "My brother James is a brave and cunning hero."

Andrew squinted at her as he chewed. "You mean that bloke who was in here earlier? The tall, pasty fellow?" He remained skeptical.

"Aye," she assured him, nodding vigorously. "He followed my captor across the whole of the Caribbean and then single-handedly defeated him and his crew of drunken whoremongers."

"Is that so?" he asked. Anne nodded again. "However did he manage that?"

Anne searched the ceiling for inspiration. "He is a master swordsman, you see. As well as a successful doctor—terribly rich, really." She decided the thicker she laid it on, the better. "Of course, now he'll never truly be happy."

"And why, dear girl, is that?"

"Alas, he has fallen in love with your daughter, though she does not give him the regard one might give a gnat. I know not why."

"He's in love with Celia?" Andrew seemed to be having difficulty grasping all this.

"Hopelessly so. If only there were a way to get her to see the depths of James's adoration for her, but she seems to only wish to spend time with the captain for some reason…most odd." She scrutinized his face for a reaction.

"Aye, most odd," he echoed with a scowl.

"I keep trying to tell my brother that if Celia will not have him, there are hundreds of genteel ladies who will. After all, is not a doctor a worthy prize?"

"You might be surprised," he mumbled into his stew.

"Pardon?"

"I have learned that money does not ensure character, my girl."

"But James simply oozes character," she blurted. "It's coming out of every hole he's got."

Andrew crinkled his nose. "I see."

She froze for a moment as she analyzed her last statement. "Let me reword that."

Just then James returned to the room carrying a bucket of soapy water. "Ah, greetings, Anne. How fare ye?"

"Quite well, brother dear," she replied in a singsong voice. "He does worry about me so," she explained to Andrew offhandedly. "His heart is so full of compassion."

James frowned and put the back of his hand to her forehead. "Are you ill?"

"No."

"Had a little too much of the demon rum?"

She laughed in embarrassment. "You're so amusing, brother. He has a wit that rivals no other," she boasted. "Mr. Pierce and I were just speaking of how wonderful you are."

James was obviously befuddled. "Oh?"

"Aye," Andrew added. "You fence?"

"Not at all, I fear, sir. I'm completely useless when it comes to anything of a physical nature."

Anne put her hand on James's shoulder and gouged her fingernails into his flesh through the fabric of his shirt. He shrieked in pain like a little girl.

"He's so modest," she explained insincerely, continuing to purposely maim him. "I've already told of your master swordsmanship, James, so don't deny it."

"You great bitch!" He wrung himself from her grasp, completely oblivious to what she had just said. "That's bound to leave a mark."

Andrew seemed baffled and amused at the same time. "Tell me, sir, is it true your sister was abducted by slavers?"

He looked as though he were going to answer the question, but when Anne reached for him again, he spun away defensively. "Aye," he finally replied, while staring at Anne in great annoyance. "Captain Malvern was good enough to liberate her at my behest. Though now I'm beginning to question my judgment."

"A *woman* saved your sister from slavers?" Andrew appeared both horrified and incredulous.

"Aye, but you'll find the captain is no ordinary woman." Anne made an angry face at him. "As my sister can most heartily attest," he added. "She's quite taken with her."

CHAPTER TWENTY-ONE

Twilight was descending around *Original Sin* as the ship rushed to catch up to the *Belladonna* to retrieve both capital and comrade. Gayle stood on the quarterdeck, staring to the fore and hoping to catch a brief glimpse of their quarry—any sign they were on the right track.

"How fare ye?" came a concerned inquiry from behind her.

Gayle turned to see Celia—wind whipping her chestnut hair behind her and pressing her billowy blouse to her body in all the right ways. "The shoulder still pains me, though you gladden my mood. How is your father?"

"He is well, for a man cast o'erboard and left to perish in the depths of the sea."

"And did you explain to him all that has betallen you in these last fortnights?"

"I started to—"

"And how far did you get?"

"He became extremely angry when I told him of Phillip's acquiescence during my abduction. So I told him to lie down and rest, and I would come to him later and continue the tale."

Gayle was stunned. "You've a mouthful or two more to regale him with, wouldn't you agree?"

"I would…I do," Celia admitted.

"In fact, I daresay that you've left out the most noteworthy parts. Did you even reach the point where you were brought on board?"

Her eyes darted heavenward. "Not as yet, per se."

"Do you mean to tell him the story by giving him a new word each day? At this rate you'll be fifty before you get to the naughty bits. Is that your plan? You hope to outlast him?"

"It's not that," Celia said, with a heavy sigh. "Would you not agree that the man has had a rather unpleasant day?"

"An understatement, I'd say. But mightn't what he is *not* hearing be even worse than what you might tell him as the truth?"

"What do you mean?"

"Imagine it, love. He has heard many an unsavory rumor. Couple with this, your frank admission earlier of lustily tumbling into the licentious dog days of summer." Celia bit her thumbnail and groaned. "What amoral and wanton depravity do you think he has envisioned? Would most people not assume the very worst?"

"You make a viable point."

Gayle eyed her lustily. "Though you are a most libidinous wench, 'tis true."

Celia bit her lower lip provocatively. "You somehow bring that out in me, my Captain."

"So go tell your father all that has transpired, though you may wish to leave out a detail or two—anything that involves nudity or carnal hunger. Come to my cabin and we shall sup. Then after feasting *with* you, I will feast *on* you."

"You make it all sound quite uncomplicated."

"The feasting?" Gayle asked in confusion. "I thought I had already aptly demonstrated that. The trick is effectively staving off a jaw cramp."

"Not that part. The telling-everything-to-Father part. You seem to think he will not be troubled at all by this."

"He is no doubt already troubled, Celia. But I can only hope that both assuring him that I have treated you well, in addition to saving his life, will mean more to him than the loss of his daughter's chastity. It certainly would to me."

"Well, it makes so much more sense when you explain it. I think you should be present—to help me tell him the whole story."

"Have you gone completely fuckin' mad?"

"What happened to all your confidence and reason? It was here just a moment ago."

"You honestly believe that your father will want to hear the story of his daughter's abduction and ravaging from the individual who committed the acts?"

"I wouldn't use the word 'ravaging' if I were you," Celia suggested, her index finger extended. "Besides, if you want to be particular about the details, is it not truer that *I* 'ravaged' you?"

"Aye, 'tis true, though it may prove imprudent to share that bit o' news with your father."

"You see how much better you are at this than I?" Celia implored. "And if we're somewhere communal, perhaps at the supper table, Father dare not become hostile. He is, after all, a civilized man."

Gayle said nothing, instead gazing at the stars as they dimly faded into view above her. Celia kissed her exposed neck, sliding her tongue playfully up to her earlobe.

Gayle shivered at the sensation, then kissed Celia softly. "One of these days woman, I plan to tell you 'no.'"

"Fair enough. Just not today, if you don't mind."

On board the *Belladonna*, Molly lay in the cargo hold in shackles. It was her understanding that she was being held for the pleasure of Captain Fuks—as was customary. No crewman could lay his hands on her before the captain did.

Her attempt to flirt with Cabo, the largest sailor in the crew, had unfortunately come to naught. The lad who had brought her some water and biscuits earlier had helpfully explained to her that "Cabo" was Spanish for "stub." Apparently Cabo had received this nickname after an unfortunate knife fight with a much shorter opponent. Under these circumstances, Cabo was no longer a man Molly felt confident that she could adeptly woo.

The runner-up was a burly fellow named Cruz. He seemed less angry than many of the other seamen, but his size was imposing. He was dark-skinned and had enormous hands with impossibly thick, meaty fingers, which Molly hoped was a clue that Cruz would amply make up for what Cabo tragically lacked.

She had made eye contact with him earlier, and he appeared transfixed by her—especially after she lifted her shirt up and licked her own nipple. Men did seem to like that for some reason, she thought with a shrug.

At last, Cruz ventured down to the hold. She looked about to see if anyone else was nearby.

"There is only you and me," he said, his voice deep, with a hint of a Spanish accent. "Do not worry."

"Look at your bloody hands," she couldn't help but say aloud. "You're a fuckin' work of art, you are."

He beamed at her compliment, displaying a gold front tooth. "I could say the same of you, *amorcita*. Never before have I seen a woman do that with her own breast."

"Just a li'l trick I picked up in New Providence, love. Would you like to see more?"

"I fear who might discover us," he confessed, glancing over his shoulder. "Should anyone catch us, I will surely be keelhauled. The captain would not stand for it."

Molly felt more confident with each utterance from Cruz's mouth. "But you are the only man I can imagine touching me," she lied, and for greater effect she ran her hands leisurely over her breasts. "I shall die if your horrid captain shoves his ghastly member into me. Then you shall never have me."

It appeared that Cruz was both erotically charged and in a quandary. Molly could only imagine the questions that must be racing through his mind. Was this woman and all the pleasures of her eager, nubile body worth the wrath of the cat-o'-nine-tails? Would a quick tumble with her be enough to sustain him through torture and the possible depths of the briny sea itself? Would this lass's quim be the last flesh he'd meet before shuffling off to meet old Davy Jones himself?

And his expression revealed his answer. You bet your arse it would!

Cruz lunged for Molly hungrily, like a bird of prey might dive upon a hamster. Their mouths met impatiently, and he made quick work of finding her right breast and kneading it like dough.

She feigned inability to reach his groin. "These manacles," she complained huskily. "They keep me from feeling your tremendous shaft."

Cruz, proving to be as gullible as he was easily aroused,

immediately withdrew a dagger and began to pry open the shackles at her wrists. When they were at last off, she cast them aside and leapt at him, exploring his body eagerly.

In no time he had her shirt unbuttoned, and as he kissed her breasts, Molly claimed his own dagger and, with it, bisected the length of his gullet—slicing his vocal cords and rendering them useless.

He recoiled and fell backward, clutching his hemorrhaging throat. She moved over him quickly and, feeling some compassion for this amorous lummox, hastily grasped his head and snapped his neck.

Dragging his lifeless, massive body out of plain sight would prove the most difficult part for her.

As Gayle, Celia, and Andrew took a seat around the supper table in the captain's quarters, an awkward silence fell over the room. Hyde ladled hot soup from a tureen into three bowls and set one before each of them.

"Thank you, Hyde," Gayle said softly.

"Aye, miss. I'll return shortly with the next course." He hurriedly exited and shut the door behind him.

Celia tasted the soup. "This is lovely, Gayle. What kind is it?"

"Oyster and clam, I believe is what Cook said."

Andrew sat stoically, neither eating nor joining in the conversation.

"And I thought I didn't care for oysters."

"They are a bit of an acquired taste, I find." Gayle tasted another spoonful.

"Is someone finally going to tell me what the hell has been going on?" Andrew shouted.

"Are you sure you don't want to try the soup first, Father?"

He answered her with an angry glare.

"All right," Gayle conceded. "What would you like to know?"

"Who has deflowered my little girl? Was it you?" He shook his fist angrily.

Gayle mulled this question over for a moment. "I prefer to think of it as helping her realize her natural sexual endowments."

Andrew jumped to his feet and his eyes flashed. "You depraved bitch! I'll have your head on a pike for bankrupting my daughter's virtue."

"Father," Celia said, standing as well. "Don't blame Gayle for this. Sit down and I'll tell you everything you wish to know."

"Start by how you decided to have carnal relations with another woman."

"Only if you sit, Father."

To Gayle's surprise, he did so.

"Now try the soup," Celia directed.

Andrew complied with this request as well, albeit grudgingly. He murmured something unintelligible into the bowl.

Celia nodded to him in approval, then noted Gayle's puzzled expression and shrugged. "You see, Father, after I was brought here to help tend to the crew's wounded, the ship had already set off toward New Providence to get further medical care."

He glowered at Gayle over his spoon. "And that's when you manhandled my Celia?"

Celia answered for her. "No, Father. That was much later."

Gayle's eyes flew open wide. "She doesn't mean there was manhandling later," she explained, fidgeting. "She means there wasn't any handling of any kind at that point."

"Right," Celia answered. "That's what I meant. Neither of us handled anything." Andrew slurped some more soup and scrutinized Celia with one eyebrow raised. "Once we arrived in New Providence, we met the gypsy. It really was all her doing."

"You were defiled by a gypsy?" he asked incredulously.

"No," Gayle interjected. "I can attest that the gypsy was on her best behavior."

"Father, the gypsy read my palm. She told my fortune—and that's when I knew I needed to help the doctor find his abducted sister in Jamaica."

"That pretty blond thing I met below deck who gets everything all wrong?" he clarified, waggling his spoon.

"Aye. Though this was before I realized that Anne was a bit of a slut."

"Celia, you bedded her too?"

Gayle cleared her throat. "I think she's referring to Anne trying to bed me."

"By the wounds of Christ," Andrew bellowed at Gayle. "It's a wonder you have time to sail this bloody ship, as much as you're busy rubbin' up on everyone. Is there anyone on board you haven't ruined?"

"I haven't ruined anyone but your daughter," she spat back. There was a palpable silence. "Wait a moment. Allow me to rephrase that."

"Father, listen to me. Do not think that Gayle took advantage of me or compromised me in some way. It was I who seduced her."

He gawked at her spellbound for what felt to her like hours before he turned back to Gayle. "What, my daughter isn't good enough for you? She had to throw herself at you like a common strumpet?"

"Trust me," she argued. "It was not for lack of trying on my part."

"Succubus," he shouted back defiantly.

"Good God, old man. Is there no pleasing you? I'm not sure what else to tell you that will not make you want to eviscerate me. Let me lay out the truths for you. Truth—I find your daughter extremely comely and desirable. Truth—she did seduce me, and it was ten of the most extraordinary hours of my life. Truth—I would willingly stay with her as long as she can tolerate me. Truth—I would never knowingly allow anyone to harm her. I would sooner perish. I am sorry if you wish to hear none of this, but it is all factual."

Andrew said nothing.

Celia smiled broadly and was filled with affection. "Well, I enjoyed hearing it, at any rate."

Gayle exhaled slowly. "Now, does anyone still insist on disemboweling me?"

Andrew seemed uneasy. "Girl, do you care for this woman?"

Celia stared at her ardently. "Aye, Father, more than I could ever care for Phillip."

He sighed and refilled his spoon with soup. "Then provided she does nothing to hurt you," he threatened, his eyes downcast, "I shan't kill her."

"Well," Gayle whispered. "Saints be praised."

CHAPTER TWENTY-TWO

Gayle, Churchill, and Abernathy were seated around the captain's table in her quarters scrutinizing a map of some kind while Celia sat in the only other chair, sipping her flip—a concoction that contained several things, from what she could discern, though the most notable ingredients were ale, sugar, and some sort of brandy. This mixture had definitely become her intoxicant of choice.

Because the officers had been discussing all things nautical since supper had adjourned, Celia was now thoroughly bored and well on her way to inebriation. She took another sip of her aqua vitae and sighed.

"So according to Mr. Pierce," Gayle was saying, "the *Belladonna* outmans us by at least thirty men, perhaps more."

"But we have surprise on our side," Churchill noted. "They have no idea that we pursue them, let alone that we picked up someone who has been able to tell us so much about their ship and crew."

"Aye," Abernathy said. "If we come in with the big guns, they won't be outmannin' us for long."

Gayle shook her head. "But if we come in with the big guns, we run the danger of sinking her, mates. And that would include Molly and the whole of Father's hoard. We need to attack under cover of night, and keep the destruction to a minimum."

"The captain's right," Churchill said. "There's no point in trying to liberate anyone or anything from that vessel if it all ends up at the bottom of the ocean."

"Verily." Gayle put her chin in her hand. "I just worry that we may already be too late. To execute this plan, the soonest we would be able to approach would be tomorrow evening." She searched Churchill's face as she ran her hand over the chart before her on the table. "You feel fairly certain, based on this course, that we will sight them sometime on the morrow?"

"Aye, based on how long Mr. Pierce had been floating in the water after being jettisoned, what he was able to tell us of the size and structure of the *Belladonna*, and the type of wind and water current we look to have, I'd say her lead is a small, dwindling one. We may have to spend a good deal of the day tomorrow trying to stay out of her sightline. If so, we can use a drogue to slow us down a mite."

"Abernathy, can you get the crew together and ensure that they understand the plan as it currently stands?" She paused. "And make sure they're prepared for potential last-minute changes."

"Aye, Cap'n."

"Then we are agreed." The two men nodded. "Begin the preparations. Make sure whoever mans the crow's nest tonight vigilantly watches that we do not happen upon the *Belladonna*. We must ensure we are not seen until we mean to be seen."

"It shall be done," Abernathy answered.

"And if anything changes," Gayle instructed solemnly, "wake me immediately."

"Aye, Captain," the men said in unison.

After they left her quarters, she sat back down at the table, her concern evident.

"What's a drogue?" Celia asked from her corner of the room.

Gayle seemed surprised at the question, as though her worry and apprehension had made her forget that she wasn't alone. "Well, a drogue is an anchor made of cloth that we drag off the aft end to slow our speed."

"Ah." Celia nodded as though she understood perfectly. "Why would you do that?" she asked, still for some reason nodding in the affirmative. She set down her drink, stood, and sauntered over to Gayle. The liquor made her feel warm and flushed.

"At times you may not wish your opponent to realize how fast you're capable of traveling," Gayle explained as Celia slyly sank onto her lap and began to nibble her left earlobe. "If they think they can outrun you, they are much more inclined to take you on... Love, whatever are you doing?"

"You have the most luscious bloody ears," she said. "I've wanted to put my tongue in them all evening. They're like ambrosia."

"You've obviously been enjoying your spirits." Gayle shuddered, as though Celia's warm, heavy breath sent a chill through her.

"Aye, and now I'd like to enjoy you," Celia purred, moving her pliant kisses to Gayle's jawline and finally to her mouth. She ran her hands through Gayle's loose, crimson tresses as she pulled her closer.

"You taste sweet, love," Gayle murmured, and kissed her deeply again.

"Just so you know," she whispered, "it's not just my mouth. I taste that way everywhere."

Gayle's eyebrows rose. "How saucy you've become, woman. Were you not, just weeks ago, a virginal maid brimming with chaste and wholesome virtue?"

Celia considered this question. "That was simply because I had not met anyone that I desired."

"No one?"

Celia shook her head in response but maintained her heated gaze.

"So you would have me believe that before you and I met, you had never once had a sexual thought or inclination?"

Celia leisurely brought her mouth to Gayle's and slid her tongue lightly along her lips. She then softly bit the lower one and retreated again. "Not once," she lied huskily.

Gayle looked amused. "You've never even had a sexual fantasy before?" Her hands caressed Celia's waist and lower back.

Celia ran her hands across Gayle's breasts lightly and felt the nipples contract in response. She smiled at the feeling of power that reaction gave her and she stood, pulling Gayle to her feet as well. "I would not even have known what to fantasize about." She kissed her again and began to unbutton Gayle's shirt.

"Perhaps a daydream here and there?" Gayle suggested playfully. Her hands found Celia's bottom and she murmured as she squeezed it. "Thankfully this is just as I left it—round and as though forged by the gods themselves."

"Not I." All buttons now successfully unfastened, Celia pulled the garment away from Gayle's skin eagerly, lingering over the feel of her warm flesh, newly exposed.

Their mouths met hungrily and Gayle began to follow suit with Celia's shirt—though she took a much more unhurried pace in doing so, as if she was determined to caress every inch of her in the process.

"So then you met me, though you were painfully modest and pure. What exactly happened?"

Celia nudged Gayle closer to the bed and pushed her down onto the muslin sheets. With her shirt completely unbuttoned, she straddled Gayle and began to gyrate against her erotically while she unfastened her lover's breeches. "I saw you, Madam Captain," she rasped, consumed by her want. "And all I could think of from that point on was the taste of your mouth, the feel of your hands on me, my hands on you."

"My God, but you make me want you so completely." Gayle kicked her boots off.

Celia pulled Gayle's breeches down and slowly kissed her breasts and stomach. "Tell me how much."

"What?" Gayle was too enraptured to fully comprehend the request.

Celia sat back again, her smoldering gaze making Gayle's body ache for her touch. "I want to hear how much you want me. I just shared how very much I want you, after all."

"But—"

"Tell me," she whispered, kissing Gayle with renewed fervor, then cruelly pulling back again.

This was driving her absolutely mad, Gayle thought, and she loved every damned minute of it. "I want you absolutely and utterly," she professed with some difficulty in concentration. "I want nothing more than the touch, taste, and scent of you. I need you to possess me, to take me, beloved. If you want to know how much I desire you, give me your hand."

Celia's eyes darkened further with passion, and she did as she was told. With great care, Gayle pulled Celia's fingers along her silky wetness.

"This is how much I desire you," she whispered. "You leave me with a want of nothing and no one else." As Celia's hand began to move, Gayle gasped and closed her eyes at the sensation. "I need nothing but the release you can bring me."

Celia leaned in closely, her lips only a breath away from Gayle's. "And if I tell you that you must beg?"

Gayle groaned in frustration as Celia's hand stopped moving. "Then I shall supplicate most humbly."

Celia grinned mischievously then, and kissed Gayle fully and powerfully. "You need not. You have suffered my torment long enough. Give me your mouth, love."

Just after dawn the cabin boy ran up from the hold, past the orlop, past the gun deck, and to Captain Fuk's quarters. He beat on the door frantically. "Captain! Cruz…*está muerto*."

In a matter of seconds, several crewmen had gathered and Fuks had opened his door. "What is it, lad?" he asked groggily.

"Cruz is dead," he answered, his Spanish accent thick. "He is in the cargo hold, Captain. The prisoner…she is gone."

"What?" Fuks stormed out to the main deck, practically sprinted down to the cargo hold to verify this report, and confronted the brutal truth. At least a dozen crewmen rapidly fell in behind him, and they too beheld the sight with exclamations of amazement. "So, somehow, I am to believe that this tiny slip of a woman overpowered Cruz, viciously killed him, and freed herself from her chains."

"Captain," a crewman shouted from above. "The starboard skiff is gone."

Fuks felt as though he was straddling the fine line between openly weeping and decapitating everyone on board.

"So somehow…" his voice cracked with rage, "this dark-haired pygmy not only freed herself and killed Cruz without anyone hearing so much as a bloody whisper, but she also rowed away in my skiff without any crewman noticing? How the fuck does that happen?" He could feel the arteries of his neck bulge and pulsate. "The gold," he suddenly gasped, darting back up to his quarters to see if somehow, though it had been beside him while he slept, she had miraculously taken the treasure with her.

He arrived, out of breath, to see that both trunks were still exactly where he had left them. The treasure remained his. Fuks sighed in relief.

He cursed that he had not ordered her brought to him the night before. He had not really been very interested in her sexually, as he preferred conquests under the age of eight. Though, he reasoned, she was of small stature, and he would more than likely have been able to convince himself that she was a poor, hapless orphan that he had caught panhandling in the street. Damn his exacting tastes.

Well, he thought angrily, at least she had left him with his wealth—the filthy whore.

Below deck in a hammock, Molly rocked peacefully. She hoped that jettisoning one of the ship's two skiffs would convince the crew of the *Belladonna* that she had slipped away overnight. True, she had needed to send a couple of troublesome crewmen overboard with it, but her scheme had luckily gone quietly, and no one else had awakened.

Besides, she had played this game before. Posing as a young lad shouldn't be too difficult with this many men at sea. She merely needed to pull her weight and stay out of sight—whatever it took to call as little attention to herself as possible.

Molly sadly contemplated the fate of Captain Malvern. She doubted that she had survived the gunshot wound the other night on the beach. And she felt fairly certain that the other members of the party had shared her fate, leaving her more than likely as the only survivor. She wondered if *Original Sin* had been attacked as well, and what had befallen the rest of the crew.

No, she decided, there were far too many unknown factors to proceed any other way. And based on what she had overheard from the crew regarding their current course, had she actually set out overnight in the skiff, she would have been rowing for weeks before she hit land, leaving her fate to the whim of the weather—or worse, to be happened upon by another ship and taken aboard, more than likely as cargo. Her best course was to sail aboard the *Belladonna* to the next port and slip away there.

She contemplated the vast treasure brought on board along with her, dismayed that her heroic captain would now never be able to deliver it to her father as promised. The thought of leaving all that wealth with that whoreson Fuks filled her with contempt.

Perhaps Gayle wouldn't be able to return it to Madman Malvern, but that didn't mean someone else couldn't. If the loot was to slip away with her—to be returned to its rightful owner—then all the better, she reasoned.

CHAPTER TWENTY-THREE

Y ou need to be more fluid," Gayle said, slowly swinging her cutlass to illustrate her point. "When you halt your blade's progression like that, you betray your next action."

"So your blade moves constantly?" Celia held a cutlass before her defensively as they faced off on the main deck.

"Not constantly, but nearly. Here, advance toward me offensively. Come swinging, as we practiced."

As Celia's blade slashed aggressively, Gayle's repeatedly swatted it away, the picture of mercurial poise.

Andrew Pierce leaned on the deck rail watching his daughter and the captain spar. He had never noticed how naturally athletic Celia was. He had always deemed her a fine dancer, and in general quite graceful. This type of pursuit, however, was a completely different matter. She seemed almost predisposed to fencing. Perhaps if he himself had thought to teach her the sport, she would never have been abducted in the first place. She could have defended herself, since that dunderhead Farquar had been incapable of doing so.

Of course he himself had never been much with a sword. He had always used intimidation rather than actual force. Before now, he had never realized how powerful a woman with fighting skills could truly be, how imposing simple physical prowess was.

Gayle spun away from Celia's attack, her blade always deftly blocking his daughter's. Finally they stopped, their swords crossed before them. Both were breathing heavily, and their eyes locked intently.

"Gayle?" Celia panted, not lessening her pressure on Gayle's blade even one iota.

"Aye?"

"You're bleeding, love." Her eyes darted briefly to Gayle's shoulder.

Gayle immediately withdrew her cutlass and assessed her still-healing wound. Indeed fresh blood had begun to seep through her shirt. "Buggar," she muttered.

"I should not have tried you so. You are not completely recovered."

Gayle seemed amused, her golden eyes squinting. "Are you saying that you should have gone easy on me?"

"Perhaps a bit."

"Such bloody grandeur." She smoothly returned her cutlass to its baldric. "Two fortnights ago you didn't even know how to hold the soddin' thing."

Celia smiled back with some degree of cheekiness. "It's that you are so adept a tutor," she said. "Were you not so skillful, I would never have been so able to utterly thrash you."

"Thrash me?" Her voice was tinged with indignation. "You've a thing or two to learn of thrashing, I'm afraid."

"Is that so?"

"'Tis so, aye. For you to thrash me, you would need to draw my blood—not have me draw my own."

"A modest formality." Celia's blue eyes were flashing. "You were the first to bleed. You lose." She sheathed her cutlass.

"Do make sure you establish these rules before you engage your next foe," Gayle replied. "Should you battle someone during her menses you'll be the winner before you even draw your blade."

"Let us get you to the doctor, shall we?" Celia examined Gayle's shoulder with some concern. "How do you hope to engage Fuks this evening if you cannot even weather a duel with me?"

"It just needs to be sewn up, I'm sure," she said, as they headed below deck to see James.

Andrew remained deckside as he watched them depart—somewhat amused yet somewhat disturbed.

Celia made certain to knock loudly on the doctor's door—wanting never to see him *in flagrante delicto* for the rest of her natural life and well into the afterlife.

"Enter," he called. They did so, and James immediately stared at the blood on Gayle's stark white shirt. "What has happened?"

"I was fencing." Gayle turned so he could examine her wound. "And I must have re-opened it."

"So it would seem." He peered beneath the fabric. "Strip this off, Captain." Gayle removed her shirt and sat on the table. James dabbed the wound with a rum-soaked cloth, and she winced. "You could possibly do with a stitch or two, if you're planning to continue this manner of exertion."

"I am. So have at it, Doctor."

James threaded his needle with silk. "I suppose it would be completely pointless to try and convince you to refrain from such mêlée until you are healed."

The corners of Gayle's mouth shifted upward slightly. "I suppose it would."

"I know you are eager to attempt to rescue Molly," he continued, apparently ignoring her answer. "And you feel you have an obligation to your father to fulfill. But couldn't this skirmish wait a day or so?"

"'Tis the waiting that's eating at me."

"We'll reach her in time," Celia said. "You yourself stated that Molly is a testament to strength and cunning."

"She is quite a hardy lass," James chimed in, inserting the needle and pulling the thread through the skin.

"As you, above all, can attest," Celia said.

James said nothing in response, but blushed quite visibly and continued to sew.

"You do have a remarkable knack for conjuring awkward silences," Gayle remarked to Celia.

"Have I?" she asked, playfully.

"Like none I've ever seen. You could make the devil himself contrite."

Celia considered the possibility. "Perhaps that trait will come in handy someday."

"Doubtful. But I suppose if you're trying to make someone openly weep—"

"There you are," James said, snipping the end of the silk with small scissors. "That should hold you together through even the most raucous fray."

"Which is just what I anticipate," Gayle answered with a nod, reaching for her shirt.

"For everyone's sake," he said, "I hope that isn't the case."

"As do I, Doctor." Gayle put her shirt back on and stood, moving her shoulder to assess its limitations. "Thank you."

"Good day, James," Celia said as she moved to the doorway.

"Um, Celia, might I have a word with you?" he asked in an uncertain tone.

Celia glanced to Gayle for a reaction, but she merely shrugged. "I'm off to change," she said, and headed back up to her quarters.

A long pause ensued, making Celia feel quite uncomfortable. "Well?" she finally asked, coolly crossing her arms in front of her.

"Well," he echoed. "I simply thought that you and I might converse for a moment."

"About what, exactly?" she said, feeling too ill at ease to actually walk from the doorway back into his quarters.

"About you and the captain," he stammered.

Now her curiosity was piqued. She took a few steps toward him. "What about us?"

"Well, I can't help but notice that you and she are, well, intimate."

"Aye. We are."

"Intimate in the way in which lovers are."

"Easily explained."

"Is it?"

"Aye. We *are* lovers. See how it all fits together nicely now?" She interlocked her fingers and held them out for him to study.

James's brow creased. "I suppose. Though I am surprised that you do not mind being, well, one of many, shall we say."

"What are you implying?"

"That the captain is not the sort to limit herself to just one companion."

"You know what sort she is?"

"I think I do. Ask her if she has ever been true to someone, Celia. And if her answer is what I expect it to be, is that the kind of person you want to give yourself to? Don't you think that you deserve better?"

Celia narrowed her eyes as she scrutinized his expression and tried to sense his motives.

"I think I deserve to be happy, which means more than simply finding someone to be faithful to me. It means finding someone whom I truly love—beyond being merely a suitable match. I know now that I am worthy of someone who completely adores me, not someone who simply endures my company so that he might bed me. Therefore, if you're trying to tell me that I would do better to be with you, James, then I'll have to disagree."

"Oh." He looked crestfallen.

"You are a very pleasant man. But you and I are not meant to be."

"I do think I could make you happy, Celia."

"You couldn't, because I don't love you."

"So you love Gayle, then?"

She paused and felt suddenly flushed. "I do. And if that's a mistake, then I'll just have to jump in headfirst and completely bungle it."

"And if she perishes tonight in the skirmish?"

"Then I'll go to my grave with naught but my memory of her."

James stood there silently staring at the floor, his face twisted in something akin to dejection.

"I *am* sorry."

"Go," he muttered, waving her away. "Be with her. But know that I will always be here for you, no matter what happens."

Celia found these words strange and vaguely malevolent. With a niggling hint of suspicion, she made her way back topside.

As Gayle strode into her quarters to change her bloodied shirt, she was entirely taken aback to see Anne strewn across her bed, completely naked. "God's gullet," she exclaimed, unable to draw breath and frozen in her footsteps.

Anne ogled her seductively and slowly ran her hand between her own breasts. "Do you like what you see, Captain?" she asked in a sultry tone. "Because this is all for you."

"Are you stark bloody mad?" Gayle asked finally.

"Aye. Mad for you." Anne shifted so that her legs were opened slightly and her wares more evidently on display.

"Put that away," she said, covering her agape mouth with her hand in consternation.

"But it's my endowment to you, Gayle. I want to give it to you... all of it."

At that precise moment, Celia stepped into the cabin, shutting the door behind her. "Holy Mother of God."

Anne quickly moved to cover her nudity with her shift. "We have been discovered," she exclaimed dramatically.

"What exactly is this?" Celia asked.

Gayle, who was still horrified, was unable to do anything except shake her head.

Anne stood and slipped her shift back on. "You assured me that we would be alone," she said to Gayle. "I shan't bed you both at the same time."

"Can you explain this, please?" Celia calmly asked again, arms akimbo.

"I wish I could," Gayle answered. "I arrived here about one minute before you did. She was just lying there, bared and brazen, offering me her goods like a sluggish fishmonger."

Anne was obviously livid. "Who are you calling 'sluggish'?"

"Would you prefer the term 'whoring'?" Celia suggested.

Anne stormed over to Gayle. "Are you going to let her speak to me this way?"

"Absolutely. In fact, I'm going to encourage her."

Anne scowled and picked up the rest of her clothing. "You know," she said, stopping only a few inches from Gayle's face, "this simple girl will never give you everything that I can."

Celia squinted angrily. "Like chancre sores?"

"You horrid bitch!" Anne spun and pulled her arm back to strike Celia.

Gayle caught Anne's wrist in motion and jerked it, throwing Anne off balance. "Look here," she growled. "You're just a passenger on this ship, one that I am increasingly regretting rescuing. But I have no problem securing you in the hold in a barrel full of bilge water if you can't behave."

"Oh, really?"

"Or I could let Celia knock you out again. She's quite a brute when she's angry."

"What do you mean 'again'?"

"Go on, woman. Off with you." Gayle shoved Anne toward the door. "You've worn out your welcome." With that, she opened the cabin door, pushed Anne out in just her underclothes, and shut it behind her.

"Today is becoming extremely bizarre," Celia said.

"Verily. And what did our good doctor want with you?"

"To tell me that you would be unfaithful to me and that I should consider being with him instead."

Gayle sat on the bed and began to remove her stained shirt. "It seems there's some fuckery afoot here."

Celia approached her. "Hmm. It does seem a most remarkable coincidence, doesn't it?"

"Those two siblings are up to no good. I'm not sure what they gain by dividing us, but clearly that is their plan."

"If the gypsy were here, perhaps she could tell us."

CHAPTER TWENTY-FOUR

As darkness fell over the quiescent sea, *Original Sin* began to methodically close in on her prey. It was decided that the best time to strike would be around midnight, when the majority of the *Belladonna* crew was asleep.

Gayle, Celia, and Andrew ate supper in uneasy silence, dispelled only by periodic bursts of cordial small talk. Gayle advised that they should all have no more than a single glass of wine with their meal, as they would most assuredly need their wits about them later.

When they had finally pushed their empty plates away and were somberly pondering their fate, Gayle finally addressed something that she had procrastinated in doing all day.

"All right, it's time for the unpleasant bits."

Celia seemed concerned. "How unpleasant?"

"I have made sure that the skiff is loaded with provisions. Should things this evening take an unfortunate turn, I need you both to be on it."

"On it and headed where?" Andrew asked.

"The provisions include a compass and a map. If it appears that *Original Sin* will either be taken or sunk, cut the lines, drop the skiff into the sea, and row east toward the islands. Your chances of reaching land safely are about sixty to sixty-five percent."

"Is there a plan with slightly better odds?" Celia asked, her chin in her hand. "Something in the eighty-five percent, or better, range?"

"These are the best odds I can get you, *amor*. If you stay on board and the ship is taken, you would be giving yourself over to being violated in a myriad of ways."

"Lovely folk, these pirates," Celia muttered.

"Now for the troubling part."

"So, being 'violated in a myriad of ways' is the *good* part of this proposition of yours?" Celia asked. "I can't wait to hear the troubling part." She swigged back the last sip of her wine. "Might I get devoured by wolves?"

"Unlikely. I need you to take Anne with you." She said the words hurriedly, trying to lessen their bite.

After a moment of silence, Celia appeared horrified. "You expect me to look after that debased and vulgar trull?"

"That is precisely why I deemed this the troubling part. I had a feeling you might take exception to this request."

"Take exception? I'd sooner see that common slattern ignited and heaved over the side."

"Celia, mind your words," her father told her.

She looked sheepish for a moment. "Well, fine. We need not set her on fire first. But she'll not share my seat in our voyage to safety."

Gayle gazed at her warmly. "Even if her only other option is death?"

Celia blinked twice. "Am I supposed to find that thought distasteful?"

"Aye, a bit."

"Well, it *is* filling me with some emotion, but I believe it's amusement."

Gayle arched her eyebrows in surprise. "I understand how you feel. I hold many of those opinions myself. But I can't simply leave her on the ship to perish when the whole reason she is here is because we brought her. She is by and large one of the most vexing women I have met, and I'd certainly trust her no further than I could throw her. But I likewise cannot abide her imminent death when I can do something to prevent it."

Celia was silent for a while, then said with a sigh, "All right. I'll take the witch along with me. But I make no promises about the condition that she arrives in."

"You've a deal. Just don't kill her. That's all I ask."

"Then the bargain is struck. And will you, in turn, promise me that you'll take no careless chances?"

"I, careless?"

"You question it as though you have never taken an unnecessary risk, Captain. And you are well aware that I know better than that."

"You, madam, have my word. I have no desire whatever to sup with Hades before my time has come."

Their eyes locked for a palpable moment. "That is good to hear," Celia replied. "For I have not yet tired of your company."

Andrew awkwardly cleared his throat, and Gayle looked at him in chagrin, abruptly reminded that they were not alone.

As the moon rose higher in the sky, a thick fog began to roll in. Gayle recognized this occurrence as providence and knew that the time to strike had arrived. If ever *Original Sin* were to be able to advance, it would be now. Stealthily they quickened their pace and the crew prepared for their attack.

Gayle took Celia by the hand and pulled her into their quarters before the battle began so she could ensure she was completely prepared for all eventualities.

"We have only a matter of minutes. Did you inspect the skiff as I asked?"

"Aye, I did." Celia slipped her arms around Gayle's waist and gazed into her eyes. "You seem to have it well stocked, though it is missing one thing."

"And what would that be?"

"A captain. I never travel without one."

"I see." She pulled Celia to her and caressed her back lovingly. "Any captain in particular?"

"I suppose not," she murmured, moving under her touch. "Though it should be a woman. With smoky eyes that cast come-hither glances. And she should have a thoroughly wondrous mouth, one that I'll have need of on a very frequent basis." She kissed Gayle deeply. "Mmm, you're hired." She pulled her mouth away and held her even closer. "You meet all those requirements nicely."

"I do love you quite thoroughly," Gayle said.

"Do you?"

"Aye, Celia. I ache for merely a glimpse of you, or the sound of your easy laughter. You have completely bewitched me."

"I love you too. And though it is the most unfamiliar sensation, it now feels as compulsory to me as breathing in and out."

They kissed again, but a knocking interrupted them. "The *Belladonna* is in sight, Cap'n," someone called softly through the closed door.

"I'll be there presently," Gayle called. She tried to quash her feelings of worry. "'Tis time, *amor*." Celia nodded solemnly, and Gayle reached onto her thumb and removed her silver dragonfly signet ring. "Here, take this token from me. Wear it until the battle is won." She slipped it on Celia's thumb.

Celia stared at it but said nothing in return. Instead, she pulled off her opal ring and slipped it onto Gayle's ring finger. "And you hold this for me. Let its enchantment guide your sword, my love. I need for you to stay safe, as I cannot bear the thought of this world without you."

"I need the same from you. Protect yourself and your party, and God willing, I will come to collect you all."

"I promise."

They kissed again, this time tentatively and with great heavyheartedness. Gayle pulled away, but Celia captured her hand and tenderly kissed her palm.

With enormous reluctance, Gayle turned and left the cabin. As she strode out to the deck to meet her crew, she took stock of her own weaponry. In her baldric she had her cutlass, as well as two loaded flintlock pistols and a blunderbuss. At her waist was her trusty silver dagger, and another was tied to her left forearm, ready to be drawn. She was resolute that she not be caught unarmed.

"Diego," she called quietly. "Have you caught sight of their lookout?"

Diego, as accurate an archer as he was with both a cannon and a rifle, stood off the starboard bow with a large, ornate recurve bow and a quiver of broadhead arrows. Aside from the sheer beauty of the inlaid wood, this bow was equipped with an impressive range, as well as remarkable power and accuracy with which it struck its targets. "Not yet, Cap'n," he whispered back, peering through the fog.

The crew stood at the ready as *Original Sin* silently skulked closer to its quarry. Gayle watched as Diego peered off through the darkness. Finally she could periodically spy, between patches of fog, the crow's nest, as well as the lookout in it. With great artfulness, Diego pulled his loaded bowstring back and took aim and an arrow sang through the air.

With as much discretion as possible, Molly pulled her breeches back up and buttoned them, scurrying deftly down the rigging. Her time aboard ships disguised as a man had taught her that the easiest time to tend to the call of nature was when it was dark—especially on ships like the *Belladonna* that had no indoor privy, just seats of easement mounted directly off the bow for sailors to sit on and defecate through.

She did love the sea, but the life of a sailor could certainly be a shitty one. She chuckled at her unintentional pun.

Just then, a strange noise came from above—a muffled gag, followed by a resonant thud. Peering upward to the crow's nest she saw the arm and head of the lookout limply dangling over the platform, his body seemingly caught in the rigging. It was too dark to make out any more details, and pockets of fog further impaired her view.

Tense, Molly began to look about for the crewman's assassin. Now, drifting into a swatch of mist so thick she could not see more than a few feet, she strained in the hopes of hearing another ship. She snatched up a belaying pin in case she needed a weapon and slowly crept toward the aft of the ship, the hairs on her body standing on end.

"Lad," a sailor on guard duty called to her. "Did you make that sound?"

She shook her head, all the while still trying to glimpse the origin of the danger. "It came from up there," she said nervously, gesturing behind her.

Before the guard could even turn in the direction Molly was pointing, the bow of a large ship broke through a wall of fog, appearing as though it had just manifested from thin air. Molly knew at her first sight of the prow, with its figurehead of Eve holding out an apple, that it was *Original Sin*.

"By Satan's bollocks," she murmured, as the ship closed from about a hundred yards away.

"Jesus, Mary, and Joseph," the guard cried. But before he could list off anyone else from the New Testament, Molly cracked the belaying pin into the back of his head. It took her no time to rid the unconscious man of his cutlass and his pistol, then begin to wave her arms wildly at the approaching ship.

"Cap'n," Gleeson whispered to Gayle as he peered through a spyglass at the *Belladonna*. "Someone on deck is wavin' at us."

Gayle looked through her own spyglass. "Trice me, I believe it's Molly," she exclaimed under her breath. "Blimey, she's a wily scrapper."

Suddenly, the posted helmsman of the *Belladonna* began to loudly ring a brass bell and call, "Beat to quarters!" He shouted the command only once before an arrow sailed through his chest and he tumbled backward onto the deck. But the alarm had been sounded, and the crew was already starting to pour out from below decks.

"Blast. Gleeson," Gayle commanded, "fire the swivel gun at their decks, but mind Molly. She's there at aft."

"Aye," he said, lighting the breech-loaded gun with his linstock. With a flash, grapeshot filled the air and began to rain on the *Belladonna* crew to the fore of the ship.

Their screams filled the damp night air as the shrapnel cut them down.

"Starboard battery," Gayle called. "Mount the muzzles."

Twenty-four men manned the six cannons on the starboard side of *Original Sin*, and at Gayle's command, they took aim as their ship continued to close the gap between it and the *Belladonna*.

Molly sprinted from the aft of the ship to the bow, wanting to get as far from the line of fire as possible and hoping that as soon as they were positioned, *Original Sin* would board them.

Though about eight *Belladonna* crewmen had been either killed by the first strike or left so maimed that they could do little but writhe on the deck in pain, others rapidly dashed out topside to replace them. They scrambled to load their cannons so they might fire back.

The gunner's mate appeared from below deck, looking somewhat inebriated as well as completely panicked. Molly sneaked up behind him, glanced quickly about her, and ran her cutlass through his chest. In the pandemonium, no one seemed to notice.

As Molly peered over to those now manning the guns, her heart lurched when she saw one gunner loading a fire cannon. This small device launched burning projectiles solely intended to ignite the sails and rigging of the target ship. "Lucifer's bumhole," she exclaimed.

Three of *Original Sin*'s cannons launched more grapeshot at the deck of her prey, and again it ravaged the exposed crew of the *Belladonna*. But not all crewmen were incapacitated, and as the attacking vessel got within twenty-five yards, a single heavy cannon fired back at them.

Gayle and the gunners on deck ducked quickly at the sound of the cannon blast, though many men were struck by shivers—the jagged pieces of flying wood caused from the impact of the shot.

She commanded that the sails be furled and three more cannons discharged at their foe. Another round from the fire cannon was unleashed on *Original Sin*, and within a matter of moments, the searing projectiles had done their job and the ship was ablaze.

Andrew quickly pulled Celia by the wrist to the waiting skiff. "Come, daughter. We must flee."

"But, Father," she said, not wanting to give up so quickly. "The fighting has only just begun."

"Our ship is in flames. For us, it is over." When they reached the skiff, Anne was already seated in the vessel, quietly crying. Andrew picked Celia up by the waist and put her into the rowboat.

Celia realized that her father was right. *Original Sin* was on fire near the bow, as well as farther back on the starboard side. She frantically searched for Gayle, but saw only smoke and heard nothing but pandemonium.

"Sit down, Celia," Andrew said, and worriedly she did so. Slowly, he began to apply slack to the rope that suspended the skiff over the sea. As the boat gradually descended, Celia's heart was nearly breaking.

She and Andrew each manned an oar, with Anne continuing to sniffle and openly cry, but no one spoke. They rowed east, as Gayle had instructed, while the sounds of battle continued in the distance—growing ever fainter. The fog remained thick and oppressive.

When at last Celia could hear only the slapping of the oars on the water, she wanted to join Anne in weeping.

CHAPTER TWENTY-FIVE

The crew of *Original Sin* swiftly cast their grappling irons, pulled the two ships together, and began to board the *Belladonna*. The younger lads carried loads of grenades—wooden orbs filled with bits of iron and gunpowder. One by one, they lit the fuses and lobbed them any place the enemy crew began to gather, such as by the cannons. Gayle watched Hyde cleverly drop several down the hatches to slow the pace of their foes' emergence on deck.

The smell of sulphur and the cry of the wounded filled the air as the battle raged. Gayle had already fired and discarded both her pistols, and was now deftly wielding her cutlass as another man emerged to take her on. Several yards away, Molly fought at her side.

"Good to see ya, Cap'n," she called, kicking her adversary in the genitals and then running her cutlass through his breastbone.

"I see you're managing well." Gayle struck at her sweaty opponent.

"Been getting by, I have." Molly turned and swung her blade at another *Belladonna* crewman.

Gayle's foe lashed out at her, and his blade sliced the air loudly, forcing her to leap backward. "You great prick!" With renewed anger, she swung back, causing her adversary to stumble and fall in his haste to position himself. She thrust her blade through him before he had even fully landed on the deck.

Behind her, she saw *Original Sin* ablaze. "Churchill, get everyone onto the *Belladonna*. The flames are too high to fight."

"Aye," he called from the opposite deck, and darted off to gather all remaining crewmen.

"If I didn't trust my own eyes, I'd swear you to be a specter," Crenshaw hissed, appearing before Gayle with his blade drawn. "Haven't I already killed you once, you piddling whore?"

She narrowed her eyes in recognition and assumed a defensive stance. "It seems there is no limit to your failure." She arced her blade at him aggressively.

"I would have thought the taste of your own blood would have curbed that insolent tongue of yours." With that, he lunged at her expertly, his cutlass narrowly missing her as she spun away. "But apparently not."

"It's only insolence if it's not true. And when I say that I'm going to carve out your heart for killing my crewmen, believe every fucking word of it."

Their blades clashed, and Gayle advanced on Crenshaw with renewed fervor. He frowned. "What bravado you possess." He swung at her three times in succession, and she adroitly blocked each blow. "No wonder the wenches vie for your attention. Pity you have no member to properly service them."

"Shed no tears for me," she countered, a bit out of breath. "I manage well enough. Better than one who has a member that lies feckless in his breeches."

She sliced across his groin, cutting through his pants and catching him off guard. His eyes flashed angrily. "Bitch!" He advanced on her, but she countered him again. "It's a pity for you that tavern wench sold you out. But I'll enjoy returning to her and regaling her with the story of your death."

Gayle's cutlass struck his as she recognized the weight of his heated words. "Desta," she murmured. "Of course." She swung her blade into his again, spun quickly away, then struck once more, this time slashing his left side open.

Crenshaw cried out and moved his hand protectively over the wound as blood began to color his shirt.

"Are you even trying?" she taunted him.

He screamed wildly and launched his body at hers without heed.

Gayle evasively crouched, bringing her cutlass up only as he moved within range. She angled her blade upward, and it ripped through his lower abdomen, embedding itself in his lower pelvis.

Slowly standing, she pulled the blade up into his body even deeper as his shriek intensified. She stared him in the eyes malevolently as she sawed up even higher—the cutlass now well into his rib cage. His arms lay at his sides limply as his blood poured onto the deck and his blade fell from his weakened grasp.

Crenshaw's eyes grew glassy, and blood slowly trickled from the corners of his mouth. He made unintelligible sounds as Gayle's sword nearly cleaved him in two.

She refused to stop. "This is the pain Nichols and Caruthers felt, you vile piece of shit. Feel it."

When blood began to bubble more quickly from his throat, Gayle pushed his body backward and he fell heavily into his own pooled blood. He visibly stopped breathing.

As Gayle darted off to aid her crewmen, James warily stepped onto the deck of the *Belladonna* carrying his medical bag. The explosions and screams utterly panicked him, but he knew sailors needed medical attention.

"Doctor," a fallen sailor called weakly from the port side of the deck.

James inched over and recognized the lad who called to him as Gleeson. "How fare ye?" he asked, nervously looking about him to ensure he had not called any undue attention to himself. All about him sailors continued to brawl mercilessly, and metal clashed violently as the smoke from the cannon and fire burned his eyes.

"I've taken a bullet in the gut, Doc," Gleeson replied, moving his bloodied hand so James could examine it more closely. "It burns like a son of a bitch."

"I've seen worse," James remarked, trying to assess if the bullet had passed through the lad's side or still resided there, and if any clothing had possibly been pulled into the wound, which, if so, would almost guarantee infection.

He poured rum on the wound, and Gleeson cried out.

"Save some o' that fer yer own wounds," a booming voice called from behind him. "Yer gonna need it."

James turned and fixed his watering eyes on a tall, imposing sailor—his cutlass drawn and his gaze murderous.

"I—I'm not armed," he sputtered.

His adversary brandished a toothless sneer. "Good."

"But I'm a doctor," he said as his mouth became dry. "I can tend to your wounded."

"Not if yer dead, ya can't," the brute explained matter-of-factly. He slowly approached James, who stared at the fresh blood clinging to the sailor's blade.

Suddenly, after only two strides, his attacker froze, his eyes growing wide. As James watched, a sword blade burst through the sailor's chest and began to wriggle lethally. As life left his body, he collapsed roughly onto the deck, the assassin now fully revealed.

"Molly?" James was stunned.

She stood clutching her sword, breathing heavily but looking invigorated. Blood spattered her face and clothes, but her cheeks were flushed. "Yer welcome," she said, then paused to spit.

James was delighted to see her. "I'd thought you as good as dead, lass."

"Piss," she responded dismissively. "I'll not be goin' to the great beyond until I'm damn good and ready, mate."

"I should have known better."

"You can make it up to me later, Doc," she said with a naughty wink, then headed back into the mêlée.

After over two hours of rowing east, Celia, Andrew, and Anne finally hit land, then dragged their skiff onto an uninhabited quay. They had broken out of the fog almost completely, and moonlight now bathed the beach in its pale glow. Though Andrew was thoroughly fatigued, and Anne was still beside herself, Celia found that focusing on settling in and waiting for their rescue was just the diversion she needed to keep from breaking down.

While her father rested in the sand, breathing heavily from the extreme physical exertion of their long trip, Celia methodically unloaded the supplies from the skiff. The muscles in her arms now twitched in exhaustion, but she set up camp under the balmy night sky, with the Caribbean winds whipping her dark hair.

"Here, Father." She offered him a wooden ladle full of grog. "Drink this. Refresh yourself."

Eagerly, Andrew did so. He sighed deeply and handed the empty ladle back to her. "We're in a right mess, I fear." He removed his spectacles and rubbed his eyes wearily.

She sat down next to him on the beach. "That has been my location for the last several weeks, Father. It's not so bad once you get used to it."

He chuckled and searched her face. "You are amazingly courageous, Celia. I don't think I've ever been more proud of you than I am right now."

"Thank you, Father." She brushed her hair from her eyes. "It was terribly bold for you to venture out to sea to find me."

"Well, child, I needed to know that you were safe." He coughed. "And word had traveled back to me that you had taken up with a pirate captain. Not exactly the news a father yearns for."

"I'm sorry for that," she said, staring at the breaking waves. "But given the circumstances, I was hesitant to share that news in a letter." She picked up a handful of fine sand. "I suppose too I was still sorting through it myself."

"Well, it's quite a lot to sort through, Celia. That's a certainty."

"But I can't set aside the insight that I've never felt more alive than I have since I've embarked on this very bizarre journey."

Andrew sighed again. "You've grown into a remarkable woman, lass, and you did it while I was looking the other way."

"Well, you did play a significant role, Father."

"Perhaps, but I never saw it until now." His expression became darker. "I hope this isn't the final macabre realization of a cursed man, trapped forever on this isle."

Celia studied the way the moonlight illumined his features. "You need to have some faith, Father. If I believed Gayle to be vanquished I'd not be able to muster the strength to go on."

Behind him, Anne was rummaging through their provisions. When she discovered a bottle of rum, she removed the cork with her teeth and spat it into the sand, then wandered off, alternating between drinking the kill-devil and wiping her teary eyes with the back of her hand.

"Hmm." Andrew seemed to share her wariness.

"Aye. I have no desire to end up like our girl back there—crazed and now well on her way to becoming soused. I prefer to remain hopeful."

"You're certain they'll come for us?"

"I'd wager my left teat," she said, with an affirming nod.

Andrew flinched. "This life at sea has certainly added color to your lexicon."

Celia smiled. "Aye, that it has. Will you help me start a signal fire?"

Back on board the *Belladonna*, Gayle drove her cutlass past the breastbone of her attacker and, with a rather inelegant kick, sent his gasping body soaring over the railing into the seas below.

She snapped her head around to see if anyone else was immediately upon her to fight. Winded and weary, she was relieved to see no one but her own crewmen. She inhaled vigorously to try and catch her breath, and quickly examined the sword wound she had sustained what now seemed like hours ago. Her shirt was stained with blood on her left side, and, under the sliced fabric, the bleeding had started to dissipate on its own—a very good sign.

Dowd jogged over, the dried blood of his foes generously spattering his face and chest. "Cap'n. We believe we've handled the last of 'em."

"And Fuks? Was he taken alive?"

Dowd shook his head. "We gathered the survivors. None o' them have 'is scar. I have Hyde and Frederick combing through the dead for 'im."

Gayle and Dowd headed below deck to survey the captain's quarters. Inside she was pleased to find the two chests of her father's wealth that had been purloined from them. She opened first one, then the other, and discovered at least the vast majority of the items to still be there. "There's sweet succor," she murmured in satisfaction. Glancing about the rest of the cabin she saw no signs of life, either past or present. "Where is the bastard?"

Abernathy entered, his cutlass drawn. "The prisoners say they thought their cap'n was below deck guardin' the treasure."

"There's no bloody sign o' that," Dowd replied.

"We'll search this vessel from stem to stern," Gayle said. "If he's on board, we'll find him."

"Cap'n," a crewman bellowed from above deck.

"Aye?"

"The *Belladonna*'s skiffs are gone."

She stared at Dowd and Abernathy in chagrin. "Would a pirate captain row away when boarded? What kind of nerveless, prancing fop is this Captain Fuks?"

"Faster, Logan," Fuks demanded, glaring at his crewman, who was rowing the skiff unassisted.

Logan, a broad-backed and sinewy man, was wheezing loudly, but still pumping the oars as fast as he could. "I can't go much farther, Cap'n," he rasped in his thick Irish accent. "I'm all but dead."

Fuks squinted hopefully through his spyglass. He had spotted small quays in this direction. "Ah, well, buck up, lad. Not only are we close to land, but it looks as though there are some provisions ripe for the pickin'."

"Huh?"

"Directly east. Someone's made a nice welcome fire for us."

CHAPTER TWENTY-SIX

A nne sat dejectedly on the quay, her knees pulled up under her chin, staring into the now-dying signal fire. She drank from the nearly empty rum bottle as the sound of rolling waves lulled her into a state of unqualified despair.

How had she ended up here? Everything that she had initially thought was going to be wonderful had ended up being totally horrendous.

Her trip to the brothel? As promising as that had seemed, it had only gotten her kidnapped by a slave trader and dragged all the way to the Caribbean.

Being rescued by a dashing and sexy female pirate captain? Well, that had proceeded no better—no lusty tumbles, losing Gayle's affections to that buxom bitch who had also somehow captured the heart of her own brother—the Judas. Now she was stranded here in the middle of nowhere.

Why was God punishing her? Surely he had bestowed exquisite beauty upon her so that she might take pleasure in the passion of others. It was almost as if he was somehow trying to tell her that was not the case.

Anne took another gulp of her only friend, which warmed her extremities like a toasty blanket. She sighed loudly before someone violently slammed her backward onto the sand, the wind knocked from her lungs.

"You must be one o' them sirens o' the sea," a man with a thick Irish accent cooed malevolently as he pinned her to the ground. Anne struggled to inhale, but was unable. "And you're quite a comely one," he added, his sweaty face within an inch of hers.

She gasped, struggling to regain the ability to breathe freely and speak. Turning her face to the left to determine where Celia and Andrew were, she saw what appeared to be Andrew's body lifeless in the sand not far away. There were no signs of Celia.

"A lively little lass ye be, too," the bastard added as Anne continued to wriggle against him.

Finally, she was able to draw a small amount of breath. "Get… off," she wheezed.

He laughed menacingly. "Keep moving under me like that and I will in no time, lass."

As Celia approached the camp with more firewood, she suddenly sensed that something was amiss. A faint cry made the tiny hairs on the back of her neck stand up, and she stopped, wary.

Quietly, she set the firewood down and continued toward the beach. Another noise came, a muffled scream, and adrenaline raced through her body.

To be less visible she crouched in the sand, creeping toward camp and listening intently. Anne was pinned beneath a behemoth of a man, but, curiously enough, she did not appear to be enjoying it.

Simultaneously, beside the dwindling fire, another smaller man was digging through their provisions. With great concern, Celia scoured the dim night for her father. What had they done to him? Who were these men? Were there more than the two she could see from here?

In her possession she had a loaded pistol, but unfortunately no powder or shot to reload it; a silver dagger strapped to her thigh—she had learned a thing or two, after all; and little else of value. She had not thought to grab the cutlass Gayle had packed with their provisions, and she was now regretting her carelessness.

"Why don't you help me a mite, lass?" Logan pleaded as he tore the blonde's dress. "I'm plenty tired from the trip here, you know. If you were to be a bit more cooperative, I might work harder to help you to enjoy it."

"God's teeth, Logan," Fuks cursed, using the hilt of his dagger to break the neck off a bottle of rum and then pouring some into his mouth. "Just get it over with. How long is it going to take you to fuck that girl?"

"Stop fightin' me," Logan implored again. "I can make this good for both of us."

"No, you can't," the blonde spat back. "Stop bloody mauling me."

"Fine," Logan replied with a grimace, holding both of the hellcat's small wrists securely with one of his large hands. "Have it your way, then."

Fuks turned away again to further rummage through the wealth of goods on the beach and heard a gunshot. When he spun back around, he discovered that another young woman had apparently leapt from cover somewhere, placed a pistol to the back of Logan's head, and shot most of it clear off. His lifeless body, his head now a red, pulpy mass, lay burdensomely on the blonde—who finally lay still.

"Bloody hell," he shouted. "What have you done, you silly bitch?"

Celia's heart was beating so frantically her pulse was pounding in every part of her body. She glanced down at the smoking pistol in her hand. She had definitely made her one shot count. "I blew your friend's ruddy head apart."

Anne struggled under the dead body pinning her to the sand, but as he was well more than twice her weight, she made little progress in moving him.

The small man drew the cutlass from his baldric, tilting his head appraisingly to the left. "Your name wouldn't be Pierce by any chance, would it?"

"It might be. Yours wouldn't be Anus, would it?"

He squinted at her in disdain. "Fuks," he said.

"Ah, yes, I assumed you were called something vile. I was right." Anne was still unable to move, so she attempted to assist her by shoving Logan's body with her foot.

"That's enough of that, whore," Fuks snapped. "Leave your friend where she belongs—rutting with the dead." He waved his cutlass at her.

Celia did as she was told, glancing at the dead man to see if he had any weapons she could snatch up. Seeing nothing more lethal on him than a dagger, which did her no good, she then looked toward the provisions in hopes of spying her cutlass there. She didn't see it, but just beyond Fuks's left shoulder, her father lay stretched motionless in the sand. "Father?"

"I don't know how that lubber kept from drowning when we sent him overboard," Fuks said. "I was shocked to see him still drawing breath."

With no other thought than ensuring her father's safety, Celia threw her spent pistol to the ground and dashed past Fuks, just beyond his grasp. She dropped to her knees in the sand beside Andrew's body, relieved to see his chest rising and falling. "Father," she called, shaking him gently. He didn't stir at her touch, and a large gash on his head spilled blood freely.

"Leave him," Fuks commanded. "You're the last one to be givin' aid to anyone else, as you'll be dead shortly."

Celia slowly pulled her hands back, disappointed that Andrew had no weapons on him. There was at least one more loaded pistol in the provisions, and she had hoped that he had grabbed it. The only potential weapon nearby was a plum-sized rock, which she covertly grasped with her right hand.

"Now get up and turn around," he barked.

Slowly, she did so.

Meanwhile, Anne had continued to gradually struggle free of her gory restraint. Pushing mightily, she shoved the dead body several inches, expelling a loud grunt as she did so.

Fuks turned. "I told you to leave him, bitch."

Celia saw his averted attention as an opportunity she dared not waste and hurled the stone in her hand at her captor as hard as she was able. It struck him sharply in the left temple, and he cried out, drawing his left hand up to it.

Celia lunged toward her cutlass then, knowing this was her only chance to defend herself. Fuks was clearly too distracted to stop her, and she drew the weapon quickly from its sheath and brandished it defiantly.

"How's your head?" she asked flippantly.

"Bloody harridan." He held up his fingers covered with his own blood.

"Well, don't worry about the blood too much," Celia said. "I plan to hack that melon of yours right off your putrid shoulders."

He squinted as warm blood ran into his left eye from the gash above it. "The day a woman bests me is the day I cut my own fuckin' throat."

"How chivalrous of you to offer to help," she said through clenched teeth.

Fuks clearly was not amused by her threats, and he charged her, emitting a savage cry of anger. His blade slashed down at her once she was within reach, and she blocked the powerful strike only by clutching her weapon tight with both hands and parrying.

He seemed momentarily stunned that she had deflected his violent blow, and he struck at her again, but his weapon again glanced off. His face turned red, and the veins in his neck and forehead became visible. "You fuckin' whore," he screamed.

Celia defensively stepped backward, unable to anticipate his moves while he was in such a frenzy.

"There's no gettin' away now, lass," he shouted as he advanced on her. "I'll slice you a thousand fuckin' ways to Sunday."

As Celia continued to retreat, their blades clashed again, though this time the steel remained joined, as though their weapons were embracing. Suddenly, Fuks reached out with his left hand and grasped her right wrist. Though the cutlasses were still entangled, he had complete control of hers, as she was now unable to move her sword. "This skirmish is over," he muttered, his disfigured face only inches from hers. With that, he yanked her wrist savagely to secure an opening to run her through.

Anticipating his fatal strike, Celia let go of her cutlass and tried to spin away from him. This sudden motion caused her to lose her footing in the sand, and she fell backward, landing dangerously near the fire, now prone and disarmed.

Fuks laughed darkly and stood over her. "Where's your saucy chaff now, lass? How are things looking from down there on your arse? They look pretty good from up here." He stepped directly over her, letting his blade touch the ground.

Celia glanced to her right at the dying signal fire and, without hesitation, grabbed the unlit end of a burning log. He raised his blade to slash at her, but first she was able to ignite the bottom of his black, knee-length coat.

Fuks screamed and bolted toward the ocean to douse himself—the rush of air that hit him only making the fire surge and intensify. His coat was now completely ablaze, as well as his breeches. Torn between trying to remove the blazing garment or simply jumping directly into the sea, he chose the latter, diving face-first into the rolling waves.

The sting of salt water on charred skin and blisters almost immediately replaced the sudden abatement of the pain of his burning flesh. "God's bunghole," he yelled, anguish racking him. He struggled to remove his now-scorched coat, though in just the attempt he felt as though some of his skin was coming off as well.

His lungs filled with the smell of burning hair and hide, and again fury consumed him. He flung his coat into the darkened swell of the seas and spun back around to the beach, to kill the bitch that had done this to him.

"You bloody—"

As he turned, he focused on the pistol barrel now pointed toward him. The hellcat stood just where the waves were breaking, only a few feet from him. She was clearly aiming at his head. Fuks inhaled to speak, but the pistol discharged before he was able to utter a syllable in his defense.

The shot blew most of the bastard's face away, and he fell backward into the surf, motionless. Celia watched as the tide carried Fuks farther ashore, and once she was convinced that he was no longer breathing, she ran to help Anne finally free herself.

Dropping the spent pistol, Celia grabbed the dead body of Anne's attacker and began to roll him over. After a minute or two, Anne was at last unconstrained.

"My God," she cried as she sat up. "Thank you so much."

Celia and she uncharacteristically hugged each other tight. "Are you all right?" she asked softly, holding her close and rocking her back and forth.

Anne could only continue to weep.

By the time the *Belladonna* had sighted Celia's signal fire and sailed inland, Gayle was frantic with worry. Yes, that appeared to be one of Fuk's skiffs moored there on the quay, which now confirmed her building fears.

With no skiff to disembark onto, Gayle, Abernathy, Diego, and Dowd were hoisted one at a time by the remaining crew directly into the surf. Gayle sprinted through the waves toward the beach, her cutlass drawn and her pistols reloaded and at the ready. She suppressed the desire to call out to Celia, on the slight chance that perhaps someone on that quay did not see their ship's approach in the cover of darkness.

First she saw a body—possibly Captain Fuks, but who could be certain?—washed up on the shore, lying on his back, his face blown completely apart.

"*Madre de Dios*," Diego gasped, nudging the corpse cautiously with his foot.

The group moved slowly toward the light of the fire, and from a distance they saw Andrew, seated in the sand with his head bandaged. Beside him was Celia, who had her arm around Anne and was humming to her. Just beyond them was a large dead body with the back of its head utterly and irreparably decimated.

Celia looked up from the fire as her rescue party stared at her.

"Gayle?" Her eyes and face lit up in jubilation.

Gayle cocked an eyebrow. "So your journey was uneventful, I see."

CHAPTER TWENTY-SEVEN

F ather," Gayle called as she entered The Bountiful Teat. "Have you moved a bloody inch since we left you?"

Malvern the elder turned from his stool to see his daughter in the doorway with Abernathy and Celia. "You bleedin' marauders," he called, standing and moving to embrace her. "You made it back."

Gayle hugged him tight and kissed his cheek. "You look well."

Abernathy found a table with several chairs and directed they sit there.

"So, did you find it?" Malvern asked as he sat.

"Aye. Then we lost it, and took it back again."

"You lost it?" he stuttered. "What do you mean?"

"A freebooter by the name of Fuks followed us to the quay, killed Nichols and Caruthers, and stole the loot."

"The bastard. How'd you get it back?"

"Followed him and took his ship," Abernathy added.

"Did you, now?" Malvern felt both proud and relieved.

"Aye. But in so doing, we lost eight men—including Sully and my good friend Churchill—and *Original Sin* herself."

"No, lass. Say it ain't so."

"'Tis the truth, Father. I'm so very sorry."

Malvern downed what was left of the rum in his tankard. He took a deep breath and tightened his jaw. "Did you kill the son of a bitch?"

Celia blurted, "I did."

Malvern assessed her in a whole new way. "*You* killed him?"

"Aye."

"You've got a great bloody eye for the ladies, Gayle. Have I mentioned that?"

"You have, old man."

"So what ship are you sailing now?"

"The *Belladonna*. I can't say it's the best ship I've ever sailed, but it kept my feet dry."

Malvern looked about the tavern. "Where is that serving wench? We should drink to our fallen comrades."

Gayle nodded toward Abernathy. "Get us all some drinks, will you?"

"Aye, Cap'n." He stood and went to the bar to order from the barkeep.

Diego appeared in the doorway and Gayle waved him over to sit with them. "Is it done, then?"

"Aye, Cap'n."

"Is what done?" Malvern asked.

"Your little tavern wench. She's who sold us out to Fuks."

"Desta? Are you certain?"

"Heard it from their own bloody mouths."

"Pity. She wasn't too hard on the eyes. I'll let Smitty know he'll need a new girl."

Celia studied Gayle's father. Beyond his somewhat glib comment about Desta's appearance, it did not seem that anyone would miss her much. "What did you do with her?" she asked Gayle quietly.

"She's on a voyage."

"To where?"

Gayle shrugged and deferred to Diego. "To where?"

An expression of evil amusement came over Diego's face. "Madagascar."

Abernathy then arrived at the table and put drinks in front of everyone. "That's four rums," he said, setting the tankards in front of Diego, Malvern, Gayle, and himself. "And one flip," he added, giving Celia her drink.

"Thank you, Abernathy," she said with a wink.

The crewman blushed and took a large swig of rum.

"Gayle?" Celia asked.

"*Amor?*"

"Isn't Madagascar off the eastern coast of Africa?"

"That it is." Gayle nodded, her bronze eyes alight with mirth.

For a long moment everyone was silent and simply looked at each other with knowing glances.

Celia picked up her drink and held it up. "Well, let us drink to her *bon voyage.*"

"*Bon voyage,*" they all called in unison, their tankards clanking together.

A beam of hot sunlight punctured the clouds, pierced the porthole, and fell directly on Desta's face. After several moments, the bright light beating on her left eyelid brought her back into consciousness, and her eyes fluttered open.

"Where the hell...?" She looked about her. She was in a ship's hold—of that she was fairly certain. She lay in a hay-strewn heap, amidst a collection of chickens, pigs, and goats.

A man poked his head in at the sound of her voice. He was short and round, but didn't seem threatening. "Ah, you're awake. *C'est bien.*"

"Where am I?" She tried to stand and realized that her head was throbbing mercilessly.

"You are on the *Yvette,*" he answered politely. "And we are a merchant ship bound for Madagascar."

"Bound for where? How did I get here?"

"Ah, your friends booked you passage, *mademoiselle.* I assured them you would be safe even though you are traveling alone."

She held her head tight, trying to keep it from splitting open. "My friends, you say? What friends?"

"The crew of *Original Sin.* They said they owed this trip to you."

"Bastards."

"They must care for you very deeply," he prattled on in his thick French accent. "After all, this trip will take months."

"Months?"

"*Oui, mademoiselle.* We must sail south past the coast of Brazil and around the southern tip of Africa to reach the island of Madagascar. *C'est très jolie.*"

Desta sat back down in the hay. That really was too much for her to wrestle with all at once. "Do you have any rum on board, Frenchy?"

His eyes lit up at her question and he clapped his hands together quickly. "*Mais oui.*"

EPILOGUE

As the cool autumn breeze drifted through their bedroom window, Celia ran her hands appreciatively along Gayle's naked body. "Damn, but I could do this all day," she murmured into her lover's shoulder.

Gayle rolled over in bed to face her and kissed her passionately. "So you haven't tired of me yet?"

Celia gazed into the amber eyes before her. "Are you missing the sea, love?"

"No. Though some days I miss the roll of the ocean under my feet."

"Are you regretting giving over the *Belladonna* to the crew? She could have been the flagship of your ever-expansive fleet."

"No, I'm glad I let her go. And I was damn proud that they elected Molly as their next captain. She earned it, she did. With her cut of the loot, she could easily have walked away from sailing forever, and she decided to stay."

"I'm sure she's a fine captain."

"I think it's just *Original Sin* I miss, and that crew and that ship are gone forever. The others who lived to tell of it took their cut and settled down."

"As you did, love." She kissed Gayle—a long, easy kiss that said more than mere words could convey.

Life had certainly taken a favorable turn for them. They now lived on a beautiful estate in Jamaica that overlooked the ocean. Occasionally, old friends like Abernathy or Diego would visit and stay with them.

Molly and her crew had even docked there once for a few days, and it had nearly been like old times, save for all the new faces on board.

Gayle's father now lived only a short distance away, and Celia's parents planned to make a trip out that way to winter with them.

Both Anne and James had left the *Belladonna* after the loot was divided up. Molly had mentioned something about James moving back to England and marrying a cobbler's daughter.

Anne was never really the same after the unfortunate altercation with Captain Fuks and his Irish crony, and apparently she had found comfort from the Lord. They had heard that she was now in a nunnery in Wales somewhere, but Gayle suspected that it was probably just so she could have all those virgins to herself.

Celia turned onto her belly, and Gayle began to softly trace the outline of the tattoo on her right shoulder. It was the familiar image of a dragonfly lighting on the blade of a cutlass, and it matched the one Gayle had gotten on the inside of her left forearm.

"You're an excellent catch, Celia."

"Mmm, and are you glad you are the one who caught me?"

"Verily."

She turned back to face her. "That's nice to hear," Celia whispered seductively, nibbling on her ear.

"And who knew when I caught you that you'd turn into such a formidable, fearsome pirate?"

Celia rolled Gayle onto her back and straddled her. "Prepare to be boarded."

About the Author

Colette Moody has long been an avid bibliophile and fan of history (and swashbuckling). When she isn't doing research or crafting scenes for her next romp of a novel, she can be found doing one or more of the following: trying to best her high score on Wii Tennis; sequestered in the kitchen eagerly trying to prove that everything DOES taste better with bacon; meticulously recreating classic cocktails from the 30s and 40s; or planning her next trip to Disneyland. While waiting to be generously (and inexplicably) remembered in some wealthy stranger's will, she begrudgingly bides her time as a corporate lackey, working for the man. She lives in Southeastern Virginia with her beloved dog and her equally Wii-addicted partner.

The *Sublime and Spirited Voyage of Original Sin* is Colette Moody's first novel. She is currently working on her second for Bold Strokes Books, *The Seduction of Moxie*.

Books Available From Bold Strokes Books

The Sublime and Spirited Voyage of Original Sin by Colette Moody. Pirate Gayle Malvern finds the presence of an abducted seamstress, Celia Pierce, a welcome distraction until the captive comes to mean more to her than is wise. (978-1-60282-054-8)

Suspect Passions by VK Powell. Can two women, a city attorney and a beat cop, put aside their differences long enough to see that they're perfect for each other? (978-1-60282-053-1)

Just Business by Julie Cannon. Two women who come together—each for her own selfish needs—discover that love can never be as simple as a business transaction. (978-1-60282-052-4)

Sistine Heresy by Justine Saracen. Adrianna Borgia, survivor of the Borgia court, presents Michelangelo with the greatest temptations of his life while struggling with soul-threatening desires for the painter Raphaela. (978-1-60282-051-7)

Radical Encounters by Radclyffe. An out-of-bounds, outside-the-lines collection of provocative, superheated erotica by award-winning romance and erotica author Radclyffe. (978-1-60282-050-0)

Thief of Always by Kim Baldwin & Xenia Alexiou. Stealing a diamond to save the world should be easy for Elite Operative Mishael Taylor, but she didn't figure on love getting in the way. (978-1-60282-049-4)

X by JD Glass. When X-hacker Charlie Riven is framed for a crime she didn't commit, she accepts help from an unlikely source—sexy Treasury Agent Elaine Harper. (978-1-60282-048-7)

The Middle of Somewhere by Clifford Henderson. Eadie T. Pratt sets out on a road trip in search of a new life and ends up in the middle of somewhere she never expected. (978-1-60282-047-0)

Paybacks by Gabrielle Goldsby. Cameron Howard wants to avoid her old nemesis Mackenzie Brandt but their high school reunion brings up more than just memories. (978-1-60282-046-3)

Uncross My Heart by Andrews & Austin. When a radio talk show diva sets out to interview a female priest, the two women end up at odds and neither heaven nor earth is safe from their feelings. (978-1-60282-045-6)

Fireside by Cate Culpepper. Mac, a therapist, and Abby, a nurse, fall in love against the backdrop of friendship, healing, and defending one's own within the Fireside shelter. (978-1-60282-044-9)

Green Eyed Monster by Gill McKnight. Mickey Rapowski believes her former boss has cheated her out of a small fortune, so she kidnaps the girlfriend and demands compensation—just a straightforward abduction that goes so wrong when Mickey falls for her captive. (978-1-60282-042-5)

Blind Faith by Diane and Jacob Anderson-Minshall. When private investigator Yoshi Yakamota and the Blind Eye Detective Agency are hired to find a woman's missing sister, the assignment seems fairly mundane—but in the detective business, the ordinary can quickly become deadly. (978-1-60282-041-8)

A Pirate's Heart by Catherine Friend. When rare book librarian Emma Boyd searches for a long-lost treasure map, she learns the hard way that pirates still exist in today's world—some modern pirates steal maps, others steal hearts. (978-1-60282-040-1)

Trails Merge by Rachel Spangler. Parker Riley escapes the high-powered world of politics to Campbell Carson's ski resort—and their mutual attraction produces anything but smooth running. (978-1-60282-039-5)

Dreams of Bali by C.J. Harte. Madison Barnes worships work, power, and success, and she's never allowed anyone to interfere—that is, until she runs into Karlie Henderson Stockard. Aeros EBook (978-1-60282-070-8)

The Limits of Justice by John Morgan Wilson. Benjamin Justice and reporter Alexandra Templeton search for a killer in a mysterious compound in the remote California desert. (978-1-60282-060-9)

Designed for Love by Erin Dutton. Jillian Sealy and Wil Johnson don't much like each other, but they do have to work together—and what they desire most is not what either of them had planned. (978-1-60282-038-8)

Calling the Dead by Ali Vali. Six months after Hurricane Katrina, NOLA Detective Sept Savoie is a cop who thinks making a relationship work is harder than catching a serial killer—but her current case may prove her wrong. (978-1-60282-037-1)

Shots Fired by MJ Williamz. Kyla and Echo seem to have the perfect relationship and the perfect life until someone shoots at Kyla—and Echo is the most likely suspect. (978-1-60282-035-7)

truelesbianlove.com by Carsen Taite. Mackenzie Lewis and Dr. Jordan Wagner have very different ideas about love, but they discover that truelesbianlove is closer than a click away. Aeros EBook (978-1-60282-069-2)

Justice at Risk by John Morgan Wilson. Benjamin Justice's blind date leads to a rare opportunity for legitimate work, but a reckless risk changes his life forever. (978-1-60282-059-3)

Run to Me by Lisa Girolami. Burned by the four-letter word called love, the only thing Beth Standish wants to do is run for—or maybe from—her life. (978-1-60282-034-0)

Split the Aces by Jove Belle. In the neon glare of Sin City, two women ride a wave of passion that threatens to consume them in a world of fast money and fast times. (978-1-60282-033-3)

Uncharted Passage by Julie Cannon. Two women on a vacation that turns deadly face down one of nature's most ruthless killers—and find themselves falling in love. (978-1-60282-032-6)

Night Call by Radclyffe. All medevac helicopter pilot Jett McNally wants to do is fly and forget about the horror and heartbreak she left behind in the Middle East, but anesthesiologist Tristan Holmes has other plans. (978-1-60282-031-9)